Also from G.C. McRae

Picture Books
The Cannibal Anaconda
The Tooth
Pretty Ballerina

Fiction
Kana and the Red Pilot
Seven Tales

Free Pizza

by

G.C. McRae

MacDonald Warne Media

Free Pizza, by G.C. McRae
Published by MacDonald Warne Media

Copyright© G.C. McRae 2019
All Rights Reserved

Edited by Marg Gilks

ISBN: 978-0-9939183-8-4

Fiction

Visit us at: www.gcmcrae.com

For Claude
My sides still ache
from laughing so hard,
so often, all those years ago

Chapter 1

You ever have one of those life-changing experiences? You know, where you're just a happy kid, bopping along, la-la-la, and all of a sudden somebody kicks you off a cliff? You're like, *Whaaa?* wagging your arms and legs, wondering where the ground is? Yeah, that was me, for like, two whole weeks last year.

By the way, my name's Brian McSpadden. My story is completely weird. It's all about potatoes and snot and people falling out of trees. It's about stamps and boobs and it even has a farmer from Alpha Centauri. Well, not really. But he sure looked like it.

My story has almost nothing to do with pizza, tragically. It's mostly about me getting to meet my birth mom, which was like, wow. It's also about my friend Danny, how he threw a grenade into my life, and how I threw a few back into his.

I'm not anybody special. We live in this nothing neighbourhood on the west side of Edmonton, not too far from Westmount Mall. I'm not fast or slow; I'm not super smart and I hope I'm not an idiot. (Do idiots know they're idiots?) I basically go through life trying not to get beat up and trying not to be boring.

The center of our house is not my parents and it certainly isn't me. The center of our house is my horrible little brothers, Kyle and Jayden. Kyle is the older one. He's five and he comes into a room nostrils first, on account of his drippy nose. Jayden is simply cute and he knows it. But when he doesn't get his way, he has a whine that makes your eyeballs want to trade places.

I'm not really part of the game in our house. I'm way older and like, independent, which I think kind of ticks my mother off. She's a control freak and she has lost control of me. Besides, being the only adopted kid, I was never totally under her control to begin with. I'm a stranger who got made by strangers and the only instruction book that came with me was in a foreign language.

The way Kyle and Jayden rule over the house is with their constant complaining. Stuff like, "But I don't like that itchy sweater! It hurts my neck! Ow-ow-ow!" If you cry that long enough, I guarantee you'll get what you want.

In the morning I like to hunch over my breakfast bowl and read from my phone. That way, if I slob milk or cereal, it just drips back into the bowl and I don't waste anything. (I need all the calories I can get.) In the summer I get up later than anyone else so I can have peace and quiet. But that first morning, my mom wandered in to put the dishes in the dishwasher away. That made me groan inside because Kyle wandered in behind her.

"Morning."

"Morning."

"Are you going to be here this morning? I have to bring Kyle to the doctor."

That's all she had to say to launch Kyle into full complaint mode. "Do I have to get another needle? I don't want another needle!"

I didn't even get a chance to answer. The conversation had been hijacked.

"I told you," Mom said, "we're just going to our own doctor. The needles are finished. And where's your kleenex?"

Kyle had plunked himself into a chair across from me. Two big globs of snot were oozing from his nostrils. "But I don't wanna go to the doctor!" He held up a gnarly wet ball and dabbed at the drips, which came away in strings. I had to look away.

And there was Jayden coming into the kitchen, sucking his thumb. The kid was four and he sucked his thumb so much, it wrinkled and cracked. And he cried constantly. Well, not that morning. But like, often.

Even though it was July, both of my little brothers were in pajamas, tartan slippers, and flannel dressing gowns with the belts cinched tight. They looked like a couple of miniature seniors, ready for their evening tea.

Jayden came and stood next to his brother, looking extremely concerned. He put his free hand on Kyle's arm, trying to calm and comfort him.

"Listen to me," said Mom. "There aren't going to be any needles today. We're just going to talk."

"About what?" Kyle asked, shaking off his brother's hand. "Can I wear my shorts?"

"Don't be silly; it's raining. And get yourself a new kleenex, would you? We're going to talk about your nose. Remember, we saw the doctor last fall?"

"Yeah."

"And we went to the allergy clinic last week?"

"They gave me all the needles!"

"Well, they didn't find anything, did they? We don't know what's causing your drippy nose."

It had been ten months of that drippy nose. The kid produced mucus the way sugar maples produce sap—in a slow, constant drip. So far the experts had determined it was not a cold, it was not allergies, and it probably was not asthma. Now they had to go back to the doctor and see what else it could be.

"And get a fresh kleenex! Ugh!" Mom launched herself off the counter toward the kleenex box by the stove. "You're making me crazy."

Zip-zip—she pulled two kleenexes from the box and covered the bottom half of Kyle's face with them. With two twists and a scrunch, she had all the snot off his face and half the next batch squeezed out of his little honker. Then she grabbed the wet ball he'd been holding and all three tissues went into the garbage.

Before she returned to the dishwasher, Mom had time to pull Jayden's hand away from his head. The kid was covered in mosquito bites and wouldn't stop scratching them. This woke Jayden from his trance and he yanked his thumb out of his mouth long enough to say to me, "We get to go on the bus!"

"No, sorry," Mom told him. "Your dad took the bus to work this morning so we could have the car."

Jayden had not taken his eyes off me. "We get to go in the car!"

I nodded, swallowing a mouthful of cereal. "I don't have to go with you, do I?"

Mom closed up the dishwasher. "Brian, what have I said about that phone at the table?"

"There's nobody else eating."

"I was hoping you'd watch Jayden while I go in with Kyle."

I scooped up my phone. "I'm pretty sure I'm going out."

"Since when?"

"Since…Danny texted me," I lied. "We're gonna hang

out." I began typing a new message to Danny:

sup

Mom looked at me suspiciously. Danny Cheevers was the only kid on my mom's list of approved friends. She had met his mother at some parent/teacher thing and the two had hit it off. Little did she know, Mrs. Cheevers was at work all day. Mr. Cheevers worked at home and barely ever left his office. And Danny...let's just say he was a bit of a wild man. "Well," she said, "we won't be back till after twelve."

"That's fine." I kept staring at my phone, waiting for an answer.

This was about as exciting as things ever got in our house. Well, unless you counted vanilla pudding for dessert once a week or my brand new armpit hairs. In our neighbourhood, there were two kinds of people: old ones and young ones. My family was no exception.

My parents—my adoptive parents—were old. They got me when I was a baby because they thought they couldn't have kids. My dad was so old he even got a pension. But it wasn't much, so he worked as a security guard downtown. When I was little, my mom stopped bringing me to the park because the other moms thought she was a grandma. Then, *spang!*—she got pregnant with Kyle. She was like, forty-two or something. And a year later, *spang!*—freako number two, Jayden was born.

My parents and the boys were a single unit. They were all the same: short and skinny. And they all had the McSpadden nose, which looked too small for their faces. Me, I was taller than all of them, even though I wasn't that tall for my age. So at school, I was normal. At home, I was Frankenstein.

"Jayden!" Mom barked again.

The fingernails crept down his neck to his lap. His lips closed around his thumb and he gave it a few quick sucks.

I tried to concentrate on my Bran Flakes. Yeah, I said it. I was eating Bran Flakes. It was either that or Bran Buds. It was what my dad liked, and my mother refused to buy sugary kid cereals. Bran was good for our guts, she said, and it wouldn't make us hyper.

Finally I got an answer from Danny: *sup w u*

I quickly typed: *wanna do something?*

The answer came like lightning: *come on over got new video game*

when

I laughed at his response: *soon b4 I kill something*

Oh, thank god, I thought. But two seconds later came another message:

after 9:30

I glanced at the time—8:51—and typed back: *k*

Kyle's chin had stopped quivering. He had gotten up to get himself another kleenex and now sat there staring at it on his lap.

"Were you up in the night, Kyle?" Mom asked.

"Huh?"

"Last night, did you get up?"

"I couldn't find no kleenex in the baffroom."

"Why didn't you use toilet paper?"

"Toilet paper is for poop."

"Well, what are you going to do in September when school starts?"

"Huh?"

"What if that's all they have at school?"

Kyle was offended and folded his skinny little arms. "I'm not pooping at school."

"That's not what I—oh my god, I give up."

Kyle looked over at me. "Do people poop at school, Brian?"

"Sometimes," I told him.

"Well, I'm not."

All this poop talk, apparently, was Jayden's cue. His lips made a squelching sound as he released the suction on his thumb. He looked at me. He tipped his head slightly and let out a little *putt* of a fart. He immediately burst out laughing, thumb poised to return to its face hole.

"Je-de!" I shouted, my mouth full of cereal.

"Gross," said Kyle, sliding off his chair.

The thumb went back in and he laughed around it.

Mom spun around and gave Kyle and Jayden a shove toward their bedroom. "That's enough of you two. Go on to your room. I'll be there in a minute to pick out your clothes."

As the two shuffled off, I stretched the text on my phone to giant size and kept eating.

Mom discovered a couple more balls of wet kleenex on the floor, scooped them up and pitched them into the garbage. "You know it's your birthday tomorrow," she said to me. "Anything in particular you want for dinner?"

My answer would have been pizza. But she never got delivery pizza, ever. Only the crappiest freezer pizza, and I couldn't handle that.

"I don't know. Not really."

She went to the sink to rinse her hands. But something went goofy and she ended up spraying her flowered shirt and had to dab it dry with a paper towel. Mom's style was thirty years out of date. Even when she got new glasses or a new hairstyle, she still looked like her high school pictures, except wrinkly. She even prided herself on being able to get into pants she wore in grade ten. Yeah, great, Mom, except for the granny butt.

She folded the paper towel and placed it in the garbage. When she got back to the sink, she looked like she was doing a bunch of things that didn't need doing, just to talk to me. "You'll probably get a card from Aunt Rita. And maybe some cash, eh?"

"Yeah."

"What do you think you'll buy?"

"I don't know; stuff for my phone?"

She gave me a look like I was crazy. "Stuff? What stuff?"

My phone was a sensitive subject. The year before, I had convinced her to buy me a phone so she would always know where I was. The thing is, you need another phone or a laptop to do the tracking. Duh. By the time she figured that out, it was too late. I had an awesome phone and she refused to spend the money to buy another one.

"Like, apps," I said. "And maybe game things like armor and weapons."

"I don't even know how you would do that." She folded the dish cloth and draped it over the tap. For sure, she had something practical in mind for me to buy. Socks or some stupid thing. But she was done with me and sailed past, heading to the boys' bedroom. Two seconds later, she was giving them heck for unfolding shirts from the drawer. "Look at the mess you've made! You're just making more work for me!"

Ugh, I thought. Nine thirty couldn't come soon enough.

Chapter 2

Ordinarily, I would have lazed around till it was time to leave. But I was going to Danny's and he had an older sister named Cindy that I didn't want to stink out, so I had a shower. After that, it was still early and, on my way downstairs, I discovered something cool.

If I stood at the top of the stairs and reached down the wall and handrail, I found I could jump like, 80 percent of the way. I even went back up and tried again, and the result was the same. Someday, I thought, I would perfect that and make it all the way down.

When I got to my room, I played games for a bit on my phone. Then I got bored and started goofing around with this lump of blue plasticine I'd stolen from the boys. I wasn't really that good at making anything and all my modelling tools were homemade—toothpicks, popsicle sticks, a pencil where the eraser had dried up and fallen out. I liked making heads, even though they all ended up looking like rock monsters. This time, I made a sort of duck-billed guy and stuck a toothpick in his mouth. When it was time to go, I laid him on my dresser and headed up to the landing to put on my shoes.

That's when the house phone rang.

I did not know it was going to be the most important phone call of my life. I wasn't even there to listen to the conversation. All I heard was my mom answering, "Hello?" and then waiting like, fifteen seconds before speaking again. By then I had my shoes tied up.

Into the phone, she said, "Yes, he'll be turning twelve tomorrow."

I figured she was making some kind of birthday arrangements for me, which was weird. Nothing special ever happened on our birthdays. But hey, miracles happened.

I leaned into the kitchen, waved, and said quietly, "I'm going to Danny's."

Distracted, Mom waved back and kept listening to whoever was on the other end of the phone. I didn't think anything of it and pushed the door open and stepped outside.

At least it wasn't raining hard anymore. But wow, the drizzle was incredibly annoying. It was like fizz floating in the air and no matter which way you turned, you got it in your face.

Danny's was about two blocks away. It was an old two-storey house with yellowing siding, the most boring cube you've ever seen. But in the last few years, somebody figured they'd make it look "modern" and stuck this huge ugly porch on the front. It had big honking pillars, as if it was the entrance to a mansion. Too bad they forgot to paint it. And too bad nobody ever mowed the lawn or weeded the flower beds.

I usually went around to the back, but this morning, Danny must have seen me through the front screen door as I was coming up the sidewalk. "Get in here!" he yelled. I could tell from the reflections that he and his younger brother, Randy, were playing a racing game in the living room. Maybe having pesky little brothers was why we got along so well. Who knows?

I put on a chilled face and went in. "You got a new TV?"

The thing was almost too big for the stand it was on. The box it came in was shoved off to the side.

"Huge, eh?"

"No! No!" Randy yelled at the giant screen. "You're cheating! Stop that!"

Even though it was still morning, the place smelled like Pizza Pockets. As I took off my hoodie and threw it on the nearest chair, I found myself wondering a) were there any left and b) could I get like, a nutrition boost by inhaling the air in here?

Danny and Randy had pulled the couch away from the wall and moved it in front of the TV like, six feet away. If I did that in my house I'd be grounded for a century. I didn't know where their older sister Cindy was, but I could smell her candy lip gloss.

"Oh my god, I hate you, Danny. No! No!"

"Randy!" came a voice from the second floor. Their mother came down the stairs, her heels clomping noisily. She and all three kids looked like they'd popped out of the same mold: blonde, narrow head, big front teeth. On Danny, I called them Bugs Bunny teeth.

Randy looked up at his mom. "Yeah?"

Clomp, clomp. "You left half your bedclothes in the hallway. I nearly tripped and killed myself. That's your job today." I don't know how she did it, but she came down the stairs putting on earrings while holding a laptop under one arm and a big purse and raincoat over the other. When she got to the bottom, she peered into a mirror beside the front door. "Cindy!" she called. When her daughter didn't instantly appear, she called even louder, "Cindy!"

Cindy came flying around from the kitchen sounding annoyed. "What? I'm busy!"

I liked Cindy. A lot. And not just because she had boobs.

Their mother wrapped her laptop in her raincoat and swished a finger at the two boys on the couch. "These two," was all she said, making a fierce face.

Cindy rolled her eyes. "Of course!" she said. "I know. I know. Have a nice day at work."

"Whatever," said Mrs. Cheevers. "I'm so late." And she burst out the door into the drizzle.

Cindy rolled her eyes and disappeared back into the kitchen.

Randy played the game in silence for a minute. He was one of those kids who got tense and held the controller out in front of him, hoping it would work better if it was closer to the TV.

"Guess she didn't smell the pee," said Danny.

Randy's face was twisting in every direction as he tried to beat Danny at the game. "Shut up."

"At least you got the stink out of the bedroom."

Randy tried to bash Danny with his game controller. Danny just leaned out of the way.

"Do I get to play sometime?" I asked.

"'Course," said Danny. "Soon as I whoop this guy's butt."

Three-quarters of the main floor was living room and kitchen. The last quarter was a dinky bathroom and Mr. Cheever's office. The guy practically lived in there. I heard him laugh just before he flung the door open. He was pretty bald and had a shiny phone headset on, so he looked kind of sci-fi. He must have been able to see Cindy in the kitchen because he waved his giant coffee mug at her and closed the door again. I had seen inside his office once. It was a total disaster area—books, papers, crap everywhere. The only thing neat and tidy was his desk, which had two giant monitors on it. I had no idea what Mr. Cheevers did, but he was always on the phone.

"I thought you said you had a new game," I said to Danny.

He looked wide-eyed at me and nodded. "*Shh.* In a sec."

"Oh, god..." Randy whined, slamming his controller down on the couch. "You totally cheated. How'd you know about that jump?"

"Practice." Then in a lower voice he said to his brother, "Dude, go distract Cindy." And he showed him the corner of a metal DVD case stuffed down the side of the couch. "I want to show Brian the demons game."

Randy whispered, "*She's totally going to hear it.*"

"I'll keep the sound off."

"Okay!" He jumped up and swung around into the kitchen. The kid had a bit of a permanent limp from a fall when he was little, but he was too annoying for anyone to feel sorry for him. "Hey, Cindy," I heard him say.

I got up and moved over to where Randy had been sitting. I didn't know if it was my imagination, but the couch cushion felt slightly damp. So I shifted over and picked up the controller. It felt sticky.

Danny was watching me. "What's with you?"

"Some kind of ick," I said, wiping my hand and then the controller on the couch.

Danny had fished a disc out of the metal case. He dropped to the floor in front of the TV and hunched over the game box under it to eject the racing game. He inserted the "demons" game, whatever that was.

"*Dude!*" he whispered to me, wagging a hand at the remote on the couch. "*Kill the sound!*"

I picked up the remote and pressed Mute.

The game loaded. *War Demons* it said in big black letters. Then *splat!* The whole screen was covered in blood and brains dripping down in glorious grossness. "Oh, no way..." I said. "Where'd you get this?"

"Tyler Lupul. We trade games all the time."

13

"I thought he was on holidays in like, Mexico or some-thing."

"He is. He let me borrow this while he's gone. It's his brother's. He'd kill him if he knew. It's like, off the charts for gore."

"Awesome."

We had just picked our characters and started playing when Cindy came around from the kitchen. Or rather, tried to. Randy was blabbing his face off and trying to block her. "It's fine. No! Just go back! Cindy! Come on!"

She easily shoved by him and looked at the screen. "I knew it was too quiet in here. What the hell is this?"

"It's just a game," Danny told her.

"You keep that damn sound down, or else. If Dad hears you he's gonna blame it on me."

"Yeah, yeah."

"Don't friggin' yeah-yeah me," she said. "What's Cindy's Rule?"

"Oh, whatever. Just let us play."

She leaned over and ripped the controller out of Danny's hands. "What's Cindy's Rule?"

"Don't bug Cindy."

"Thank you. And keep it the hell down." Cindy threw the controller back at him.

Randy was about to sit down on the floor to watch, but Cindy picked him up by the arm. "Hell, no," she said, dragging him back toward the kitchen with her. "You have enough trouble at night without *that*. You come and help me. I'm making stuff for Auntie."

"I just want to see!"

"Whaa-whaa," she said, imitating a baby. "Give it another century and you'll be old enough."

We played for the next five minutes. We could hear Cindy banging pots around in the kitchen and telling Randy what to do. Then Randy snuck around into the living room with his mini-limp.

Danny yelled at him, "Get outa here, rheumatoid!"

"Randy!" Cindy barked from the kitchen.

The kid went running back into the kitchen with a stupid giggle.

I couldn't help asking, "You call him 'rheumatoid'?"

Danny snorted. "Yeah. We just found out he's got arthritis."

"I thought that was for old people."

"Yeah, well, so did we."

Playing the game, Danny showed absolutely no mercy toward me. He had obviously played it before and would not show me anything. I fumbled along with him either laughing at my mistakes or getting miffed when I got killed too quickly. Thankfully, I caught on pretty fast and started to beat him. That *really* got him annoyed.

"How'd you learn that?"

"I don't know. I just tried it."

"Well, calm down or it'll be no fun to play."

"Yeah." I laughed. "For *you*."

About ten minutes later, Cindy swung around the corner from the kitchen. She was holding her phone and literally skidded to a stop as soon as she could see out the front screen door.

"What's going on?" I asked.

Cindy started stabbing at her phone. "Oh my god, somehow those freaks got my number. They are *so* blocked."

Danny and I both leaned forward to see outside. Two guys with their hoods up were huddled around a phone on the city sidewalk, cigarettes sticking out of their faces. They were kids, but way older than us.

"What the—?" Danny started to say. And then, "Oh my god, it's Ordry Bruce."

"Yeah?"

"The other guy must be Morgan," Danny continued.

"What are they doing right in front of our house?"

I knew their names and I'd seen them around the neighbourhood. They were two grades higher than us, same as Cindy, but probably three or four years older. Basically, they were cavemen who should have been in high school by now but were too stupid to get out of junior high. Not just bullies. Not just known for fighting and selling dope, but like, super rough and violent. We didn't really know them or anyone who hung out with them. It was freaky seeing two hooded figures standing right outside the house.

"Whoa!" said Randy, coming around to see what was going on. The two hooded figures must have been able to see us looking at them. I could tell they were laughing. Randy hid behind Cindy. "You know those guys?"

Cindy rolled her eyes. "No!" She spun around, grabbed Randy by the shirt, and hauled him back into the kitchen.

Ordry Bruce obviously worked out. He was solid and meaty and looked like, dirty. He shoved his hood back to see us better. He had curly blonde hair that hung over his face. Morgan was almost the same build, but a little taller, with totally scruffy facial hair.

The next thing I knew, Danny had jumped off the couch and was pushing out the front door. "Can I help you?" he asked.

I stood up and followed, holding the door open to watch. Danny was halfway down the steps to the pillars.

Bruce pocketed his phone and pulled the cigarette out of his mouth. "Yeah!" he yelled back. "When can I hump that sister of yours, Cindy?"

I didn't think Danny would answer. I thought maybe he'd like, laugh it off. Oh, no...he had to open his big mouth. "Ha!" he called back, "Maybe when you grow a wiener to go with those little beans of yours."

Even though I was perfectly safe in the house, my heart jumped into my throat. I blinked and looked to see Bruce's reaction. By the time I opened my eyes after the blink, Bruce and Morgan were halfway up the sidewalk.

"Wha!" Danny yelped in surprise, and came tearing up the front steps. He bashed me out of the way and hauled the screen door closed with a huge *slam!* Then he flung the storm door closed with another *slam!* and stood there with his back to it, eyes and mouth wide open, shocked at what he'd done.

"Oh," I told him, "you are so dead."

He tried to shush me, but Cindy raced back from kitchen. "What's going on?"

She was followed by their father, who emerged from his office, looking none too happy with all the door slamming.

"What was all that?" asked Mr. Cheevers, who stopped in the archway to the living room.

I was trying to see out the window of the storm door. "Are they gone?" Danny asked me.

By then, Cindy was at the window with me circling wide behind her to look out. "It's those jerks," she said. I could see the two figures crossing the grass back to the city sidewalk. "What did you do?"

Danny was all grins. "Nothing."

"Just keep it down, eh?" said their dad, returning to his office. "Or there'll be hell to pay."

Danny waved at him, "Sorry!"

"Well, that was bright," I said to him.

Cindy turned to go back to the kitchen. "Danny, can you *please* mind your own business?"

"Whatever. They asked for it."

"And I'm asking you to stop!"

"Whatever. You shoulda seen his face."

When everything settled down and the two of us were on the couch again, Danny seemed like he was in a great mood, muttering happily, bopping along with some made-up tune.

I just shook my head. "Those guys are going to kill you, you know."

Danny just snorted. "Yeah, maybe."

An hour later, we were still sunk into the couch, nothing moving but our thumbs. I don't even know where the time went. Cooking smells wafted in from the kitchen. Then, Cindy came sailing through the room and went upstairs. She wasn't there more than five seconds when she came thundering down and blasted into the kitchen. "Are you kidding me?" she yelled at Randy. "They're stinking up the whole place! Get up there and deal with it! Now!"

Randy came slumping past us and just to be a jerk, walked real slow in front of the TV.

"I will pulverize you if you don't move," Danny told him.

Randy didn't move any faster. But the instant Danny's butt left the couch, Randy ran to the stairs and went up, sticking his tongue out at us the whole way. He came down a minute later with his arms full of old sheets and blankets that absolutely reeked of pee. Again, he took his time passing in front of the TV.

"Really? *Really?* You are *such* a little dinkus!"

Randy stepped closer and shook the pee smell at us.

Danny picked up the metal DVD case and winged it hard at his brother's head. It missed, banged into the TV screen and clattered to the floor.

Randy raced into the kitchen. Danny jumped up and went over to examine the TV. Even from where I was sitting, I could see a bright vertical line that had appeared on the screen. It was like a frozen lightning bolt, sort of wiggling with electricity. "Oh, great," he said. "I guess the TV ain't new anymore."

Chapter 3

Cindy had heard everything. She came into the living room just as Danny was rubbing his thumb over the silvery crack in the TV screen. "That better not be what I—oh my god. Did you just do that?"

Randy appeared in the archway with his heap of bedclothes. "He tried to bean me with it!"

Cindy turned on him. "Get that stinking mess down to the laundry! Now! And you guys. Seriously. When Dad sees this—" She swore, ejected the game disc, and stabbed it at Danny. "Hide it. Now! I don't want Randy getting hold of it."

"Yeah, yeah."

"You are so dead. You know how much that TV cost?"

"Whatever."

"Whatever? Really?" Cindy's voice went into a high-pitched screech. "Mom is going to kill you when she sees this! How's she going to watch her shows?"

Danny flung a hand at the TV. "You can still see fine! It's just a line! It's not broken!"

Right then, Randy's shouting voice came from the kitchen, "Cindy! Something's burning!"

"What?"

By the time our heads had turned toward the kitchen, a cloud of white smoke with wispy black flecks in it came rolling along the ceiling out of the kitchen.

"No!" Cindy went tearing around the corner toward it, Danny following. I didn't know whether to go and help or get out of the way of the toxic cloud. It smelled like burning plastic. "Look what you made me do!"

I pulled my shirt up to cover my nose, ducked low and went to see what was going up in flames. The kitchen was filled with smoke. Harsh, bitter smoke that got into the back of your throat and snapped it closed.

Mr. Cheevers barged out of his office. "What's going on? What is that?"

Cindy had an oven mitt on and knocked something off the stove. It was a large pink plastic bowl—or rather, part of it. The bottom was melted off and flames were shooting up one side as it hit the floor. Danny stomped on it with his socked foot to put the flames out.

"Don't do that!" his father yelled.

But it was already done. The flaming plastic was stuck to his sock and Danny went straight into panic mode and kicked it off. It went flying against the sink cupboard, leaving strings of melted plastic everywhere.

Cindy pried the rest of the melted bowl off the stove. It stuck to the oven mitt and she dropped the whole thing off her hand.

"What the hell happened?" asked Mr. Cheevers. But he did not wait for an answer. He went tearing back to his office to pull the door closed. "Burnt plastic is hell on computer equipment."

By then, the smoke was unbearable and I went back into the living room. I opened the storm door. I couldn't get the screen of the screen door all the way up, so I opened that door too and held it wide with my body.

I could hear Mr. Cheevers. "Cindy, Danny, everybody out. Get the back door open. No! Leave it! Wait till the smoke clears."

Danny was coughing.

Cindy said, "You made me do this! Go on! Do what Dad says, get out!"

Danny came back into the living room, shirt up to his face, same as me. "That sucks."

"Yeah, no kidding."

"Let's go outside. I can't take this." He put his foot on the screen door and shoved the little metal disc on the plunger thing to keep it open.

I grabbed my damp hoodie and pulled it on. Danny picked a few bits of plastic from his sock and stuck his feet in his runners. Then he fished around in the heap of coats and sweaters draped on the big bottom post of the stair railing, found a jacket that was too small for him—probably Randy's—and we headed outside.

The rain had gone from fizz to an annoying drizzle. I followed him around the side of the house. "What do you want to do?"

"I don't care. It's only going to be a minute before the smoke clears."

The back door was propped open. I couldn't believe how much smoke was leaking out of it. Cindy was on the landing, yelling downstairs, "Randy! Randy! Don't cram them in a ball. And do the short cycle thing! I need the washer right away!"

At home, my backyard was like, perfect. The lawn was always the same length, the fence nicely painted, the maple tree trimmed. The Cheevers' yard was like an abandoned lot.

The sidewalk was choked by grass. On the left was a really old garage and Mr. Cheever's black jeep sitting in deep, mud ruts beside it. On the right was a huge poplar tree that was awesome for climbing.

"So what do you want to do?" Danny asked me.

"Wanna go raid your neighbour's garden? He's got like, raspberries, right?"

"Grantree?" he exclaimed. "No way. Last time I even stepped in his yard, he totally threatened me. Says, 'I'm gonna have you sent to juvie, kid.' I was like, get a grip, ya old fart. It's just dirt. He does have awesome carrots and stuff, though. And last year he had tomatoes and like, cucumbers in his greenhouse."

The greenhouse was just on the other side of the fence, which was very obviously Grantree's fence and not the Cheevers'. The greenhouse was tall and the top was covered in leaves and gunge from the poplar tree.

I was getting impatient. "Can we get out of the rain, at least?"

"Yeah, yeah."

Shoulder to shoulder, we headed into his garage, if you can call it that. It was from the days when cars were a heck of a lot smaller. The roof was even made of these ancient wooden shingles, going all black and mossy. The little people door was stuck open and sometimes you'd find whiskey bottles left by drunks hanging out in there. There was an old workbench covered in random pieces of bikes and cars and like, water heaters. The whole place reeked of oil and wet wood.

Danny began rooting around in a box at the back of the garage, muttering more to himself than to me. "Who threw this out? Hey, this is mine!" A sock went flying over his shoulder onto the dirt floor.

I wandered around, looking at things and swatting mosquitoes—who didn't want to be out in the rain either. I found a busted frisbee, a jar of nuts and bolts spilled out over a metal shelf, a beer can that somebody had squashed flat.

Suddenly Danny said, "Ow!" and straightened.

"What happened?"

"There's broken glass in there!" he said, wagging his hand in pain.

I just looked at him. "I don't know how you do it."

"Do what?"

"Dude, every time I see you, you get mangled. I haven't hurt myself in weeks. Maybe months."

"Whatever. You never get injured 'cause you never do anything."

"No, it's because I'm careful."

Danny rolled his eyes. "Yeah, right. My dad always says careful people never get to be heroes or like, inventors or anything. You gotta take chances!"

"What is he, Philosopher Dude?" I said sarcastically.

"Shut up," said Danny. "You just wish you had a cool dad." He walked around sucking his injured finger, picking things up with his other hand. I leaned against the workbench, trying to think up a good reply. But the moment passed and I ended up just staring out at the rain.

Then Danny exploded again. "No way!" I looked over to see what he'd found. It was an old roast knife with half its wooden handle missing. "I totally know what I'm doing with this."

"What?"

He stood up, walked over to the door and pointed outside with the knife. "See that?"

Up in the poplar tree was the most pathetic tree fort you've ever seen. It was just three or four boards hammered on for a floor and sides.

"That's mine," said Danny firmly. "I made it when I was like, seven. Now Randy thinks he can do whatever he wants in it, the little twerp. Last week when it was sunny, he burned his initials into the main board with a magnifying glass. I been looking for something to chisel it out with."

"Nice," I said, seeing it was raining harder now. "I'll stay here."

Danny felt the edge of the big knife with his thumb, "I'll be back in a sec." Out he went into the rain.

By the time he'd climbed up the slippery tree trunk and hunched down to scrape off the initials, I was bored. I went poking around the garage some more, spending as much time swatting mosquitoes as I did checking out the junk in the dark corners. Danny was really taking his time out there.

After like, five minutes, I heard this, "Ow!" and went to the doorway to see what had happened. "You okay?" Danny was busy swearing and looking at the back of his hand. "You cut yourself?"

"No," came the reply. "Stupid mosquitoes."

I went back to the dark corner where I'd left off my survey. There was a doll head mounted on bike handlebars, but no bike. And some weird paper mâché blob that was probably a Halloween costume at one point. There was more swearing from Danny up in the tree and when I wandered back to the door, I could barely see him through the leaves. The guy was like, fifteen feet up and way the heck out on one branch.

"What are you doing?" I laughed.

"Ungh! I lost my knife! When that mosquito got me— ungh!—I got ticked and threw it away!"

"That was dumb."

He was way out over his neighbour's yard, hugging a thick branch with his arms and legs. I had to stretch my neck to see what he was doing. At his fingertips was the knife, resting on the fork of a branch just above him. "Ungh! Almost there!"

The next moment was so shocking, so stupid, I had to blink like, sixty times to make sure what I was seeing was real.

There was this huge *crack!* that sounded like a gunshot and the branch Danny was on swung down, carrying him with it. Then I heard this, "Nooo!" followed by a massive *Smaaash!*

when the branch crashed onto his neighbour's greenhouse and Danny fell through the roof and out of sight.

I stood in the doorway blinking, too stunned to move. The only sounds were the wimpy patter of rain and the swish of traffic from 111 Avenue. Then my mouth made some words, all by itself: "Wow, what an idiot."

Chilled with shock, I raced out into the rain and straight for Grantree's fence. I had realized that Danny might be dying in there with a big shard of glass stabbed into a neck artery. The fence was tall, but I hiked myself up, ready to throw a leg over. But down below, on the neighbour's side, the whole length of the fence was these glass cold frames, like little mini-greenhouses made out of old windows. I didn't trust myself to be able to jump over them, so I dropped back down and tore into the alley and around the neighbour's garage, all the time imagining gushers of Danny's artery blood spraying the greenhouse walls.

Mr. Grantree's garage was one of these perfect double things with carriage lamps and not even one dead leaf on the concrete. His back fence was just the same—perfect—and for me, totally confusing. Where the heck was the gate? I couldn't see a latch or hinges or anything. Finally I just gave up and started to climb over it, and the part I was on wiggled as only a gate would wiggle. I jumped back down, found the stupid latch and flung the gate open.

The whole yard was full of garden, from one side to the other, with a perfect sidewalk down the middle. I raced past the garage and saw the branch lying on the greenhouse. It was huge and—duh—totally dead. The top of the greenhouse had gone from a nice A-frame to a glass and metal crater. When I got the door open, I found Danny knocked out cold. Thankfully, there were no gushing arteries. His forehead was bleeding and his legs were all wonky. He had obviously hit his head on this little metal table while his body landed on a square bale of peat moss. Chunks of glass lay all around—

flat, jagged shards from little tidbits up to like, dinner plate size.

"Hey, bud," I found myself whispering, "you all right?" I couldn't tell if he was dead or unconscious and looked for signs that he was breathing. I didn't even clue in that I should be calling for help. I just kept hoping Mr. Grantree wasn't home.

Through the rain-soaked glass I saw movement and spotted Cindy climbing the fence at some kind of super speed, leaping over the cold frames with no problem.

I felt bad for Danny and tried to wake him before she got there. "Dude, you okay? Dude?" But it was pointless.

Two seconds later, Cindy swung around into the greenhouse. "Oh my god, he's just knocked out, right?"

"I think so."

Cindy leaned over her brother and smacked him on the face. "Danny! Hey! Wake up!" For the first couple of slaps he didn't make a sound. I just cringed, thinking she might actually be swatting a dead person. "Hey! Come on! You all right? Danny!" *Smack!*

He groaned and began to roll off the bag of peat moss. Cindy caught him and pushed him back. Danny snorked a big red spray of blood onto his upper lip and croaked, "I'm sorry I'm dead."

"You're not dead, Danny. Please don't say you're dead. Come on, wake up, will you?" She leaned over him and shoved his eyelids open with her thumbs.

"Aaah!" he bellowed, and pushed her hands away. "Okay, okay, I'm not dead."

In the middle of this, the tree above let go with a ton of big, heavy water drops that rattled off the broken glass.

Suddenly the muffled sound of a cell phone broke the unreality of it all. Cindy dug into a pocket and pried her phone out. "What?" she barked into it. "Why are you calling me right now? My stupid brother's almost killed himself. Yes! He fell through the roof of the neighbour's greenhouse. What?"

As Cindy listened, Danny half-opened his eyes, squinting and blinking up at his sister.

"What are you talking about?" she said into the phone. "That's ridiculous." Then to Danny she said, "You all right? Can you see this?" She snapped her fingers.

His mouth twisted with pain and frustration. "'Course I can see it." He looked up at the crater he'd made of the roof of the greenhouse. "Ugh. Now I'm really dead."

"Oh, shut up," said Cindy. "No, not you," she fake-laughed into the phone. "Text me later." She hung up and shoved the phone back into her pocket. Then she opened up with both barrels. "What the hell were you doing up there? You got a death wish?"

"Wha...?"

"Last week you were spitting over the fence at Grantree. Now you trash his greenhouse?"

In a slow, groany voice, Danny replied, "I didn't spit. It was cherry pits."

"Who cares!" Cindy yelled. Then she looked down at the busted everything. "How'd you even—? I mean, what the heck were you doing?"

Danny grimaced in pain, so I answered for him. "He found this old knife in the garage. He was going to dig out Randy's initials up in the—"

"Dad told you you couldn't go up there!" She sighed heavily, as if she had six million better things to do. Then she spotted the knife on the floor and picked it out of the glass. "Is this it?"

"Is there any blood on it?" I asked.

"You shut up," she said to me. And then, "Not that I can see."

"Good," said Danny. "I thought I was gonna land on it."

"You better hope Grantree didn't notice."

"Ha!" I put in. "I think he's gonna notice this freaking

giant branch lying on his greenhouse."

"Oh, god…" Cindy moaned.

"What?" said Danny. "Is he home?"

Cindy exploded. "For sure he's home! He had surgery last week! He had his whole hip replaced!"

"Oh no."

"When he sees what you did—oh my god, I can't even think about it. And that's nothin' to what Mom's going to do. First the TV and now this? Oh, man, when she gets home, she's gonna—"

A door slammed outside and Cindy and I looked to see who it was. *Great,* I thought. It was the neighbour himself. He was one of those thick old men who looked like a snarly bulldog: face drooping over his shirt collar, huge round chest, saggy-crotch pants. He was leaning on this rolled up umbrella like it was a cane.

"Oh, no…" Cindy mumbled. "Danny, can you get up? Can we get out of here? Grantree's coming."

That got Danny moving. Or rather, trying to move.

Cindy got her arm under his neck to support him.

"No! No!" Danny said, pushing her arm away. "Don't help me. I'm okay."

"You don't look okay. Do you think you broke anything?"

"Ungh, I don't know…"

"Let's get going. If you can move, let's move it."

Danny got himself into a sitting position. "Ow! Ow! Ow!" Once he was up, he rocked his head slowly back and forth, like he was getting water out of his ears. He wiped the blood off his top lip and smeared it on his pants.

"You got a gash on your forehead. But it's not so bad. You, kid," she said to me, "gimme a hand, would you? What are you standing there for?"

I squeezed around to Danny's far side to help, but Danny insisted, hands out like he was trying to balance, "No! No! I'm good! Let me do it!"

By then, their neighbour was trying to get down the two steps from his deck. He was having real trouble, wincing in pain and trying not to let his crappy slippers fall off. "Who's in there?" he shouted, all red around the eyes. "Hey, hey! HEY!"

I moved my head back and forth to see what Grantree was yelling at. It was Randy. He had managed to boost himself up to the top of the fence and was just swinging a leg over. When Grantree yelled at him, he stopped and dropped back to the Cheevers' side.

By then, Cindy and I were following Danny out of the greenhouse, the three of us headed for the sidewalk. Mr. Grantree had gotten down from his deck and was moving slowly toward us, squinting like every step gave him a stab of pain. "Hey," he said, his back teeth clenched with hidden fury. We stopped where we were on the sidewalk. "You, uh... you all right, kid?" There was a total disconnect between his words and the expression on his face. He sounded calm but you could totally see he wanted to rip the three of us limb from limb.

Cindy blinked a couple of times. None of us expected Grantree to be concerned. "He's okay, I think," she said. "Hey, I'm really sorry. Whatever he has to do to fix this, you bet he's gonna do it."

"That's fine," Grantree forced out. I had never seen someone talk with their back teeth clenched. "You go take care of him. Kid's gonna be sore in the morning."

"Thanks, sir. Really, I promise, whatever it takes to make this right."

Grantree's eyebrows lowered menacingly. "Yeah," he said, real slow. The whole thing was too weird for me. Mr. Grantree stood there wobbling on his umbrella, looking way more hurt than Danny.

When we got out to the alley, we ran into Randy. The kid walked backwards in front of us and spat words into Danny's face. "Who is the dinkus now?"

Danny tried to kick him, but just ended up grunting in pain as Randy spun around and jogged ahead. "And you broke the TV," Randy taunted. "Ha!"

"Randall!" Cindy snapped. "Get the hell in the house. You hear me?"

Randy went skipping ahead, singing, "TV! TV! TV! TV!"

"He's not wrong," said Cindy, taking hold of Danny's arm to steady him. "The hurt is just starting for you today."

"Oh, shut up," said Danny. And he yanked his arm out of Cindy's grip and pushed her away.

Cindy stood there, shocked for a second. "Really? You don't want my help? And you're telling me to shut up? So much for Cindy's Rule, eh? You are so dead. I can't wait till Mom gets home. Actually, I'm gonna phone her right now and see what she wants to do."

Danny took a limping step toward her. "No-no-no! Don't call!"

But Cindy had walked away, her phone out, stabbing numbers with a thumb. We watched her stride toward the house with the phone up to her ear, stomp in through the open door, and step up into the kitchen.

I could see Grantree, still out on his sidewalk. He wasn't doing anything. It just looked like he was hanging around, making sure we were no longer a threat to his yard.

"What do you want to do?" I asked.

"I gotta sit down. Or lie down. I really hurt my back."

"What about your head?"

"It's just a gash. I'll live."

"You want me to help you?"

"Yeah," he said, and put one hand on my nearest shoulder. We headed toward the house, him shuffle-limping the whole way.

"I'm good from here," said Danny, clinging to the door handle. "I'll talk to you later, okay?"

"Seriously?"

"Yeah, yeah. I'll call you later."

As I started away, I looked back to see him easing himself inside. Wow, I thought, wherever he went, the guy left a trail of disasters behind him. I didn't realize then, but I was already his next victim.

Chapter 4

When I got home, my mom didn't say anything about the phone call—which kind of confirmed it had something to do with my birthday. She didn't say anything about anything, for that matter. She was too busy stomping angrily around the kitchen.

"How'd it go at the doctor's?"

She stopped in her tracks, mouth firmly set. "What?"

My mother never said "what?" It was always "pardon me?" or "excuse me?"

"Oh, nothing."

"Fine." *Stomp, stomp, stomp.*

"Can I put the groceries away?"

"No!"

There were about six grocery bags still on the kitchen floor. She must have gone shopping after the doctor's. My mom always shopped at this horrible discount place that had like, rubbery carrots and cans of stuff that were probably made in the last century. My dad didn't mind. He even made it worse by bringing home stuff his "clients" brought him. His clients were just people visiting his building. But there were regulars. Some farmer guy kept bringing him bags of crappy green potatoes every Thursday that my mom had to peel. And there was always stuff that somebody just wanted to get rid of, like rhubarb or zucchini or bags of crab apples. We weren't actually poor, but wow, my parents sure acted like it.

I did my special Brian lunge down the stairs, trying to make it all the way to the bottom without touching any steps. I was sooo close!

Even though my mom had just bought groceries, lunch was horrible. She served the boys their sandwiches first.

"Where's the top bread?" Kyle asked.

My mom set their sippy cups down in front of them. Yeah, they had sippy cups. Not that they needed them. Mom just hated the idea of wasting milk if they ever tipped. "What?" she said, still distracted and annoyed. "It's called open-faced."

I just stared at it when she served me. It was a piece of bread with pickles barely hidden under a melted processed cheese square. The boys each got half a slice. I got a whole one. "That's all I get?"

"Don't be greedy. If you eat that, I'll make more."

The boys picked at the cheese. Just to prove how hungry I was, I folded the bread and ate the whole thing in two bites.

"Bri-an!" Jayden scolded me, as if I'd done something against the rules.

Mom had cut an orange into quarters. "You ate that fast," she said, dropping two pieces of orange onto my empty plate. The other two went to the boys.

"Uh-huh." She was in a freako mood. I didn't want to risk angering her even more, so I kept my trap shut.

Making a whole bunch of noise, she made me another

open-faced sandwich. That got devoured, same as the first. When she finally sat down to eat her own lunch, I was getting up.

"Are you finished?" She seemed genuinely surprised.

"Yup." She was in such a weird, angry mood, I couldn't wait get out of there and back downstairs.

I spent the afternoon on my bed, playing games and posting stupid comments online. I didn't hear a thing from Danny. I couldn't believe how dumb that whole greenhouse thing was. And the TV. And what was he doing, spitting cherry pits over his neighbour's fence? Seriously, the guy was trouble with a capital T.

Around five thirty, I got off my bed and went upstairs to see if supper was ready yet. Mom had calmed down a bit by then, but I could tell she was still in a twist about something.

"Oh, there you are," she said. "Were you sleeping?"

"Not really," I said. I'd been messing around with my plasticine and playing games on my phone.

She was setting the kitchen table. "Your father will be home in a minute."

I didn't know what she meant. He was always home at this time. "Yeah?"

"He's very disappointed in you."

"Huh?"

"Breaking that man's greenhouse? Now I know why you've been hiding out in your room."

I was so stunned, I couldn't get my mouth to work properly. "What? I didn't—no, it—"

"I just got off the phone with Mrs. Cheevers. What's his name? Graintree? He's threatening to call the police."

"What?" For a second I could not wrap my brain around what she'd said.

Mom was angry. "Yeah, my day just keeps getting better and better. She said the man is home recovering from surgery. What on earth were you two thinking?"

I finally found my words. "Us two? I didn't do anything! Danny climbed up his stupid tree and fell down without me being anywhere near!"

"That's not what I heard."

"What? What did you hear?"

She pursed her lips in a way that always made me completely crazy. "We'll talk about it when your father gets home."

I tried getting a crowbar of words back into the conversation, to pry it open so I could defend myself, but she wouldn't budge. So I threw my hands up and went around into the living room where the boys were watching cartoons. For the first time ever, Kyle's nose did not seem to be dripping. And Jayden's mosquito bites were covered in animal band-aids.

They have the worst taste in cartoons I've ever seen. They liked every piece of crap I hated. Being ticked and not caring what they thought, I grabbed the remote and changed the channel to something random.

"Hey-ey!" they said in chorus. "What are you doing? That was our show!"

"Tough."

"Mom!"

I slumped into an easy chair and looked to see if there was any good stuff recorded. Nothing new. Nothing good. So I switched it to football, which I never watched. The boys went flying into the kitchen to whine their complaint. "He changed the channel! Now he has the remote! We were watching Mitzy Pits! It's not fair." I'd heard the same garbage about a bazillion times and today, they could drop dead.

Apparently Mom thought so too. She sent them to their room and left me alone. I had no idea why. So I watched the football game for the next twenty minutes, till Dad got home. By then it was close to six.

My dad is one of those old-school dads who goes to work, makes money and leaves everything about house and kids to our mom. His main job was being tired. And he was an expert at it.

As soon as he was in the door, the boys came tearing out of their room and went for the hugs and their daddy time. That meant that as soon as he sat down in the kitchen, they climbed up onto his lap and hijacked his first half an hour at home. Today they got to him down in the landing, before he had his shoes off.

"We went to the doctor!" Kyle announced.

I was way too antsy to sit there. So I got up and went around into the kitchen and slouched in Mom's chair to listen.

"I know," Dad said. "Are you all right?"

Mom was at the kitchen counter. "Oooh, I've had a day of it. It was a complete waste of time. We already knew it isn't allergies."

"No? What is it, then?"

"He doesn't know. He's sending Kyle for more tests. To a nose specialist. They got us in next Monday. At least we don't have to wait too long."

"So what's wrong with him?" Dad came up into the kitchen. He pushed through the boys and went straight to the fridge for his after-work beer. Whenever he took his hat off after work, he always had a piece of his white hair sticking out in some weird direction. He never noticed and he never cared. Today, it was a bunch of jagged spikes veering off to the left.

"They have to do a scope thing up in his sinuses or whatever. Polyps. He might have polyps. That's what's making his nose run."

It was Kyle's turn to interject. "I got plops, Daddy!"

Dad laughed.

"Paul-ips," Mom corrected him. "Like Saint Paul?"

There was silence in the kitchen, as if no one knew what she was talking about.

Dad cracked his beer and sat down opposite me. The boys piled onto his lap. Out of habit, Dad tried to keep Kyle's nose away from the white shirt of his security guard uniform. "So what do they do about 'em?"

"Well," Mom huffed, furious, "he wasn't going to do anything! Ten months of this nonsense. With the drugstore full of things we could use? Then he says, oh no, not till after we see the specialist. I got so angry! I told him I wasn't leaving without a prescription."

"Okay…"

"Then we stood in line forever. It's a spray."

"It goes up here!"

"Kyle, get your finger out of there."

"Did it hurt?"

"No. Yes! But it tickled."

"Did you ask about Jayden's tummy pains?"

Jayden had been having stomach troubles on and off for the last couple of weeks.

"Oh, he poked him in the side and looked down his throat. Then he says, 'It's probably gas or growing pains.' I swear we need a new doctor. All morning, for what?"

"That's too bad."

"That's not the half of it," Mom said.

"Oh?"

"I asked Dr. Tan how Kyle could have gotten these polyps things—if that's what he has. You know what he said?"

"No."

"He asked if there was dust or cobwebs or dirty carpets in our house. I was so insulted. Of course not, I told him. I clean every day. Their clothes are spotless. And my house is immaculate. And you know what he says?"

"What?"

"He says, 'Well, perhaps your house is too clean.' Can you imagine? I just about packed up the kids and walked right out of there."

Jayden decided to steer the conversation back to hilarity. "And Kyle's got pull-ups in his nose!"

"That's nice," Dad said. Then to Mom: "I imagine you were upset."

"Oh, like I said, that's not the half of my day. You have to hear about Brian."

That got me out of my slouch in a hurry.

"Why? What's up with him?" Dad just stared at me, blank-faced.

"Apparently he was over at Danny Cheever's house and—"

"Can't I tell it?" I barged in.

Dad held up a hand to tell me to keep quiet.

Mom continued. "The two of them broke into a greenhouse."

"No, we didn't!" I said. "I wasn't even—"

"Hey, hey!" Dad stopped me with a pointing finger.

But he couldn't stop Kyle. "He broke all the glass and nearly died!"

Dad clutched his beer and shook his head slowly, as if he had the weight of the world on his shoulders. "Really."

Mom was over by the sink drying cutlery, trying way too mildly to get the boys' attention. "Kyle, come on now; Jayden, you too."

"Yeah, but—"

"That's enough there," Dad snapped at Kyle. "I need to hear this from the beginning."

"Brian started it!"

"What?" I managed to squeak in.

"Yeah! And he broke everything! *Pechew-bala-kshsh!*"

"Boys, boys!" Dad said. "Let your mother speak, would you?"

"How does she know?" I said. "Why can't I tell it?"

Dad gave me a look to shush me.

"Thank you," said Mom, wagging her dishtowel for effect. "Apparently they were out in the backyard, up in this tree, and Danny got pushed down and broke through a greenhouse."

"Wait. What? No!" I said, nearly jumping out of my chair. "That's not even close to what happened!"

"*Pechew!*" Jayden said, copying Kyle.

"All right now," Dad said, attempting to calm everyone. "I still don't know who we're talking about."

"It was at the neighbour's!" shouted Kyle.

"Whose neighbour? Ours?"

"No! It was—"

"Kyle, stop," said Mom.

"I didn't push anybody!" I said. "You guys don't know anything!"

"Well, that's what Mrs. Cheevers told me," said Mom. "Didn't Danny fall through the roof of it?"

"*Daaaddy*," Kyle whined and began picking at the buttons on his shirt.

"Shush, shush," Dad said calmly. I could tell that all he wanted was his dinner and some TV time. "Just let one person speak. And not you," he said to Kyle with a wink.

"Yes, Daddy."

"We got suckers at the doctor's," Jayden announced. "Mom says we have to save them till after supper. Wanna see?"

"Sure, yeah." He set Jayden on the floor and as he toddled off toward his bedroom, Dad asked, "So, Brian was over at the Cheevers'?"

"Yes," said Mom.

"And he broke somebody's greenhouse."

"Apparently," Mom said.

"No!" I shouted.

"Well, if that's not what happened, what did? You were there, weren't you?"

By then, I was red-faced. "I was the only one who saw it!"

"Danny saw it," whispered Kyle.

"That's ridiculous," said Mom.

Dad moved Kyle's hand away from his shirt buttons.

"Please, no one speak but Brian. I want to hear this."

Thank god, I thought. *Finally!* But luck was not on my side. The moment I drew breath to start speaking, the phone rang. Dad turned around to reach for the phone on the counter behind him.

Mom rushed toward him. "It's for me. It's for me."

"Yeah?" Dad asked. "Okay."

She waved her hand in a "gimme" gesture and he passed it to her. Stepping back to the sink, she said, "Hello?"

Dad looked at me. "So?"

But I couldn't not listen to Mom. It might be Mrs. Cheevers calling again.

"Yes, hi. Um, yes, he's home. But I haven't had a chance to discuss it with him." We all sat in silence for a second. The only one who moved was my dad, prying Kyle's fingers off his shirt buttons again.

In a really quiet voice, I said to Dad, "I didn't do anything."

"Wait," he said, pointing his beer bottle at me.

I sat back, ready to explode.

Mom listened for a bit. She had the phone tucked into the crook of her neck as she opened a cupboard and began fishing around at the back for something. Her hand came out with birthday candles. Must be for the next day, I thought. "Of course," she said into the phone. "Absolutely. No, he's right here, I can tell him… All right, that should be fine." She listened for a while longer, dumping the candles out onto the counter to count them. Then she said, "A website? Yes, of course." She motioned for my father to give her a pen and paper. Birthday candles rolled off the counter onto the floor. Dad reached into the drawer under the phone cradle, then handed her a pencil and a white envelope from the counter. I jumped up to see what she was jotting down. In her old-fashioned writing, it looked like *Mrrmmrrmm dot org.*

Jayden had toddled back into the kitchen with two suckers, a red one and a blue one. "Who's that?" he asked. "Who is she talking to?"

Kyle lifted his shoulders. "I don't know. Who is she talking to, Daddy?"

"I guess we'll see in minute."

Jayden returned to his perch on Dad's other knee. "Don't touch mine!" Kyle ripped the blue sucker from his brother's hand. Dad plucked both suckers from them and laid them on the table. Jayden stuck his tongue out at Kyle.

"Perfect," Mom said, looking like she was going to hang up the phone. "Oh, no problem. I was just getting dinner ready... You bet. And thank you so much for this. It's going to change Brian's life, I'm sure." *Click.* She bent to pick up the fallen candles without even thinking about me.

"Change Brian's life?" I said. "Who was that?"

I startled her out of her thoughts. "Oh, sorry." She handed the phone to Dad to return it to the cradle and said to him, "We have to talk after this."

She took so long spitting it out, I actually shouted, "What???"

"Hey, boy," said Dad. "That's enough of that."

I took a long, slow breath so I didn't completely lose it.

Mom stood up and began laying the candles in a row on the counter. But with so many things to think about she got flustered and wagged her hands. "Okay. First things first. This Graintree business."

My mouth opened to scream but I caught myself. "Grantree."

"Pardon me?"

"His neighbour's name. It's Grantree."

"Lovely," Dad said to me. "Weren't you about to tell it? You were there, right?"

"Ugh," I groaned. "Yes." I felt so torn and frustrated, wanting to know what this life-changing thing was, that my words came out in a muddle. "Of course I was there. I saw the whole thing. I didn't even leave the garage. He was up in the tree before I even knew what he was doing and *bam!*—he crashed down and nearly killed himself."

"Well," Mom said to Dad, "apparently this Graintree fellow—"

"Grantree," I corrected her again.

"Grantree," she said. "He says the greenhouse can't really be fixed. It was some kind of kit and they don't make them anymore." I got my hopes up right then. But they were dashed with the next sentence. "But he can't even clean up the mess they made. I guess he's home recovering from hip surgery. So if the boys work for him for a while, the parents won't have to pay for the damage."

"Why should you pay?" I shouted. "I didn't do anything! And why should I have to work? Aaah! I was in the stupid garage the whole time! Did she say I pushed him? I didn't push anybody!"

"All right, now," said Dad. "You'd better calm down. And when's dinner? I'm starving over here."

"It will be a couple of minutes," Mom said a little impatiently. "They want him over at this Graintree's place tomorrow morning at nine."

"To do what?" I snapped.

"Hey, hey," Dad said.

Mom continued. "They want him to spend an hour or so working for him."

Dad pointed at me to stop me from interrupting. "No, no! So they're going to clean it up or whatever?"

"Among other things. They'll work it off."

"All right then," said Dad, turning to me. "Nine o'clock sharp. You get that glass cleaned up and then see what he needs doing, understand?"

There was a very long pause. My brain was so confused by the phone call and my inner volcano, I just said, "Fine. Just *please* tell me what they said on the phone!"

"What?" said Mom. "Oh." She heaved this big sigh, blinking away some strong emotion. She looked at Dad, completely ignoring me. "You have to give me a minute. To collect my thoughts." She leaned back against the counter and held it for support, taking deep breaths and blowing the air out slowly.

"So?" Dad asked. "You all right?"

Mom was so overcome with emotion, she looked from the floor to Dad, and from Dad to the floor. "They, um, called this morning."

"Okay?"

"They called...it was, um...about Brian."

"Yes?"

"An agency...a social agency...some adoption place. His mother, his birth mother was...is trying to contact him."

As I sat there listening, I felt all of the blood drain from my head and torso. "What?"

"She...um...wants to call him on his birthday." Her chin started crinkling with emotion. She was still looking from the floor to my dad. "He's going to talk to her. Our Brian. She's going to call in the morning, sometime around eleven." And her face crumpled into tears.

"There, there, now," Dad consoled her. "It's all right."

"Who's calling?" I demanded. And when nobody answered, I pretty much yelled, "The agency or my birth mom?"

Dad gave me a look that said, *You watch your tone.*

Mom got a kleenex from the counter and honked her nose. "They can finally talk to each other. For the first time. Oh, Richard..." She stepped close to Dad and pushed between the boys to put her cheek against his.

The boys began rebelling. "Mom! Ew! Stop!"

She straightened and wiped her eyes. "Are you okay with this?" she asked Dad.

He made a weird face and wrinkled his forehead. "Um... I...I suppose. I don't see why not."

Finally she looked at me. "You make sure you're here

when she phones, all right? Oh! I have to get back to them right away. She's going to call after you get back from Graintree's. Eleven o'clock."

I just looked at the whole bunch of them like, wow. Then I said in my nicest voice, "I'll be here." Well, maybe it wasn't my nicest voice. I got that eye-rolling glance from Dad again.

Mom wiped her eyes. "We'd better have dinner now. Your father's starving."

"I'm hungry too!" Kyle said.

Mom scooped up the candles and looked at Dad, her chin wobbling with emotion. "And it's going to be on his birthday. It's almost too much." Then she looked out the side window of the kitchen and wiped her eyes. "Oh, I hope the neighbours didn't see." And she adjusted the little half-curtain over the bottom of the window.

The whole thing was just beyond words. They could have their crazy town. I had way more important stuff to think about. Tomorrow, there was going to be presents, lame singing and cake. Tomorrow, I had to kill Danny. And holy crap, tomorrow, I was going to hear my birth mother's voice for the first time. And I had absolutely no idea how to deal with that.

Chapter 5

What I knew about myself, about my adopted self, you could probably fit into a sardine tin and still have room for the sardines. I knew which hospital I was born in (the Royal Alex). I knew my mom was a teenager when she got pregnant and I knew she had to hide her pregnancy from most of her family. Oh, and I knew her last name was Kelly and she was from Edmonton. That was it. The rest I had to guess, since my adoptive parents weren't exactly blabbermouths on the subject.

So that night, after the boys were in bed and my dad was asleep in front of the TV, I went into the kitchen to talk to my mom. She was sitting at the table folding a pile of the boys' little t-shirts.

I stood beside her, hands in my pockets. "So," I started, trying to be all chill about it, "what did the agency person say?"

"Brian, quit looming over me. It's spooky."

"What?"

"I'd tell you to quit being so tall, but that wouldn't work, would it?"

"Sorry." I pulled out a chair and hunched over the table. "So, did they tell you where she lives or…what she's like or anything?"

Mom was having none of it. "Oh, I'm sure you'll find out in good time."

"What does that mean? Did they tell you or not?"

She laid a hand on top of the pile of t-shirts and sighed. I could see she was upset. "Oh, Brian, how am I supposed to answer that?"

"Huh?"

"You shouldn't hear that stuff from me." And she got up and went quietly into the boys' room with their laundry.

Great, I thought. Was there some big secret I was missing? Was my birth mom like, in prison for the last twelve years?

Of course I couldn't get to sleep that night. I lay there, a pathetic brew of happy, sad and completely freaked out.

The next morning when I woke up, I was so excited about talking to my birth mom that I forgot it was my birthday. Birthdays were never a big deal at our house anyway. Nobody ever had a big party or friends over or anything. But talking to my birth mom? Now *that* was incredible.

I ran up the stairs to the landing and looked outside to see what the weather was like. If it was hurricaning, maybe I wouldn't have to work for Danny's stupid neighbour. But it was just grey and cloudy. Ugh.

When I got up to the kitchen, Mom was wiping the boys' faces with a washcloth after breakfast. "Oh, there you are, Brian. Good morning! Happy birthday."

The boys just stared at me and muttered unhappily, "Happy birthday," and went back to closing their eyes and waiting for the wash cloth to smear them, like baby birds. "Mu-u-u-um!" Kyle whined. Mom ignored him.

"You must be so excited," she said to me. "I have everything all ready for you. Look! Why don't you sit down?"

The table was set for me with a bowl and spoon and a folded paper towel. *Fancy*, I thought. *Hoity-toity. Look at me, all twelve and getting to wipe my own face.*

I did my usual thing and ate in silence, reading from my phone. Dad was already long gone to work. Mom headed off to the boys' bedroom with them. I heard her trying to talk Kyle into taking his medicine.

"I don't want no plop splay!"

"I don't care. You want to have a drippy nose your whole life?"

"But it tickles too much!"

"I don't care. Just lie down. It will be over in a second."

Through the boys' open bedroom door, I could see Kyle's legs stretched out, his slippered feet nervously paddling the air. Jayden was standing over him, sucking his thumb. I didn't even hear the squirt of the spray. All I saw was the effect. The whole lower half of Kyle's body lifted off the floor and his legs went into some kind of octopus seizure, flinging back and forth and around each other like flapping noodles. Then they thunked down like the kid was dead. Jayden just stood there, mouth open, his thumb suddenly too small for the hole.

Oh, thank god that's over, I thought. But it wasn't. She had to do the other nostril. I turned sideways in my chair and put a hand up to block the view. But I still heard the thunk of his slippered heels on the floor.

When it was all over, I was two slurps away from finishing my cereal. Mom and the boys came trooping out of the bedroom like nothing had happened. Well, except for Kyle. He looked like someone had just shot his nose full of pickle juice.

"But I wanna go outside!" Jayden was whining. He was so

close behind Mom, he bumped into her when she stopped by the kitchen table. "It's not even raining!"

"No, but have you seen yourself? You can't stop scratching those mosquito bites. I'm not letting you out to get more!"

"But Brian goes out!"

"He's older," she said. And then to me, "Aren't you, Brian? Are you ready for presents?"

"Always."

She turned around to open the hall closet, and handed Kyle a wrapped gift and Jayden two cards to bring to me. While Kyle was walking the four steps toward me, he gave a huge dry snork. I guess the plop splay was working.

Jayden shook the cards like they were full of gold. "Can I open one, too?"

"It's not your birfday," Kyle said to him.

"Can I help you open your present, Brian?"

Before I could answer, Kyle stuck his beak in again. "It's just a stupid hoodie," he said. "He's too old for toys."

I gave him a scowl. "Thanks, Kyle. I'll be sure to ruin Christmas for you next year."

"Now, boys…" Mom said. Kyle gave another huge snork. "Where did you learn that?" she asked, annoyed.

"I saw Daddy do it. And he globbed into the sink."

Mom's head whipped around. "Which sink?"

Kyle pointed like he was in trouble. "That one."

"The kitchen sink? Oh…" She immediately went over to investigate. She looked once and was about to leave, then looked again. This time, she ran the water for a second and moved the tap back and forth before turning it off.

While this was going on, I set the cards aside and let Jayden help me tear into the gift. It was a hoodie, exactly the brand I liked, dark green and smelling new. "Thanks, Mom."

"Open the cards."

I dug open the first one. There was a farm scene on the outside with the words *Dear Son* in curly letters. There was a twenty dollar bill inside. *May all your Birthday wishes come true*, it said; *Love, Mom and Dad.*

"The money's from your uncle Ford."

"Yeah?"

"He phoned and said he was too late to mail a card."

"Nice!"

"Open the other one."

"How come he gets so much money?" Kyle interjected. "Uncle Ford only gave me and Jayden ten bucks."

"You know why," Mom told him. "He's twice your age."

"So?"

The second card was from this aunt I'd never met. She lived in England and on Christmas and birthdays, she always sent us the weirdest gifts. Last year she got the family a gift certificate to the zoo. That wasn't so bad, except Jayden threw up in the car on the way and even after he got cleaned up and we saw all the critters, we had to get back into the barf car that had been sitting in the sun all afternoon. One year she sent me a purple umbrella for my birthday. I was like, nine and it was a perfect gift 'cause, you know, that's what all the guys at school were using on rainy days.

Anyway, as I was opening the card, I was thinking, *gift card*. But when I pulled it out of the envelope, my heart literally leapt for joy. The card said, in big letters, *Free Pizza*. What the heck? Was my aunt like, psychic or something? Did she know I was starving all the time? But when I opened the card up, it was not anything that I expected. My aunt had made a donation to a charity in my name. Some polar bear named Pizza had been living in an undersize cage in a Chinese shopping mall. They wanted to ship him off somewhere to give him better living conditions. Me not getting actual pizza was one thing. That was like a punch in the gut. But the picture of the polar bear totally slayed me. He was lying on his side staring like, wow, lost. "That's nice," I said and put the card face down, because it was freaking me out.

After breakfast, my Mom put the cards on the mantel in the living room and I brought my new hoodie downstairs with me. (I totally forgot to try my Brian lunge.) I wasn't going to wear the hoodie to work for Grantree, so I laid it out on my bed, still shaking my head over the disappointment of that free pizza card.

Half an hour later, I arrived at Danny's with my brain like, overwhelmed. All I could think was, in two hours I was going to hear my birth mom's voice for the first time. Danny's front door was closed so I headed around to the back. I was so distracted that when I knocked on the door, I had to remind myself to be angry.

There was no answer, which was weird. Even standing outside, I could still smell the smoke from Cindy's melted bowl from the day before. I waited a bit before knocking again and turned around to see if Danny was maybe at Grantree's already. But he wasn't. I did notice that someone had gotten the giant branch off the greenhouse.

Then suddenly the door flew open. I spun around, but there was no one there.

From ten feet away I heard Randy's voice: "Come in, already!"

So I stepped in and leaned up the short flight of stairs to the kitchen, where the smell of melted plastic still lingered. Cindy was there, talking to Danny. I could see the gash and the lump on his forehead, which was turning colour.

"I don't care what you think," she was saying to him. "Eat these." And she held out something on the palm of her hand.

"But I feel fine!" he said. "And I hate those dinky aspirins. They taste like baby barf."

"We're all out of the normal ones. Now, eat."

Danny picked up the two aspirins and popped them into his mouth. "Bleah," he said, striding over to the sink for a glass of water to wash them down. "Huh," he said to me, by way of saying hi.

"Now move it," said Cindy. "It's almost nine."

Danny limped down the few steps to the landing and pushed by me outside. He was nice and held the door for me. But as soon as he let the door swing back and turned around, I punched him in the chest.

"Ow!"—*cough*—"What the hell was that for?"

"Are you kidding?" I snapped. "Why am I even here?"

With his left hand, Danny massaged his chest where I'd hit him. With his right, he reached out and grabbed me by the hair and shook me back and forth, saying, "Don't—friggin'—sucker-punch—me—ever—again. You hear me?" And he threw me away.

The second he let go of me, I plowed him in the chest again.

"Ow!" he yelled. And the next word out of his mouth was an extremely loud swear word.

"What did you tell your parents?" I barked at him. "That I pushed you out of the tree?"

He was now rubbing his chest with two hands. "I'm gonna tear your head off for that."

"Shut up and answer my question!"

"I didn't tell them anything about you. I said I was climbing on that big branch and it broke. Duh. Nothing else."

"Then why am I here?"

"I don't know! Maybe Cindy or Randy said something. When my mom heard, she lost her mind. She went over to Grantree's and had this big confab. Then she called your place. The next thing I hear is you're coming to help me. I didn't even know why!"

"Well, tell them I didn't do anything, all right? I was standing in the stupid garage."

"I already did! They didn't believe me!"

I just stared at him, not sure if I believed *him*. "Well, try again, would you?"

"Yeah, that's not going to happen."

"Why not?"

"What? My dad's been on this video conference since like, four. And my mom's already gone to work. Besides, she's in like, total revenge mode for me busting her new TV."

"Great. I don't want to spend the summer at your neighbour's. Do you know what we have to do for him?"

"No idea. Sucks we even gotta go over there. Last night I had to saw up that stupid branch. It took me forever! All I had was this crappy little hand saw. And the old fart was watching me the whole time. Ugh. The guy creeps me out."

"Is he really gonna call the cops if we don't show up?"

"Him? Probably. Don't worry about it. How bad could it be?"

I rubbed my hair where he'd pulled it. I really did not want to be angry with anybody today. "Fine," I said. "I have to be back home before eleven."

We went around the garage and entered Grantree's back-yard through the secret gate. When we got past the garage, I spotted the jumbled pile of logs Danny had sawn, lying near the cold frames.

All the way up the walkway, I could see Grantree's face in the kitchen window, watching us. Then he looked away, probably at the clock. By the time we got up onto his deck, he had the back door open, clinging to the handle for support. His other hand held his lower back, as if the pain was killing him. The guy was wearing saggy jeans and this new work shirt, the buttons straining over his huge chest. "First things first," he said in his gravelly voice. "You clean up all that mess in there. I put a box out for the glass, and a dustpan and whatnot. There's some gloves, too. You understand?"

I was like, scared of him and couldn't even open my mouth. Not Danny. He squinted up at the man and showed his buck teeth right up to the gums. "Say again?"

Grantree lowered his eyes and pointed to the greenhouse. "Glass, box, garbage. Then you two come see me for what's after."

Danny cocked his head. "What was that?"

I could not believe Danny was being such a jerk.

Grantree looked me up and down. "Explain it to your friend, would you? It ain't that difficult." And back he went into the house, wincing, snorting and shaking his head, all at the same time.

When we got into the greenhouse, Danny burst out laughing. "D'you see his face? What a doofus!"

"Yeah," I said quietly. "Hilarious." All I could think was, Grantree might be all mean and scary, but Danny was totally kicking him when he was down.

Cleaning up the glass from Danny's disaster was fairly straightforward and it didn't take very long. Grantree had lined a cardboard box with a black garbage bag and we filled it with shards using the work gloves and the dustpan he'd left for us. After the glass was cleaned up, we sat on the little table and peat bag with our backs to the house, pretending we were still working.

Danny started gabbing about stupid stuff—game characters and some lame TV show. I was still angry with him, so I didn't say too much. It never even crossed my mind to tell him it was my birthday. All I cared about was what was going to happen at eleven o'clock.

After a bit, I spotted Grantree in the window again and Danny jumped down off the table. "I'll go see what's next." He headed toward the house.

While he and Grantree talked at the back door, I picked up this little garden trowel and began flipping it, all bored and distracted. On the third flip, I totally flubbed the thing and it went flying off my hand and banged against the glass opposite me.

"Oops."

As I picked it up, I saw Danny and Grantree staring at me from the door, Danny with his hands held out as if to say,

Seriously? When he returned, he examined the glass walls of the greenhouse. "What was that?"

"Nothin'."

"He wants us to weed his carrots."

"How long will that take?" I asked, thinking about eleven o'clock.

"Why? Are you like, allergic to them?"

"How can you be allergic to a carrot?"

"Hey, Tyler's allergic to underwear."

I just looked at him. "That's the dumbest thing I ever heard."

"No, really," Danny insisted. "They think it's the elastic."

"So what does he wear? Not-so-tighty-whities?"

"Maybe his mom makes him poop in a gerbil cage."

"What? Why? Did he poop in his gaunch before?"

"I dunno. But the gerbil's gonna be like, 'Aaah! What did I ever do to you?'"

We got out into the garden and found the carrots. There were old boards laid on the ground between the rows, so it was actually only half as much to weed, thank god. Though the tops were about a foot high, the carrots themselves were still baby, about as big as a pinkie finger. We found a five gallon pail to throw the weeds into and I started on one row and Danny worked another beside me. All through weeding, Danny kept grunting whenever he moved.

"You all right?"

"Yeah, it's just my back from yesterday."

The dirt was pretty gooey after a week of rain, so when you pulled one weed out, half the garden came with it. I clued in that I had to hold the carrots down while I weeded. Grant-ree's face stayed glued to the window for the next ten minutes. I could see him leaning against the counter, one shoulder up, like he was pressing a hand into his back. And even when he disappeared to go to the bathroom or whatever, he returned every now and again to check up on us.

I have to admit, I didn't mind the weeding. Well, except for the mosquitoes. My neck was black from swatting them with dirty hands. But being outside, doing something useful, was kind of cool. The clouds were moving in slow motion overhead. And these two robins kept hopping along the fence, checking to see if we were digging up any worms.

Danny was speed-weeding and ended up way ahead of me in his row. All of a sudden I heard him laughing to himself.

"What's up with you?"

He half turned and showed me a green carrot top with only the tiniest cap left of the orange part. His cheek was full.

"What are you doing?" I exclaimed.

"*Shh!* I'm putting them back in with just the tops. In the fall, he's gonna get a surprise. 'Ooh,' he said in a goofy voice. 'Look at all my lovely carrots! Num-num-num. *Whaaat?*'"

"You're an idiot. How many have you eaten?"

"Like, half the row."

"Oh, dude, he's gonna have your head in a bag."

"Whatever."

We got back to work. But two seconds later, Danny said, "Whoa! Who's that?" He was staring at Grantree's house. When I turned, I didn't see anything. There were only the three main floor windows, since the deck blocked most of the basement ones. I could sort of see Grantree, still in the kitchen. "Who's what?"

"I thought I saw somebody else in there."

"Does Grantree live by himself?"

"Yeah, totally."

"What did you see?"

"Oh, whatever. Nothin'." Danny shrugged and returned to weeding the carrots.

When we were done with the carrots, we swished our hands clean in Grantree's rain barrel and wiped them on our pants. Grantree came to the door and scowled at the five gallon pail, which was about half full of weeds and muck. Then he looked over our heads at the garden, trying to see our work. Without the weeds supporting the plants (and in Danny's case, without the roots), all the carrot tops had flopped over and looked pathetic. Apparently, this was normal, for Grantree never said a word about it. Instead, he rubbed his blob nose and said, "Nine o'clock tomorrow. Now get outa here."

But Danny didn't move. "Can I ask you something?"

"What's that?"

"Is there some woman in your house?"

Grantree squinted at him. "Woman? There's no woman."

"I thought I saw—"

But Grantree ignored him and let the screen door bounce closed on its springs.

"Maybe you're hallucinating," I told him.

"Oh, shut up. I saw what I saw."

At the back gate, we dumped the weeds into the box of broken glass. Then I tied up the garbage bag and left the box, bag and all, beside his two garbage cans.

We tromped up the Cheevers' overgrown sidewalk. When we got to the door, Danny asked, "You coming in? Wanna do some gaming?"

"I dunno," I answered, digging out my phone. "I gotta be home by eleven."

Danny peeked at my screen. "It's only twenty after ten. You got time."

"Naw," I said, just not feeling it. "I'm gonna head home."

"What are you doing this aft?"

"I dunno. I'll text you."

"Cool. Ciao, baby."

I left him by their back door. I was no more than two steps away when it sunk in, what was happening at eleven o'clock. My stomach dropped about ten feet and the muddy hairs on the back of my neck stood up in an electric frizz. I

56

kept thinking, *Oh, calm down, it's not that big a deal.* Then I realized, yeah, it is that big a deal. Teeny tiny me lived inside this woman for like, the first nine months of my life. Then I was ripped away from her and sent to live with creaky old gnomes for twelve years. And today, in half an hour, I was finally going to hear the sound of her voice.

Ugh. By the time I opened the back gate at home, my stomach was in knots. How on earth was I gonna be able to form a sentence at eleven o'clock? 'Cause right then, I felt like a total gibbering idiot.

Once I got in the door, Mom called from the living room, "Brian, is that you?"

My whole body was shaking by then. Sweat dripped from my armpits as I bent down to take off my runners. "Yeah," I replied, hoping she wouldn't hear me and I could escape to my room without talking to her.

But she shuffled into the kitchen and stood at the top of the stairs. "How did it go?"

"Huh?"

"Working for Mr. Graintree."

"Oh, uh, all right. We cleaned stuff up and weeded his garden."

"That's nice," she said, leaning back to look at the clock. "Are you going downstairs?"

"Yeah."

"All right, then. Um…" Her face was squinched with concern. She looked even older than usual and sort of fragile. "I'll call you when it's time."

"Okay."

I was too messed up to try the Brian lunge and almost had to go down the stairs like a toddler, one step at a time. When I got to my room and closed the door, I realized I did not want to be alone. But I sure didn't want to be with those loons upstairs. I could hear the boys running, their thumping footsteps shaking the floor above me. I didn't hate them, I just really wished they were other people.

My room felt way too small and I found myself trying to see outside. I say trying, because Mom had sprayed my bedroom windows with this fake frost stuff so pervs couldn't see in. According to her, the only thing worse than perverts spying on you was being one. With a thumbnail, I'd scraped off a little hole. But it still felt claustrophobic. I only got like, a two second glance outside and it hit me. That stupid polar bear on that card, stuck in his cage with the fake snowbanks, far from home. This room, I thought, was my cage, with strangers all around me. It was a totally lame, totally emotional comparison. But I couldn't get it out of my head.

Over the next half hour, I did everything I could to distract myself from what was coming. I changed out of my muddy jeans. I tried reading. I tried arranging my meagre comic collection. Nothing worked. So I sat there staring at my phone without really seeing it. Every once in a while I'd notice how tense I was. My eyebrows were up, my mouth stretched into cry-face. And right in the middle of it, I'd burst into this crazy, happy sob-laugh, my emotions sling-shotting between black dread and like, euphoria.

Even though I kept looking at the time every five seconds, Mom's voice calling down the stairs caught me by surprise. "Brian! It's time!"

When I got to my feet, my nerves were so wacky, my whole body was jackhammering. How the heck was I going to talk on the phone? Form words? Not puke?

I wanted to stay in my room till the phone rang. The thought of facing my idiot brothers—or being taunted by them—was devastating. I did not want them contaminating this experience.

"It's almost eleven!" Mom called. "Are you coming?"

"Yeah," I croaked.

Then I heard her say, "Boys, I want you out of here. Go to your room and get ten legos each. And no more! I don't want a big mess in there. And if I hear one peep out of you, you're grounded for a week. No dessert, no TV, no toys. You understand?"

As they complained and tried to negotiate the terms of their future punishment, I climbed the stairs one at a time, super-tense, feeling like my heart had migrated up near my tonsils.

Chapter 6

On the last few steps up from landing, all I could think was, *Oh my god, I am not prepared for this.* It was worse than going onstage. Worse than having to run naked down the street. And at the same time, better than anything that had ever happened to me.

When I got to the kitchen, Mom was back from the boys' room. She gave me a weird smile. She had taken the phone in its little base and moved it to the kitchen table. Beside it was a glass of water and a plate with three crackers on it. Again with the weird smile, she said, "I'll leave you be. Good luck, all right?"

I was so overwhelmed by what was about to happen, I couldn't get a word out and just nodded.

"What are you going to call her?" she asked.

"Huh?"

"I think her name is Alice. No, Alicia. It's Alicia, definitely."

"Okay."

Mom stared at me for a second, then left me alone. My guts were in total collapse-mode. I had to take a few deep breaths to get my act together before it was time.

The kitchen clock said one minute to eleven, but I checked my phone to make sure it was right. What should I say to her when she called? I had a million questions. But they all seemed lame and petty when I formed them in my mind. Then I got this huge jolt when I realized she might be expecting me to be a certain way. What if she was like, a world-famous singer and discovered all I could do was murder "Jingle Bells"? What if she was a math genius and found out I was just your average dummy?

At exactly eleven o'clock, I turned my chair to face the phone and sat there staring at it with my hands sweating between my knees. I was way too distracted to think of eating the crackers right then. I started watching the second hand of the clock go around, sinking like gravity was pulling it down toward the six, then watching it strain back up the other side, past the seven, the eight. By the time it hit the nine, I just about gave up. Why wasn't she calling? I wanted to stand up, knocking the chair over in dramatic movie style, and storm from the room.

But I sat there. The second hand swished past the twelve and started on the first late minute. My brain went straight to making excuses for her. She had an accident. Maybe she got stuck in traffic. Her clock probably wasn't set right.

I spotted the boys opening their bedroom door a crack and closing it again. Then Kyle came out, went into the bathroom, had a loud slurping drink at the sink and went hurrying back into the bedroom. The distraction was annoying. But it was over, I thought. Then the door opened a crack again and a little toy car came rolling out into the hallway. Over the sound of the TV from the living room, I heard their chattering voices. Then Jayden flung the door open, ran out to grab the car, and ran back into the bedroom in a flurry of giggles.

"Boys!" Mom's voice rang from the living room. "Keep that door closed!"

I leaned back in the chair to appear all calm in case Mom came into the kitchen. But I couldn't stand it and leaned forward again when the minute was half gone. *Maybe my birth mom really did have an accident,* I thought. *With her car, maybe. Or one of those freak accidents where your house explodes from a gas leak.* I realized my hands were so sweaty, if I picked up the phone right then it would squirt right out of my hand. So I got up, went to the sink and ran the water till it was super-cold, and stuck both hands into the water. I dabbed my forehead with my fingers.

As I dried off with the dish towel, I saw that the clock said 11:02. That was it, I thought. She wasn't going to call. It was past polite late and was now getting into never-going-to-happen late. I plunked myself back down in the chair and took a bite of cracker. It was so dry it tasted like sawdust. Maybe it was all a plan to torture me, right from the beginning. Give the kid up for adoption—he was ugly anyway. Then when he was old enough to care who his mother was, pretend you were going to call him, then don't. It hurt like hell giving birth to the little monster, so—ha!—get your revenge while you could. Remind him that no one cared.

Just as my brain crossed this threshold into lunacy, the phone lit up and rang. It rang so loud that I thought I was going to fall off my chair. Instantly, my guts sank. How could I talk with my mouth full of dry cracker? I tried to swallow and it wouldn't go. So I grabbed the glass of water and took a giant swig. Just as the phone rang a second time, the water and cracker ball went down the wrong way and I coughed crumbs and gooey liquid all over the table in front of me. The phone would only ring three times before it went to voicemail, so in mid-cough, I reached out and snatched it out of its cradle. With a mouth still full of goo and my throat threatening to kack again, I managed to choke out, "Haraa?"

"Hi," said a bright-sounding woman's voice from the other end. "Is this Brian?"

I swallowed like, six times, trying to clear my throat clog, before I could answer. "Yeah. Hi."

"Hi." There was this pause, which felt about ten minutes long, but in reality was probably about half a second. "Sorry," she finally said. "I'm a bit over-excited here. I've been looking for you for a long time." And she let out this little quiet sob that just about killed me. "So your last name is McSpadden?"

"Yeah."

"Is that Scottish?"

"Yeah, totally."

"Well, that's awesome. You know my last name is Kelly, right?"

I thought for a second. "Is that Scottish or Irish?"

"Irish, mostly. My family, both sides, are from Nova Scotia. But they've been here a long time."

Her family. My gut did another little flip as I thought, *They're my family too.*

"So, mostly Irish? What's the rest?"

She made a noise I'd never heard a human being make. Sort of like, "*Ah, phbb.* Hey, it's Canada. We've got a bit of everything in us. Ukrainian, French, a little bit of First Nations."

"Oh, no way. That's cool." I got up the courage to ask, "So, you're from here? From Edmonton?"

"Oh, yeah," she said, with this light, tinkling laugh that made me think she must look like a princess from a Disney movie. "I grew up just, uh—what is it?—east from you. Only a couple of miles away. Strange to think I might have seen you at the mall or something."

"Ha!" I laughed. "Maybe."

"So, do you have any siblings?"

"Yeah, two brothers, younger than me."

"Were they adopted too?"

"No."

There was silence on the other end. Then this heavy, "Oh."

I tried to pick up the conversation. "I tried looking for you once."

"Really? When was that?"

"Oh, like two years ago. I knew your name and kept googling Edmonton Kellys. I found one that lived not too far away and hopped on my bike. But I got lost. My...Mom got really ticked."

"I'll bet she did." Right then I heard this hissing whisper not far from her. She moved the phone away from her mouth and said, "Not right now. Just tell her I'm busy. I'll change her myself when I'm done." There was a complaint. "No, in a minute!" Then to me she said, "Sorry about that."

"You have other kids?"

The question seemed to catch her off guard. "Oh dear! Yes!" She laughed and her laugh totally gave me chills, it sounded so familiar. "I didn't even think of it. Yes, I have a little girl. She's just two. Her name's Maddy, like from Madeleine? You'll have to meet her. She's so cute I can barely stand it. We rent this big old house just off 95th Street."

"So you're married?"

"Oh, no," she said, as if that were an impossibility. "Me? No. My girl's father lives with us, though. You'll meet him too."

"Okay." Then I asked, "He's not my dad, right?"

"Oh, god no." She laughed. "I had you when I was sixteen. I was only in grade eleven. Whew! That was a whole different time of my life. How old are you now? Sorry," she caught herself. "What a dumb question. You're just turning twelve, right?"

"Yeah."

"So you're healthy? Everything's good?"

I had to think for a second. "You mean like...yeah, I'm okay. No diseases or anything. I always wondered about that. Does your family have any like, genetic stuff? Like, bad stuff?"

She laughed again. "I have an uncle that drinks too much. I try and stay away from him. He's always trying to borrow money. And I have a cousin that's diabetic. Does that count?"

"Is that genetic?"

"Beats me," she said. "Maybe. We all like our sweets, if that means anything."

"Yeah, me too. Chocolate especially."

"Really?" she almost screamed into the phone. "Like, dark or milk?"

"Hey, whatever I can get my hands on. In grade three I ate all the chocolate bars in my Halloween candy in one night. I thought I was gonna die."

"Oh, don't say that," she said, and laughed. "I eat a small piece of chocolate every night. The caffeine helps me sleep."

"I thought caffeine did the opposite."

"Hey, the Kellys are weird, what can I say? Listen, we should set a day to meet. Would you like that?"

"Yeah, totally."

"What's your schedule like?" She suddenly did her tinkling laugh thing. "Sorry, I guess you don't really have a schedule. I'm so used to saying that at work."

"Where do you work?"

"Oh, I'm at this cabinet place on 111th. You know, kitchen cabinets? It's just three guys. They do everything custom, from scratch. I sit in this tiny little office all day and take care of the front. I do everything. Phones, orders, all the bookkeeping. They didn't know what to do, with me taking the morning off. They make everything in the shop in back. Half the time they're out installing, so I have the place to myself.

Me and Maddy. I get to bring her to work. It's pretty awesome."

"Nice!"

"What do your parents do?"

I felt weird talking about them with my mom maybe listening in the next room. But I gave it a stab. "Oh, my dad's a security guy downtown. My mom stays home."

"With your little brothers?"

"Yeah."

"Huh. Nothing wrong with that. So you're not a latch-key kid."

"What's that?"

"Like, both parents working and you home alone."

"Yeah, no way. There's always somebody here."

There was a pause. I was too stunned to think of anything to say. But she picked it right up again. "So when would work for you? Do you want to meet somewhere neutral? Ugh," she said, "what am I thinking? Why don't you come over here for dinner one night? Would that be okay?"

"Yeah, yeah, for sure. Anytime."

"Okay. Do you have a cell? Can I text you?"

"Heck, yeah," I said, thinking, *Hallelujah, she lives in this century, unlike my ancient adoptive parents.* I gave her my number, but she sounded distracted, maybe by her daughter or something. I repeated the number like, three times, but I still wasn't sure she got it. When she gave me hers, I got my phone out and typed it into my contacts right then.

"We'll pick a day that your...parents can drive you."

"Or I could take the bus," I said stupidly.

"Of course. We'll pick a day next week, maybe?"

"Yeah, yeah."

There was a pause. "So," she said, very seriously. "It's been so great to hear your voice."

"Yeah, totally."

"So, next week, okay?"

"For sure."

"Oh my god, I forgot to wish you happy birthday!"

"Thanks."

"Okay…" There was the longest pause in the history of ever. Neither one of us wanted to hang up. "Bye…"

"Bye."

The second I hung up the phone, I wanted to let loose and cry my friggin' eyes out. But the boys' door flew open at the end of the hall and they began blabbering, "What did she say? Is she nice? What did you tell her? Can we meet her too?"

I stood up and had to steady myself. My heart was so full I couldn't even see straight, let alone talk. I completely ignored the boys and even my mother coming around from the living room. Once more the Brian lunge had to wait. I went down the stairs carefully, everything a blur. As soon as my door was closed, I dropped down on my bed and cried like a little baby for the next half hour. I had never been so happy in my life. My birth mom wasn't a freak. I was suddenly somebody, as if I'd been drifting aimless, way out in the ocean for twelve years and now, somebody had caught me and reeled me in.

Chapter 7

I was floating on air for the whole rest of the day. After I recovered from blubbering my eyes out, I went up and had a shower. Mom made tuna melts for lunch and I found myself being grudgingly chipper to her and my brothers. I say "grudgingly" because I wanted to share my experience. I just didn't want them tainting it.

"So what does she do?" Mom asked. She was at the sink, chipping at the pan from the tuna melts.

"She works," I answered.

Mom turned around and gave me a look like, *Really? That's the best you can do?*

"She's at the front desk at this like, custom cabinet place."

Mom had a strange reaction to that. "She must be pretty."

"Huh? What does that mean?"

"Oh, nothing." She shrugged.

The boys were sitting side by side across from me. Neither one seemed to be paying any attention. They were more interested in burning their mouths with the hot sandwich and blowing the heat in each other's face.

Mom half turned. "You know your father's adopted, right?"

I didn't know what to say to this, since we barely ever talked about it. All I could think of to answer was, "Yup."

After a while Mom asked, "Anything else? Is she married?"

"I don't think so."

"Kids? I mean, other kids?"

"Yeah, one." I didn't want that look again, so I added, "A little girl."

"When can *I* see her?" Kyle surprised us by asking. "Is she going to come over here?"

I was about to answer when Mom butted in. "Oh, I don't think so, sweetie."

"Take a selfie with her, okay?"

"Yeah!" screamed Jayden. "A selfie!"

I ate fast, wanting to get out of the house. Their questions and attention were becoming annoying. And worse, they were contaminating my happiness. I wanted to remember the brightness of my birth mother's voice, the sound of her laugh, and not have to think about stupid questions and my same-old life. So I texted Danny: *sup this aft?*

His answer came almost immediately: *randys gone perfect game time get here asap*

I dumped my plate in the sink and asked if I could have an apple to eat on the way.

"Have you had one today yet?" Mom rationed food as if there was some kind of shortage.

"I haven't eaten one in like, three days."

"Go ahead, then."

I grabbed the biggest one and had trouble keeping it in

my teeth while I got my runners on. I kept having to suck the juice and my spit back in.

"Oh, Brian, please," Mom groaned. "Put it down, would you?"

Five seconds later, I was up and flinging the door open. As soon as I was outside, I realized I was floating on air again. The apple tasted ridiculously good. The alley was a new alley, the trees in people's yards absolutely new trees I had never seen before. Discovering my birth mother was alive was one thing. But talking to her, finding out she wasn't a psycho, finding out she had been searching for me for a long time and gave a crap about me—well, that just made my year. I was now invincible. Nothing could crash my mood.

When I got to Danny's, he literally grabbed me by the shirt and pulled me inside. "Dude, you gotta check this level."

Since Randy had gone off to a friend's place and Cindy was visiting their aunt, Danny was all nuts about playing his freako game, War Demons.

"Look, it's rated 'I,'" he told me.

"What?"

"'I' for Insane!"

We kept the sound down really low so his dad didn't hear it. Turned out, we had only scratched the surface of the game the other day. When we got into it, I realized it was by far the most violent game I had ever played. The weapons were absurdly huge and the biggest demons were apparently big sacks of maggoty intestines. You just looked at them sideways and they popped like massive water balloons full of ick.

We played for like, ninety minutes before Cindy came home and Danny muted the sound. What was weird was, Cindy didn't come to check on us in the living room. She went flying by in the hall with a hand up to her face.

"What's with her?" I said.

From the bathroom, we could hear crap falling into the sink from the medicine cabinet and Cindy swearing. Danny jumped up to see what was wrong. "Hit Pause, would you?"

I did as he asked and sat back, wondering what was going on. Danny stood at the bathroom door, which was half shut, so I couldn't see Cindy. "You okay? What happened?"

"Just stay out of my way," Cindy said. "This hurts like hell."

"Whoa!" said Danny, his head jerking back. "Was that Auntie?"

The bathroom door suddenly flew all the way open with a bang and Cindy came charging out. There was a laundry basket on the floor at the end of the couch. Ignoring me, she went straight to it and began rummaging through the clothing. There was blood on her shirt from a gash above her left eye. The eyebrow was swollen and her eye socket was turning blue. "Ow," I commented as she dragged a rumpled pink t-shirt out of the laundry basket and headed to the kitchen. "That must hurt."

Danny followed her and I couldn't not get up from the couch. I swung around the wall so I could see what was going on in the kitchen.

Cindy was searching the fridge freezer.

"What the hell happened?" Danny asked.

She quickly found a plastic gel pack and slammed the freezer door closed. Then she began wrapping the rumpled t-shirt around it. "That old bag threw a coffee mug at me! I couldn't believe it! I spent all yesterday making her stupid lasagna and she won't even eat it. What's the point!?"

"At least Alvin will appreciate it."

"Who's Alvin?" I asked.

Danny remembered I was there. "Our aunt's son. Total weirdo."

"Be nice," Cindy snapped at him. "It's not his fault. He's the sweetest kid. And he's stuck with that freak. Oh my god, this hurts," she said as she pressed the t-shirt-wrapped gel pack to her eye.

"Mom's gonna flip out," said Danny.

"Don't you dare say anything," she threatened. Then she snapped back into caretaker mode. "Is Randy back yet?"

"Nope."

"Okay, I'm going to lie on my floor. You guys keep the sound down or I'll come and pound you out—got it?" She pushed by us, not waiting for an answer. We followed her into the living room and dropped back onto the couch as she headed upstairs.

"Well, that sucks," I said. "What's with your aunt?"

Danny picked up his controller but just sat there for a second. "Nothing. She's just really old and can't get out of bed. Actually, that's not true—she *won't* get out of bed. Lays there smoking and getting Alvin to bring her stuff. The place smells like butt crack."

"Lovely," I remarked. Danny got the game going again. After a bit, I added, "Who would name their kid Alvin?"

"Dude, if you meet her, you'll know."

I was still there at 4:30 when Danny's mother got home from work. We were both sunk deep into the couch with snack crumbs all over our chests. She came up the front steps, hands and arms full of stuff, looking at her phone. The War Demons disc got ejected and ditched in about a nanosecond. Danny stabbed the remote and some cooking show came on TV.

His mom was wearing clunky heels and a business suit and as soon as she got inside, she dumped everything she was carrying into a heap by the door: raincoat, laptop, phone, sunglasses, drugstore bags, car keys. She totally looked like a grown-up clone of Cindy; same length of dirty blonde hair and everything. She fished her phone out of the heap and flicked the screen without looking up. No hi, no hello. Just a "Where is your brother?" to Danny.

He answered with one word. "McIntyre's."

"Who is McIntyre?"

"Dunno. Some friend."

"How's Cindy?"

"Dunno. Sleeping."

"You pick up the crap she tripped over?"

"Huh? Oh, yeah. All taken care of."

His mother stood over him, peeling off her shoes. "Well, did you check to see if she was concussed?"

Danny squinted up at her. "What?"

"Oh, good god, you didn't think to check on her?" She left her shoes in the middle of the floor and hurried up the stairs. She stopped halfway up to ask, "Is your father here?"

Danny muted the sound of the TV and listened. I could hear his father's calm business voice through the closed door. "Yeah, he's there."

As his mother continued up the stairs, Danny changed channels from the cooking show to some kind of South American wildlife thing.

I couldn't help asking in a quiet voice, "So what's with your mom?"

"Huh?"

"Tripping over something?"

"Oh, long story. We're not allowed over there."

"At your own auntie's?"

"Yeah."

Between the bird calls and monkey screams from the TV, we could hear muffled voices above us. Two minutes later, Mrs. Cheevers came down the stairs with the pink t-shirt and gel pack. "Useless," she said to Danny. "Her eye is like *this*!" She held a clawed hand about a foot from her face. She went around into the kitchen, returning a minute later with the same t-shirt and ice cubes in a bread bag. "Use...less. And I'm missing my run. Thanks."

Danny began flipping the remote end to end, catching it in his lap when he flubbed it.

When Randy came in the back door a while later, I rose

from the couch. "I gotta get home."

The remote-flipping stopped. "What? No! Come on! Save me from the freak show!"

"Whatever. We can do something tomorrow."

Randy swung around into the living room right then. "Where is everybody?"

Danny got rid of him by saying, "Auntie beaned Cindy. We told Mom she tripped over some junk on our front step. She's up there." He pointed at the ceiling, flipping the remote again with his other hand. "Cindy's gonna have a black eye."

"Oh, no way!" Randy went up the stairs two at a time (tripping twice), as if the beaning were still in progress and he wanted the best seat.

I pushed out the front door and heard a big clunk behind me. Danny had missed catching the remote. It had hit the floor and the batteries had spilled out and were rolling away from him.

"Adios, freak show," I said.

"Shut up."

When I got outside, rush hour was in full swing. I went straight back into birthday mode. I don't know why I didn't tell Danny it was my birthday. I guess I just wanted to keep the secret of talking to my birth mom, and forgot. I spent the whole walk home looking up at the sky. The sun was behind some thin clouds and there was really nothing to look at. But I wanted to get that floaty feeling back. It didn't take much. After a block or so, I couldn't stop grinning.

When I got into the house, I was surprised to find Dad home early. He was sitting sideways at the kitchen table, drinking his after-work beer. Today, his white hair was sticking all forward like the front of a ship made of ice. He looked like he was gonna stab something with it. Of course, he totally didn't notice.

"You get all that glass cleaned up?"

After the day I'd had, that morning at Grantree's felt like

two years ago. "Yup."

"Oh, and happy birthday."

"Thanks."

I headed for the living room. I couldn't believe he didn't ask me about talking to my birth mom. On the other hand, I was glad I didn't have to tell him.

I sat in front of the TV to wait for supper. Dad came in to watch a bit of the six o'clock news. He was definitely a news guy. He hated sitcoms and cartoons and just about everything else. but he never missed the news. Our PVR was full of documentaries he wanted Mom to watch, but she never did. He set his beer down on the coffee table and glanced at my birthday cards on the mantel. The only one he picked up and read was the polar bear one.

He gave a snort and wagged the card in the air at me. "You aunt's a nut, you know."

I couldn't help smiling. "Yeah."

He put the card back on the mantel and dropped heavily into his recliner. Two seconds into the news, he hit pause and said, totally unexpectedly, "What are they gonna do?"

"Huh?"

"Raising money for that poor bear. What are they gonna do? Try and send him home? To the Arctic? They know it's all melted, right? There's no home left to go back to."

I nodded and laughed faintly.

"Unbelievable." He shook his head and clicked the remote.

That was my dad. Didn't mention the bear's small cage. Or the fact that he might be lonely by himself in there. And not one word about the bad joke of the card and me not getting any actual pizza to eat. Nope. His mind went straight to the melting Arctic. I did not envy his "clients" at work. I'm sure it was a laugh a minute with my dad there.

When Mom called us, I didn't have to be asked twice. I rushed into the kitchen, sat down, and waited for everyone else. Then we ate in silence. Well, except for the boys squirming and Mom telling me not to hunch over my food. Nobody ever talked at our dinner table. At Danny's, they never sat down together for a meal. But they never shut up, either. Always talking or commenting or crabbing about something. Here, the most common sound was the clank of a fork on a plate.

I pretty much inhaled dinner. The boys whined about the peas rolling off their forks. They got shushed but continued to make frustrated faces till Mom got up and fetched them spoons.

Jayden ate four peas and said, "My tummy hurts."

"That's ridiculous," said Mom. "You can't use that excuse every day. You've hardly eaten anything."

"But it hurts!"

"Fine. Just quit complaining."

"When can we have cake?" Kyle asked.

"After you finish your dinner."

"I am finished." The kid had chewed one bite of meat, which now sat on the side of his plate, mangled.

Dad had a standard answer. "You gotta eat. Don't you want to grow up big and strong like Brian?" Over the years, he had said it so many times that I stopped taking it as a compliment. I was just a lever to move a spoiled runt.

"But I don't like meat. Can I have cake now?"

"Fine. Just don't complain if you're hungry later."

"I won't."

So she brought the cake out of the cupboard. It was chocolate, one layer, and lopsided. I could see the fake brandname cake mix box sticking out of the recycling bin.

"I got to lick the spoon!" Jayden exclaimed.

"Yeah," Kyle put in, "but I got to lick the bowl 'cause I'm older."

Mom coached the boys with her eyebrows all through the singing of "Happy Birthday." Dad didn't sing. Instead, awkwardly, he reached into the drawer behind him and brought out a clear plastic bag full of gummy worms and placed it on the table beside me. That was my present from him. After the singing was over, I said, "Thanks." He nodded.

As soon as I served the cake, we ate in silence. Most of us, anyway. The boys ate with maximum lip-smacking, totally open-mouthed. I had to eat with my head down and my eyelids half closed so I didn't have to watch them turn their cake into watery pudding.

I couldn't wait to get out of there, but I made a point of thanking Mom for the presents and cake and everything.

She looked exhausted after the day. "Oh, you don't have to thank me," she said, waving me away. "It's my job."

I didn't even know how to respond to that.

I checked my phone to see if Danny or any other friend had texted me. There was nothing, so I hopped on my bike and went tearing around the neighbourhood. Well, other people's neighbourhoods. My legs took me toward the area where my mom lived. It was too far to get there and back before bedtime, but just going in that direction kept the butterflies churning in my stomach long enough for my legs to get tired.

That night, I had the most intense nightmare.

I was riding my bike around this creepy abandoned chemical factory. There were all these puddles of acid I had to steer around. The puddles kept getting closer and closer together until finally I was headed for a lake. I woke up around two in the morning, completely freaked out, and couldn't get back to sleep for the longest time.

When morning arrived, the dream quickly melted away. The sun was blazing in the kitchen window as I ate my breakfast. Dad went off to work and Mom puttered around, putting away dishes from the dishwasher and quietly sipping her black tea. A few minutes after Dad was gone, she came and sat at the table across from me.

"The boys are worried about you," she said, oddly.

"Huh?"

"They were asking if you're still going to be their brother."

"Oh." I figured I'd better pretend to care. "So what did you say?"

Her mouth tucked down at the corners and her bottom lip kind of quivered for a second. "I said you'd always be their brother, no matter what."

I shrugged and said, "That's nice." I didn't mean it to come out sarcastic. But the truth was, if my birth mom wanted me to go live with her, I'd drop my little brothers like hot potatoes.

Mom did not react well. All trace of warmth left her voice. "What does that mean?"

I shrugged and scooped the last of the milk from my bowl. "Nothin'."

"You can be mean sometimes, Brian." She stared at me. "You better watch that."

I rose from the table to put my bowl in the sink. "Sorry." For half a second I thought, *Screw you. I've got a real mom just a few miles away.* But I gave my brain a shake as I went down to my room and thought, *Wow, dude, you are totally mean.*

I farted around, getting ready to leave, thinking, *What the heck are you doing?* For years I'd been worried that my birth mother was going to be a crackhead. And now here I was, being a dick to my adoptive mother.

Just before nine, I tromped up the stairs. When I got to the landing I yelled, "I'm going to Danny's. After our work we're gonna play games, okay?"

From way off in the house, Mom answered. "Will you be back for lunch?"

Thinking about a possible marathon of War Demons, I said, "I don't know. I'll call!"

There was a pause. "All right, we'll see you later."

And I was gone. On my way to Danny's I erased everything about the morning from my brain. It was a new day. The sun was heating the street and everything seemed to be swaying in a mild breeze. I was going to be nice to everyone forever after this. No more nightmares, no more being mean. Everything just calm and nice and normal.

Everything went great with my new plan until Danny and I showed up at Grantree's. The old guy was waiting on his deck for us with a fistful of carrot tops with no carrots attached. Great, I thought, it was going to be one of those days.

Chapter 8

"You wanna explain this?" Grantree was leaning heavily on the back of a deck chair, his bulldog face sagging more than usual. We were at his mercy.

Danny immediately went into *Duh...I dunno* mode, scratching his head and looking stupid. I took his lead and my shoulders and the palms of my hands went up.

"What?" said Grantree. "You think I might have gophers? Or moles! Little creatures eating my carrots from the bottom up? *Pah!*" he suddenly spat. "You two don't fool me. No more weeding like that. You two go get yourselves a hoe from the garage and—"

Without his face moving, Danny snorked at the word hoe.

"Shut yourself up," said Grantree to him. "Now you work these beets and get all them dandelions and chickweed out. You understand?"

Silently, Danny's head started bopping.

"What is that?" Grantree demanded.

"I'm working the beats, man."

Grantree spluttered for a second like a kettle that's too full of water. Then his eyes went squinty. "Look, you," he said to Danny. "What do you got? Two months holiday, lalaing around, annoying the neighbours. Lookit me—off work, injured, in pain all the damn time. I still got a business to run. Still gotta pay the bills, still gotta buy damn groceries. What do you got? You," he said quietly, "got nothin'. Now get movin'." He waited for us to slink away before he turned slowly and limped into the house, shaking his head.

Danny looked at me as we headed to the garage. Without making a sound, he raised his eyebrows and formed his mouth around the word *wow*.

The garage of Mr. Grantree was a thing of beauty. It looked like it came out of a handyman tool catalogue. The floor was smooth concrete and there were metal shelves here and there. Fluorescent lights illuminated the tools hanging neatly from pegboard hooks on the walls. On the far side was this huge, shiny black SUV. It was so big I wondered how he even got it in there. I immediately thought of Danny's crappy dirt floor garage and his dad's jeep sitting outside in the mud ruts. One neighbour clearly needed to up his game. The other needed to calm the heck down. It was a garage, not a freaking throne room.

We found a couple of hoes and after a bunch of rude jokes, we hit the garden. In a totally amateur way, we started beatboxing as we worked. That got old real quick. But I found myself really enjoying getting the weeds out. Whenever the hoe got under a good-sized weed, it gave a pleasant little *pok!* as you chopped its head off. Then if you hooked it the right way, you could fling the weed about seven miles. Tools were my thing, apparently. Weeding by hand was for peasants.

"Hey," Danny said as we got like, halfway down our rows. "You hear about the motorcycle crash down Groat Road on Saturday?"

"Another one?" Some guy had died about two weeks before. Spun out and slammed into a power pole.

Danny's voice became excited. "The guy hit the concrete thing in the middle and launched himself into the traffic coming the other way. Got totally stuck under a Smart Car."

"Oh, no way."

"Yeah. I'm never buying a motorcycle."

"Why not? Too dangerous?"

"No, my dad says they're all wearing diapers."

"What?"

"Well, not all of them. The vibration messes up your guts. You ever see gray hair sticking out of a helmet, for sure that guy's wearing a diaper under his leather pants."

"Gross. I wonder if he has to lie down on a table and his wife changes him."

"Yeah!" Danny said, and added in a fake voice, "Here's your baby powder, my little biker-wiker."

I had to laugh. "No pee-pees on your Harley, now."

"No road rash for your little hairy bum-bum."

When he said this, I had to stop and double over, I was laughing so hard.

The old guy had a lot of beets. I had eaten a few pickled ones now and then, but geez, I couldn't imagine who would eat four rows of them. An hour later, when we were nearly finished, Grantree limped slowly outside and down the sidewalk to survey our work. He tried to find fault, stretching his neck to see between the rows. But in the end, he just stabbed at the weeds in the pail we'd used and made a weird face. "You finish up and make sure the garage is locked, awright?"

Danny stood up straight and saluted. "Gotcha."

Grantree glanced at him and went, "*Tssu.*" Then he shook his head and limped back to his house.

Ten minutes later, we were done. After dumping the weeds, we went into his garage and—well, we ended up goofing around with the tools from the wall, trying to figure out what they were for.

"Nut buster," said Danny, holding up a thing that looked like a bent clamp.

I showed him a big screwdriver. "Ear wax extractor."

He pointed to some pliers. "Nose hair tweaker."

I suddenly froze, listening. "Shh, you hear that?"

Danny looked at me. "Huh?"

I'd heard the low rumble of an engine in the alley behind the garage, then it was shut off. "Somebody's here."

Two doors slammed. I heard voices. Men's voices, by the sound of it.

There was a long, narrow window along the garage wall facing the garden. Danny moved to it and stared outside to see who was coming. Two seconds after the back gate clicked open, his eyes went wide. He flicked off the garage light and, being all dramatic, ducked down below the window.

"What are you doing?" I asked.

"*Shh! Quick!*" he whispered. "*We gotta hide!*" Still hunched over, he rushed to the back of Grantree's giant SUV and squeezed behind it.

"*What's going on?*" I asked him. But as the back gate clicked closed again and the men started to pass the window, I jogged over and squeezed in beside him.

"*Wait till you see this guy,*" Danny said.

The garage door was still wide open, so it was easy to hear the men. One of the guys, the skinny one, was saying, "I did all right, didn't I? Buy a few peanuts to go with your beer?"

The answer came from his huge buddy, in a voice that was deep and rough. "We gotta stop with the miscellaneous. I went snooping around the museum last night. They're already setting up the display cases."

"So how much time we got?"

"Dunno. I don't want to get caught before we find the big prize. Just look for the real stamps, all right? This other crap ain't worth our trouble."

Right then, the skinny guy stopped in the doorway and looked in. I had to blink twice before I could believe what I was seeing. The man had no eyes!

Behind him, the big guy spoke. "Hey, wow, lookit his greenhouse. That's too bad."

The garage door slammed closed. The voices of the men trailed away up the walk toward the house.

Danny and I stood up and looked at each other. "You see that guy?" I asked.

"Yeah; what's with his eyes? He looked like a farmer from Alpha Centauri."

"Weird, eh? Maybe it was the light or something."

"What? No! There were no whites, dude. And not even any color."

"Were they like, holes?"

"What? No. Didn't you see? They were glossy, like, all the way across."

"He's not blind, that's for sure."

A few seconds later, we opened the door and peeked out. The men were standing on the deck, the big one ringing the doorbell.

The black-eyed guy was short and was wearing brown overalls that slumped over his boots. His partner was way taller. The guy was in jeans with his huge gut hanging over them like there was a blob of lava in his shirt. He had no neck and his hair seemed to grow straight out from his forehead.

"Freakos, man," Danny said. We watched them enter the house and when we couldn't see them anymore, we got out of the garage and Danny locked the door behind us. Then we left by the back gate.

"*Grantree's Plumbing*," I read from the back of their van as we passed it. "*Residential and Commercial. Over 30 Years' Expe-*

rience. Maybe they're like, the not-so-super Mario Brothers."

"Ha! Yeah. I wonder what they were talking about with the 'stamps' thing. Do plumbers stamp stuff?"

"I dunno. In a big sewer pipe, maybe they stamp rats."

But Danny was all serious. "'Real stamps,' he said. Maybe they have like, a counterfeiting operation in Grantree's basement."

I frowned. "Something about the museum…"

"Yeah. On Alpha Centauri."

When we got back to Danny's, Mr. Cheevers was at the kitchen counter filling his giant coffee mug. He was a weird-looking man, totally their genetic father. He had a young face that was really narrow, like a hatchet. His hair was balding and he'd shaved off the rest, leaving only stubble at the sides and back. He looked exactly like Danny, only twenty-odd years older. He was staring at his phone the whole time and gave me a quick glance.

"Hey, Brian."

"Hey."

We were both dying for a glass of water and went straight to the sink. Danny grabbed two plastic cups from the drain board and handed me one.

"Where is everybody?" Danny asked his dad.

"Uh…store, I think."

There was gunge on the lip of my cup. It took a second to chip it off and while I was filling up the cup, I spotted the two men out the window, exiting Grantree's. I tapped Danny and pointed. The black-eyed guy was carrying a black and silver case, like something you'd use to store an expensive tool. Lava-gut guy had a big spool of yellow tubing or cable on a silver reel.

"Hey, Dad," Danny said. "You seen those guys before?"

His father was at the fridge getting the cream out. He leaned back to look. "Oh, yeah. They been working for him for years." He poured, literally, two drops of cream into his coffee. *Bloop. Bloop.*

"You seen that guy's eyes?"

"Sure." I couldn't tell if the black-eyed guy really was no big deal to him or he was just brushing us off. He took a long, slow sip of his coffee. "So what's Grantree getting you guys to—"

"Oh my god, dude! Look!" Danny suddenly exclaimed. He still had his cup of water in one hand and his phone in the other. He jerked the glass toward the kitchen window so suddenly that the water flew out in a shower.

I stepped over to where Danny was pointing. There was an almost identical window on the corner of Grantree's house.

"Oh, you missed it!"

"What?"

"That woman. I just saw her again!"

"What's going on?" asked Mr. Cheevers, before another long, slow sip.

Danny shook his head in frustration. "I think Grantree has a ghost."

"Yeah, that's what it is," his dad sneered. "The most impossible thing is what you think of first?"

"Okay, fine," said Danny. "But didn't Grantree's wife leave him a long time ago?"

"Oh, yeah. When you were little. So?"

"I think he might have a girlfriend or something."

Mr. Cheevers pulled his phone halfway out of his pocket, glanced at it and laughed. "Gregor Grantree? A girlfriend? I doubt it. Why?"

"I keep seeing this woman through the windows at his place."

"I didn't see anything," I put in. "I think he's hallucinating."

Mr. Cheevers ruffled Danny's hair. "Maybe that fall shook something loose."

Danny ducked away. "Oh, come on. I saw somebody. I even asked Grantree and he said there was nobody there. Could it be like, a nurse for his hip or something?"

"Why would he lie about that?" Mr. Cheevers said. "I'd believe him."

"What?" Danny said. "Fine. I'll bet you fifty bucks there's somebody there."

His dad snorted. "I couldn't care less if there was somebody there. Besides, you don't have fifty bucks."

"Yeah, well, why not? Don't I get allowance?"

"Ha! That goes to your phone bill."

That crushed Danny's enthusiasm. "Oh…right…"

"How about you do some chores and stuff."

"Like what?"

His dad laughed across the top of his coffee mug. "Have you seen this place? How about taking care of the lawn?"

"Oh, god…I hate that mower. I sprained my arm trying to start it."

"I'll get it fixed."

"Really? Okay. You pay me fifty bucks if I win and I do chores if I lose."

His dad held out a hand to shake on it. "You mow twice. Now and next time, and you got a deal."

"Yeah?" Danny slapped his dad's hand and they did one hard shake. "Oh man, I totally won already."

Mr. Cheevers stepped back to the counter to top up his coffee. "All right, but you need someone else to see her, too."

"I know."

"So what'd she look like?" I asked.

"Glasses, bangs, white shirt, this sweater with a round neck."

His dad puckered his lips and flicked his free hand. "Ghost for sure. Bangs are so over."

"Oh, whatever," said Danny. "You can kiss your cash goodbye."

Mr. Cheevers took another quick sip of his coffee and shuffled back to his office.

"Fifty bucks," Danny said to me, wide-eyed. "I so got this."

"Or not," I commented.

We headed into the living room and played games till about quarter after eleven. There was a nice breeze blowing in from the screen door. We were slumped on the couch, deep in game land, when Randy suddenly appeared in the archway to the kitchen.

"Wow!" Danny said. "Where did you come from?"

"Huh? I just got back from the store with Cindy."

"Where's she?"

"I don't know. With her friends." The kid flopped down on the floor to watch us play.

Two minutes later, a twenty-something guy in a floppy touque came up the front step carrying a big white plastic bag and knocked on the door. Randy jumped up to answer it. The delivery guy mumbled something to Randy in a quiet voice. All I caught was, "Forty-six fifty."

"Dad!" Randy shouted. And a second later, Mr. Cheevers came in, digging into his wallet.

When he paid for the order and carried the bag past us into the kitchen, the glorious smell of the food made my head turn all by itself.

"What did you get?" Danny asked.

"Jamaican. You guys hungry?"

It wasn't even eleven thirty yet, I noted. But I couldn't say no. We abandoned the game and the three of us followed Mr. Cheevers into the kitchen.

"Watch out, eh? It's hot."

As Danny lifted the lids on a couple of styrofoam boxes, I could see rice with little green peas in one and in the other, some kind of meat in sauce. I dug out my phone and headed back into the living room to call home to say I was staying for lunch.

When Mom answered, she didn't say yes immediately. Instead she asked, "Well, what is it? What are you having?"

"I don't know. Takeout."

There was a pause. I could hear her thinking it might be food prepared in Satan's armpit or something. "All right, then," she said finally. "I'll see you later."

After Mr. Cheevers took one whole box to himself and disappeared into his office, the three of us got out plates and piled them high. We headed back to the living room and started watching some crappy CGI movie. Two bites of the meat, and my face nearly melted off. I had never had anything like this food. Honestly, I couldn't tell if it was the best thing I'd ever tasted or the worst. The flavor was awesome, I just had a tough time with the heat.

Then the brothers, hyped up on spice, got into a fight. I kept watching TV while Danny tormented Randy behind the couch. Doing what, I didn't want to know. But it sounded like tickle torture. The kid screamed like a dying piglet and all their dad did was open his door a crack to see if they were still alive. He kept talking on his headset thing the whole time, then closed his door again without even changing expression.

I got bored around two and headed home. When I got in the back door, I was hoping to go straight downstairs and crash on my bed. I was glad to be home. I just needed a big dose of normal. But it was not to be.

As soon as I got inside, I heard Mom's voice. "Brian? Is that you?"

"Yeah." I'm sure I sounded disappointed.

Mom came shuffling around from the hallway. "Your, um…mother left a message for you."

"She phoned?"

"Kyle took the message. They had quite a chat."

A hand went up to my forehead. "Nooo…"

She held out a piece of scrunched-up paper. "Look what

he did! Isn't it cute?"

The paper was an old till receipt with crayon squiggles on the back. "This isn't a message," I said.

"No, but he tried and it's so sweet."

"I don't care," I said firmly. "What's it supposed to say?"

"He's trying to tell you that your birth mother called. She wanted to call your cell but she wrote the number down wrong. So she phoned here. She wants you to send her a text message."

As I was trying to hand back the crumpled receipt, both boys came tearing around from their room. Their faces were radiant with excitement. "We talked to your other mom!"

"Both of you?"

"Yeah!"

I rolled my eyes. "Great."

"She said we can have a barbecue sometime! And she has a baby! She's going to get us to babysit when we're old enough." Then they began jabbering to one another.

"We can make all the money and buy toys and candy and everything!"

"Yeah! Toys!"

I couldn't take it. I rolled the receipt into a ball and tossed it into the recycling bin. Then I headed downstairs. I wasn't sure, before this, how I could hate my idiot brothers any more than I already did. Now I knew.

Frustrated, I did a sort of half-hearted Brian lunge, just to get down the stairs faster. As soon as I got to my room, I texted my birth mom: *hi sorry I missed ur message whats up*

I tried playing a game on my phone while I waited for an answer, but I was too distracted. Thankfully, it came within like, two minutes. I think I hurt myself, I sat up so fast.

hey, she answered, *how is sunday for dinner?*

My fingers couldn't type quickly enough. I was going to meet my birth mother on Sunday! That was only three days away!

good, I answered, completely freaking out.

She sent me her address and asked if 5:00 would work.

yeah totally, I replied.

When she answered, *see you then!* I fell back on the bed and had a little happy sighing session all by myself. I tell you, come Sunday, no matter what, even if I was tied to a chair by gangsters, I would still pull myself there by my eyelids.

Chapter 9

The next morning was ridiculously hot. When I got up around seven and poked my head outside, it felt like noon. When I got to Danny's just before nine, Cindy let me in. She had been cooking in the kitchen. She had covered her black eye with a layer of makeup so thick, it looked like an android's fake skin.

"Danny!" she yelled as I stepped up the few steps from the landing. She was wearing an apron over new-looking jeans and a white top. Her boobs were very prominent and she immediately saw me checking them out. Like a doofus, I looked away and pretend it hadn't happened, but I could feel the heat in my face as it turned red.

She was about to yell for Danny again, but saw him come around from the living room, the laces of his runners flopping. "What were you doing?" she asked him.

"Nothing."

"Well, you better get going. And tell your friend to keep his eyes to himself."

Danny put his foot up on the handle of a kitchen drawer to tie a lace and looked at me. I *still* couldn't keep my eyes off her boobs. "Dude! Hey!" he waved in my face. "Gross."

"When are you back?" Cindy asked him.

"I don't know. Ask Grantree."

"You know you have to go to Auntie's."

"What? Why?" Danny complained. "I thought they had lasagna!"

"Well, yeah, it's probably done by now."

Danny pulled his foot off the drawer and groaned. "Why do I have to go?"

Cindy tipped her head so it looked like she was peering over the top of an imaginary pair of glasses. "'Cause Auntie likes *you* and she tried to kill *me*."

Danny jammed his other runner up on the drawer and started tying. "Why can't Randy go?"

"Don't be stupid."

Cindy's phone buzzed on the counter. Reaching out with a goopy hand, she flipped it roughly right side up to look at it. "What the hell is this?" she said to the screen. "Freaks! Now they're bugging my friends?"

"Problem?" asked Danny.

"Nah. Just a few people to kill. That Bruce guy and his horrible buddy. No thanks to you."

Danny dropped his foot and leaned over the counter. "What is that, anyway?"

"It's meat loaf."

"*That*? You're gonna make them eat *that*?"

"Shut up. It's not cooked yet."

"You mean it's gonna be brown, too?"

Cindy reached out with her goopy hands and Danny had to duck out of the way. "No! Don't!" He spun out of her reach and tore past me down the steps.

When we got to Grantree's, the old fart was in rough shape. His eyes were pink and he was jamming one fist into his back, hard, as if he was trying to control a muscle spasm. He could hardly move. Danny didn't even try to make fun of him. "You all right?"

The old guy basically choked on every word. "Yeah. I'm just…getting off the pain meds." He wagged the key to the garage at us. "There's some, uh…stakes for the peas and… plastic mesh. Green. You'll see."

I was all set to start, but Danny didn't move. He asked Grantree, "So what happened to the greenhouse?"

I jerked my head around. The whole greenhouse was gone. All that was left was the wooden platform.

Grantree was not in the mood to answer. "What? Oh, I had my guys…take it apart. It's over there in the garage. I guess I'll make more cold frames. Why?" he barked.

Danny held up his hands. "Nothin'. Just wondering."

When we got into the garage, we found a bundle of skinny wooden stakes and these bags of green mesh stuff right inside the door. We couldn't figure out what he wanted us to do until we checked out the bags, and realized we just had to follow the pictures printed on them.

All the stuff was for his peas. We had to pound the stakes in, then stretch out the mesh and tie it onto the stakes. We worked until after nine thirty, when I thought for sure we were done. But Grantree was just getting started.

The pea plants were about two feet long, but they were all grown into each other in these snarled balls. After we got them untangled as best we could, we had to tie them onto the mesh with little bits of string. It was like gardening torture. I swear, if I ever have a garden, I am never growing peas.

All through our work, I noticed Danny kept scanning Grantree's windows. Hey, I would too if there was fifty bucks in it for me. But it was annoying. The guy couldn't concen-

94

trate on what we were doing.

"You see your ghost yet?" I asked, a little peeved.

"What? Oh…no. Not yet." Turns out, that wasn't the only thing on Danny's mind. When we finally finished, he locked up the garage and went to give the key back to Grantree.

The old guy came to the door looking even worse, if that was possible. "You get all the uh…plants up off the ground?"

"Yup."

"Yeah?"

"Yup."

He looked over our heads to his garden. We didn't tell him there was a two-foot ball of pea plants we'd hidden in his raspberries. "Okay," he said at last. "'S good."

"Awesome," said Danny. "Can I ask you something?"

"Now what?" said Grantree.

"Do you plumbers like, stamp stuff?"

Grantree just stared at him. "Excuse me?"

"Stamp—you know. Do have stamps?"

The man blinked. "That's private," he said. "That's none of your business."

Danny gave me a quick look. "Okay, but—"

"Nope, nope," said Grantree. "We're done here. Go on now, get lost."

When we got out of his yard, Danny slammed Grantree's gate extra hard. "Did you hear that? Unbelievable!"

"Well," I said, "sounds like he's got something to hide." I was trying to be supportive, but the truth was, I couldn't give a hoot.

"Duh, you think?"

When we got back to Danny's, we guzzled water straight from the sink tap. There didn't seem to be any cups anywhere. The meat loaf was cooling on a rack on the counter, smelling awesome.

Danny wiped his mouth on his bare arm. "You're coming with me, right?"

"To your auntie's?"

"Yeah. Please? I need the moral support."

I was poised over the sink, ready to take a sip, and shrugged. "Sure. I've got nothing better to do."

"Awesome."

After I drank about a gallon of water, I said, "If I'm going, though, can I use your bathroom?"

"What? Of course. I gotta go, too, so speed it up. I could drill a hole in the bowl."

The Cheevers bathroom was, well…very different than mine at home. There was a thin layer of grime on every surface, except for the taps and where people walked. A blob of toothpaste was hardening on the edge of the sink. The mirror was sprayed with flossing-flecks and god knows what— maybe sneeze spray. And I didn't think I was Mr. Superclean, but I was sure glad the toilet seat was up, because I was not touching that without a hazmat suit.

Just as I got back to the kitchen, Mr. Cheevers came out of his office, chuckling. He was carrying his giant coffee mug, so I figured he was coming into the kitchen for a refill.

"What's so funny?" Danny asked.

Mr. Cheevers stopped and looked seriously at Danny. "You want a poke in the eye?"

Danny started to complain. "Dad—"

Without missing a beat, Mr. Cheevers tapped Danny with his elbow and said, "They're pretty good if you get 'em fresh outa Pokeny."

Danny looked at me. "My dad's got one joke. And it isn't even funny."

"Hey," said Mr. Cheevers. "To each his own. Makes me laugh."

"Yeah, well, you're the only one." Danny left me there and headed to the bathroom, while Mr. Cheevers filled his giant mug.

"You seen Cindy?" he asked me.

"Me? No, not since earlier."

"Hmm," he said. Then he chucked his chin toward the meat loaf. "Is that for Auntie?"

"Yeah, I guess." It felt weird being asked these questions as if I was part of their family. In a way, I didn't mind.

"I heard she's having trouble with her ankles or something? They're all swollen up?"

I made a face and shrugged. "No idea."

Mr. Cheevers finally pushed away from the counter to pull the cream from the fridge and *bloop* some into his coffee. By then, Danny was back from the bathroom, wiping his hands on his jeans.

"You—whoa," his father said. "Is that pee or water?"

"What?" Danny exclaimed. "It's not pee!"

"Then use a towel, would you?"

"It fell behind the toilet."

"You couldn't pick it up?"

"I just washed my hands!"

Mr. Cheevers shook his head. "Maybe you need a Pokeny eye."

Danny looked at his dad as if he was crazy. "Please, stop."

But I had to ask, "Is Pokeny a guy or a place?"

Giving his bald head a rub, Mr. Cheevers shrugged. "Who knows?"

Danny dug into a drawer and found a cloth grocery bag and shoved the pan of hot meat loaf into it.

"Oh!" said his dad. "Hang on." He set his coffee down and hurried to his office. He came back a few seconds later with a carton of cigarettes. "Here, take these too."

Danny didn't even blink. He just opened the bag and let his father drop the carton in, so I figured this was normal. Well, normal if you didn't mind meat loaf grease on your cigarette carton.

When we got outside, I couldn't help saying, "So what's with your auntie? She can't go out, or what?"

"I think she's on like, Disability. When she's really sick," he said, showing me the cloth bag, "she gets my dad to buy her cigarettes. Last time I was there, it was really grim." He rubbed his forehead as we walked, like he was trying to erase a painful memory. "I couldn't get away. She's all like, 'My little Dannikins, I haven't seen you in so long!' She made me sit and talked my ear off, smoking and coughing the whole time."

"So what's wrong with her?"

"Dude, I don't know. She's my dad's aunt, so she's like, sixty-something. What freaks me out are her teeth. They're like, rotting from the roots down. And she's *such a cow* to Alvin. Orders him around like he's two and you can see his chin wobbling like he's scared of her. Man, I freaking hate going over there."

The day was really heating up and as we headed east down 110 Avenue, there was nowhere to get out of the blazing sun. At 127 Street, we turned north up the sidewalk. There were small office buildings all along the west side. Halfway down the block we came into the shadow of these huge spruce trees on the boulevard. They were completely out of place. All the other trees on the boulevard were leafy trees.

There, squished between the cinderblock walls of two office buildings, was their auntie's house. I'd seen the place a dozen times and always thought it was weird. But now, from Danny's remarks about his auntie, I kind of got it.

The siding and porch could have used a coat of paint twenty years ago. The porch was tipped down toward the street like a ramp and the wooden screen door was propped all the way open with a rock. There were old sawn-off juice containers on the wide porch railing. All the plants inside were dead. The curtains were made of plastic and the windows were filthy. This was not the sort of house you wanted to visit on Halloween. For sure they were handing out creepy balls of puffed wheat held together with grandpa's earwax.

I followed Danny up the crappy steps and we picked our way across the porch. I say "picked" because we had to avoid holes in the porch boards where people had broken through. "Dangerous much?" I commented, peering down a particularly large hole. "There's like, a snow shovel down there."

All he said was, "Huh! You should see the rest of the house."

Danny knocked at the door. He knocked again, then turned the handle and tried to shove the door open with his shoulder. It was stuck.

Two seconds later, someone inside pulled the door open, right out of his hands, and the narrow white face of a kid appeared. "*Danny!*" he whispered loudly. "*I didn't know you were coming!*" Two seconds later, the smell of the house hit me. I could literally feel the warm cloud of it roll past us. The place reeked of urine, damp rot, and cigarette smoke.

So this was Alvin, I thought. The kid stood in the doorway, head hunched forward, arms at his sides. He seemed only a bit younger than us, but looked like he'd just climbed out of a hospital bed. He was wearing this shrunken shirt and these floppy homemade shorts. His thin hair was combed to the side like an old man's and his skin was so white, it was almost blue. But what freaked me out was his boney forehead and deep, dark eye sockets. He sort of looked like a skeleton boy.

"Who's that?" he asked Danny, almost accusingly.

Danny was calm. "Hey, he's cool. This is Brian. We go to school together." Then to me he said, "Alvin's homeschooled. His mom won't let him go anywhere."

"Sucks," I said.

The kid shook his head and said to Danny, "Huh. Tell him I got no homework."

"Alvin," Danny said, laughing, "that's all you got, is homework."

The kid made a face that truly freaked me out. From his

weird shoulder hunch, he looked up at Danny and smiled the fakest smile I have ever seen. Lips stretched, eyes dead. The kid had no idea how human beings smiled. *Wow*, I thought. *This is actually one of those people who doesn't get out much. Like, maybe never.*

Right then, a faint woman's voice came from somewhere up in the house. It sounded like every creepy witch voice I'd ever heard in a cartoon. "Aaalvin? Is there someone at the door?"

Calling out apparently made the woman cough. But not a normal *khaa*. It was deep in her throat, like she was gargling thick spit. Then she gobbed into a hanky—or maybe onto the floor, for all I knew—with a full-voiced *huh-lah!*

"My mom can't come say hi," Alvin explained. "She's not feeling so good."

"Hey, no problem," said Danny. "We just came to drop this off." And he handed over the cloth bag.

Alvin's eyes lit up but then narrowed when he took the bag. The kid could barely hold it up. His skinny arms were straining under the weight. "Oh, it smells good!" he said. "Did Cindy make meat loaf again?"

"Yeah. And there's smokes in there, too."

"I like Cindy," he said.

"So what's going on with your mom?"

"Cindy's the best," Alvin added.

"Uh-huh. So—"

"My mom's okay."

"It's her ankles, right?"

"Oh, same as before. Now she keeps rubbing her chest. Says her ribs hurt all the time."

"That can't be good."

"She likes meat loaf, though."

"Hey, it's your lucky day, then."

"Is Cindy okay?" Alvin asked. "I think my mom really hurt her. All I saw was when she yelled and went running out."

"Yeah, well," Danny said. "She'll be all right."

"My mom threw something at her?"

"Yeah. A coffee mug."

Alvin's brow wrinkled. "She's not usually like that. Just when she gets angry." More coughing came from inside, and another hard gob. "You wanna come in and see?"

"No, we're good. I gotta get home."

"Okay, bye."

Even though he'd dismissed us, and we turned and headed down the steps, the kid took a long time closing the door. One eye was still looking out when we got to the city sidewalk.

I kept quiet till we were around the corner. "Well, that was something," I said. "What's with your auntie?"

"What do you mean?"

"Her voice is like, *wow.*"

"She smokes," Danny said, making a face.

"Yeah." I laughed, remembering the cloud of stink rolling down the steps "I could tell." I found the whole thing hilarious and couldn't stop grinning like an idiot.

"Are you all right?" Danny asked me.

It took me a second to get my act together. "Yup."

When we were back on 110 Avenue, Danny said, "It's not that funny, you know. The kid practically lives in his basement. He can't hear his mom hacking down there as much."

"Okay."

"Dude, shut up," he said, giving me a shove. "Quit laughing."

I swallowed my smile. I'd never seen Danny so serious. Yeah, I thought, I was neck deep in the Cheevers world now. Freaky relatives, stinky houses, weird food. Everything seemed strong and busy and completely unlike my family where everything was boring and bland.

We were barely around the corner when I spotted someone we knew about half a block away. I had no idea at the time, but what was about to happen would trigger such a disaster, I thought I would never see Danny again. And it started innocently enough.

A kid our age was standing at the opening to the next alley, eating an orange popsicle and watching us approach. It was Noah Gulden, from school. "Hey, Dan! What's up?"

He was a pretty normal kid—not a bully, not a wimp, not a jock or nerd or anything else. I had traded comics with him once and went home with my dark hoodie totally covered in white cat hair. But that was a couple of years ago.

"Nothing. You?"

We stopped in the blazing sun.

"Hey, Bri."

"Hey."

"Just chillin' with my stolen popsicle."

"What do you mean, stolen?"

"Like, from Safeway. I got a whole box."

"How'd you manage that?"

He shrugged. "Skillz, man. I got skillz."

"You wanna share, maybe?"

"I don't know. I only got like, four left."

"Pig."

"Fine. But you gotta steal the next box."

"Yeah," said Danny. "That's not going to happen."

"Whatever. Come on. I got the box in the shade."

Danny did not hesitate. He followed Noah down the alley, with me dragging my feet behind them. I thought it was weird that Noah had been just standing there, like he was waiting for us. But Danny was already gone, with popsicle-sucking Noah jogging ahead of him. They got to the second garage and disappeared into the yard behind it.

It was right then that I got a whiff of cigarette smoke. I thought maybe the smell was still stuck in my nostrils from the auntie's house. But it wasn't. Two seconds later, I heard

Danny swear. "Whoa! No! Hey!"

There were sounds of a struggle and I went wide in the alley to see what was going on, my heart racing. The first thing I saw was Danny's bare back. He was trying to get away from someone pulling him by the shirt into the yard. It was Ordry Bruce. A great cloud of cigarette smoke floated over their heads and into the alley. Then I saw Morgan step out from the small people door of the garage. He grabbed a chunk of shirt and punched Danny in the ribs, then twice in the side of the head.

For a whole nanosecond, I thought I could rush over and help my friend. But that changed when I saw Danny skid down the stucco wall of the garage and Morgan start to kick him. This was no friendly schoolyard fight between equals. This was a beating. Right after Danny hit the ground, Ordry looked up and saw me. His face was calm and murderous, like he couldn't wait to tear me apart.

All of a sudden, every drop of blood in my body rushed to my head. The next moment, my legs and arms started moving by themselves. I was so blind with fear I couldn't have told you my own name. There was no distance between that garage and the end of the alley. Maybe I jumped, maybe I ran, maybe I sprouted rockets and flew. I have no idea how I got to the asphalt of the avenue. But I never slowed till I got there and continued to run with rubber legs for the next two blocks.

I finally glanced over my shoulder and saw there was no one chasing me. I stopped to catch my breath, bending over and gulping air like some exaggerated lung pump. It was then that it sunk in what I'd just done. And it was way worse than whatever might have happened if I'd stayed.

I was on the city sidewalk and started walking in circles, muttering like a freak. "Oh, god, what did I do? Oh, man… oh, no…"

There was no going back. In the time I had been running,

Danny would have been pulverized. I had abandoned him. And one after another, the consequences popped up in front of my eyes and exploded in my face.

What about Grantree's? What would my dad say if I didn't show up? But how could I face Danny tomorrow? One thing was certain. I was a freaking horror of a human being. What kind of friend would do that? Then I thought of my birth mother and my guts sank into the concrete. I hadn't even met her yet and I had already let her down.

Should I go home? Should I try to go back? In the end, my feet started moving toward home. I wasn't sure how I could hate myself any more than I already did, but hey, I had the whole night to try.

Chapter 10

The next morning was Saturday. When I woke up, my first thought was, *One more day till I meet my mother!* Two seconds later, I remembered what I'd done at that alley the day before and my whole body went into collapse.

I didn't want to see or talk to anybody, which was tough to do in a house with two little brothers and a mother who won't leave you alone. Around eight thirty the boys came and knocked on my door.

"Brian! Mom says you're going to be late for Graintree's!" At first I didn't answer and I could hear them jabbering to each other out in the basement: "Maybe he's gone already. Open the door and see. No! He'll be mad at us!" Then they knocked again. "Are you sleeping?"

"Go away!" I said to them and rolled over.

I could hear them running up the stairs. "Mom! He's not

getting up!" I couldn't hear the rest because I pulled the covers over my head.

About ten minutes later Mom, who got downstairs without making a single sound, rapped gently on my door. "Brian? Are you okay? You know you have Graintree's this morning." When I didn't answer, she opened the door wide enough to see me in bed. "Brian? Are you sick?"

I thought this was a perfect excuse and jumped on it. "Yeah," I groaned. "I'm not feeling well."

"Is it your stomach?"

"Yeah." Which wasn't a lie. My guts were totally in knots.

There was a pause. "Well, the boys were having trouble this morning, too. Maybe there's something going around. What about Mr. Graintree?"

It drove me so crazy to hear her mispronounce his name I had to grit my teeth to keep control of myself. "I don't know," I said. "I think we're done anyway."

My mother stood there for a second. Then she said, "Oh." Long pause. "Well, can I get you anything?"

"No..." I groaned. "I'll be up in a while."

She stood there for the longest time. Finally I thought I heard the door close and peeked out. She was gone. Ugh. This was going to be a very long day.

I did get up a couple of times, the first time to pee and the next to grab a sandwich and bring it down to my room. I didn't want to see anybody, I didn't want to talk to anybody. All I wanted was to sleep. So I figured out a cocoon where I could have the pillow over my ears and still manage to breathe. I even shut off my phone, which was a sure sign my life was over.

When Sunday arrived I was feeling a little better. I ate breakfast just to prove to myself I wasn't actually sick. But I was nearly psychotic with this weird, nervous energy. I was meeting my birth mother today! That thought almost eclipsed what I'd done to Danny, but not quite.

When Mom got back from church (she was the only one who went), she washed and ironed my best shirt and jeans. Yeah, she ironed my jeans. She even washed my runners, which I had to listen to, banging around in the dryer for like, an hour.

It was going to be another hot day. I was done faking being sick and as I sat at the table I couldn't stop vibrating. I was beyond excited. The only trouble was, if I took a breath the wrong way, a big black cloud of guilt reached down my throat and tried crushing my internal organs.

The whole house seemed glad for me. Mom was super nice and the boys came and stared at me while I was eating breakfast. I didn't mind at first, then it got creepy. So I said to them, "Don't you have something else do to?"

They had been sitting in silence. Me speaking opened up the floodgates.

"Are you gonna to go live at your real mom's house?" Kyle asked.

Mom came into the kitchen just then. I said, "It's better if you call her my birth mom. And no, I'm not going anywhere."

"Why did she give you away?"

"I dunno. I think she was too young to raise me."

"If I had a birf mom, I'd be pissed."

"Kyle!" Mom snapped. "Language."

"Sorr-y."

She was doing totally pointless stuff at the sink and dishwasher, so I knew she was hanging around to hear the jabber. Kyle's next question was directed at her.

"Did you get Brian when he was a baby?"

"Yes."

"Did you have to pay for him?"

The idea hadn't even occurred to me. Our mom's eyes blinked about fourteen times. "Pardo—what? No! There were some fees, I think. But we didn't get him off a shelf or anything."

Kyle seemed disappointed. "Oh."

I couldn't help myself. "How much were the fees?"

She looked at me like she suddenly regretted coming into the kitchen to listen. "Brian—no. I—I have no idea. A few hundred dollars, maybe. But don't ask that. That's a silly question."

I looked long at her. Things got uncomfortable and my eyes started moving around the kitchen, looking at things, wondering how much they cost for comparison. My eyes settled on the fridge. It was the only thing in the kitchen I knew the price of. And it was way more than a few hundred dollars. My guts sank. *Great. I cost less than a fridge.*

"Boys," Mom said, starting to shoo them with a dish towel, "that's enough. You two get out of here and leave Brian alone. We don't need you ruining the day for him."

The boys scrambled off their chairs and ran down the hall to their room, where they began making a racket with their toys. Mom went to close their door, then came to sit at the table, but not in her usual chair. I was expecting her to start up some kind of conversation. Instead, she sat there, looking old and kind of pathetic, folding and refolding the dish towel she'd been carrying around.

After I scraped the last smear of milk from the bottom of my cereal bowl, she said, "Are you okay?"

I shrugged, not wanting to get into a big sad blab. "Yeah, I'm fine."

"Looking forward to this evening?"

"Yeah, for sure."

"Are you angry with me?"

"Because…?"

She made a weird face and shrugged at her dish towel.

I have to admit, I was not Mr. Sensitive right then. I was way too antsy to be thinking about her feelings at that moment. I pretty much exploded off my chair. I gave my bowl and spoon a swish under the tap and dropped them in the open dishwasher. "I'm going for a bike ride."

"Oh. Okay, then. Don't forget your helmet."

When I got out to the yard, I kind of felt bad for Mom—and irritated by her at the same time. I was meeting my birth mother today. I wanted to feel all the richness of that. That's what was important. Not giving my adoptive mom a pat and saying, "There, there. You'll be fine." Gah! Sometimes it seemed like old people really needed to grow up.

When I got my bike out of the garage and my helmet on, I rode for about three blocks, south and east, not caring where I was going, just enjoying the blast of fresh air in my face. The faster I rode, the easier it was to forget what I'd done to Danny and feel the butterflies in my stomach, thinking about meeting my mother.

I ended up in this dinky ravine on the east side of Groat Road. It was too bumpy to ride down so parked my bike and walked. When I got deep into the ravine, I found this awesome gnarly maple tree and dropped myself down against it. Almost immediately I was overwhelmed with emotion. Turns out, when you mix excitement and guilt together in the same pot, you end up with this like, whole-body dread.

Yeah, I was out-of-control happy. This was the day I was going to find out who I was on Planet Earth. Why I was here. Who made me. But then, there was my freaking McSpadden mom being all emotional. And about six hundred times worse, there was the Danny thing. I was the biggest schmuck in the world and totally did not deserve any happiness. I couldn't believe fate was doing this to me. I sat there, sighing like an idiot for like, half an hour. The place reeked of green trees and damp rot from the ground. All you could hear was the leaves gently clapping all around. I just wanted to pull the earth over me like a blanket and never talk to anybody again.

But this stupid magpie had other ideas. I could see him up in the branches, hopping closer and closer, nattering at me like I was invading his space. "What?" I said to him. And I winged a stick at him to make him shut up.

That kind of broke the spell. I got to my feet and walked around for a bit, taking deep breaths, trying to shake off the tension I felt in my neck and guts. Then I walked my bike back to the street, thinking, *Wow, I really have to grow a pair and get a grip.* For sure, my birth mother did not want to meet some overly emotional kid who couldn't stop blubbering into his shirt. I sighed about forty times and hopped onto my bike. Yay! I was meeting my birth mother today! (Cue the canned applause.)

I rode back north about five or six blocks before I had to stop in the middle of the street. The way was blocked by a crappy orange car trying to park between two big commercial trucks, one with this crane thingy on it. The trucks belonged to men who were working on the roof of the nearest house, their air nailers going *Snak! Snak! Snak!*

I waited for a second, since there was no way to get by on the street. Then I got impatient and bumped up the curb onto the boulevard. And right then, I saw something that made me freeze and stare with my mouth open like an idiot. Was that—? Could that be—?

In the driver seat of the orange car was a young woman in a white shirt with some kind of dark sweater over it. The sweater had a round neck. She had bangs and giant glasses and she kept looking at me while she was trying to park her car.

I didn't know what to do, so I walked my bike farther up the walk, trying not to seem like a complete freak. I waited until she finished parking her car and got out. I leaned my bike against a boulevard tree, undid my helmet, and walked back. By then, she was around the passenger side, hauling out two giant bags of books.

"Something I can I help you with?" she asked, shoving the door closed with a hip.

I couldn't help grinning. "Maybe."

"Do I know you?"

"No," I said, laughing. She gave her head a shake and started toward the house with the men working on the roof. "Sorry!" I said. "I don't mean to be weird. Can I ask you something?"

She stopped impatiently on the city sidewalk and looked at me.

"Do you know a guy named Grantree?"

Her brow furrowed. "A guy?" she said. "What do you mean? That's my name."

"Oh! Uh...he lives over there a couple blocks." I pointed. "This old guy?"

She adjusted her grip on the heavy books. "You must mean my dad."

"He's your dad?"

"Sorry," she said, moving toward the house again. "I gotta put these bags down."

"You need a hand?"

"Oh, no, I'm all right."

I followed her up the sidewalk. "You sure read a lot."

"Huh? No, I just had to get away from this racket for a while." She tipped her head toward the workmen.

I could see the bags were from the UofA bookstore. "You go to university?"

"No, I work there. You sure ask a lot of questions."

"Sorry, I just... Are you going to be here for a while?"

"I live here."

I was afraid of annoying her more. "Okay...um...sorry. I gotta call my friend." That must have sounded bizarre, but whatever. As she brought her books up the steps, I headed back down the sidewalk with my phone out and started texting Danny. I couldn't believe what I was doing. He was either going to kill me or hug me. I had no idea which.

The message I sent Danny was: *i totally found the woman from grantrees*

As I waited, I had no idea what his reaction would be. Most likely, he'd just ignore me—which was like, the normal response to someone who abandons you. I went back to my bike on the boulevard and hunched down against the nearest lamp post with my phone, listening to the *Snak! Snak!* of the roofers' nailer. I played a game for a couple of minutes, not even really paying attention to it.

A little while later, a low-deck truck drove up, blasting music. This young guy with a super-dark tan got out. He gave me a look like I was a wart on the landscape. Then he went up the grass and joined the other guys on the back side of the roof. That's when a second nailer started up, so the sound was now like *Snak! Snak-Snak! Snak-Snak-Snak!*

The sounds must have been bad inside the house because almost immediately, the woman came out with a coffee mug and three books under her arm. She sat on the front step and began flipping through the pages. I don't even know if she noticed me.

Two minutes later, I got an answer to my text. My phone was sitting on the grass in front of me. I heard it vibrate and took a deep breath before picking it up and looking at the screen. It said: *WHAT!!!!!*

My butt slipped down the lamppost and I raked my spine on some kind of nubby thing sticking out. Through the pain of my scraped back, I got totally choked up. So far, he wasn't going to kill me.

Before I could answer, he asked: *how do u no its her?*

I typed as fast as I could: *I asked*

Then I gave him the address where I was and added: *haven't talked 2 her much waiting 4 u*

His answer came in less than five seconds: *cha-ching! b there n 10*

After reading the message, I realized every muscle in my body had been tensed for the last day and a half. I stood up and walked around, taking deep breaths to try and get myself together. What was he going to say when he got here? So far, he didn't sound like he was mad at me. How could that be?

After a while, as I was bending my neck and shaking my arms, I saw the young woman glance up from her books at me now and again. *She must think I'm some kind of weirdo stalker,* I thought, and sat back down.

When Danny arrived, I could see him coming for like, fifteen seconds. He was riding up the sidewalk, his helmet loose and high on his forehead. I got up and waved, trying to read his expression as he pedalled up the block. He spotted the woman on her front step and rode right past me and then her. She followed him with her eyes the whole way. Then he circled around on the boulevard and rode back past her.

"Can I help you?" she asked him.

"Just a sec!" he called back and came to a stop in front of me.

He was chewing gum. That may not seem important, but it was. When Danny chewed gum, he chewed it with the maximum amount of chaw, mouth open, twisting his face every direction. I still couldn't tell if he was going to kill me or hug me.

He remained on his bike seat, feet on the ground.

"Is that her?" I asked.

"Yeah, totally. How did you find her?"

I tried to be all jolly and go along with ignoring the elephant in the room. "I was just riding by. She was getting out of her car."

"See? I wasn't crazy, was I?"

"She's Grantree's daughter."

"No way." He blinked a couple of times, looking at her, chawing some more.

"I guess he doesn't think she's old enough to be a woman," I joked.

"Huh!" he exclaimed.

There was the longest pause in the history of pauses.

"Why don't we go and talk to her?" he said.

"Sure, but…"

"But what?"

I wiped the sweat from my top lip. I was so nervous I was afraid he'd notice. I let there be a little gap of silence. Then I said, "Sorry about the other day." I studied his face, trying to read his expression, the way he shifted his gum from one side to the other.

Finally, he scratched an armpit and said, "What other day?"

I did my best to hold it together. "Uh…after Alvin's? You got like, bashed by what's-his-name."

Danny shook his head, sort of wiggling his eyes in the process. "That Ordry guy? Yeah, that sucked. Look what they did to me." He lifted up his shirt and turned a bit, wincing in pain. Up by his ribs, the whole side of his back was purple with bruises. "My leg's the same," he added, lowering his shirt. "What happened to you?"

"Oh, dude, I'm so sorry. I freaked and like, took off."

"Yeah, I figured." *Chaw chaw.* "But why are you sorry? You thought you could do something? *You?*"

I was not exactly known for my fighting skills. "Well… still…"

He rolled his eyes and made a rude sound with his lips. "*Pfft.* Whatever. They just wanted to intimidate me. I lied and told them my uncle's a cop. They weren't going to do anything."

"Really? Didn't you get pulverized?"

He shrugged. "Yeah, a bit. But let's go. I wanna talk to this lady."

And that was it. I couldn't believe what I'd just heard. He didn't want to kill me. How was this possible? He was just brushing off getting beat up by two of the meanest kids in the neighbourhood. What a wimp I was! Days of gut-wrenching guilt! All for nothing. I resolved, in the future, to assume that every single person in the whole rest of the world had thicker skin than I had. Still, as I followed him up the walk, I felt a six thousand pound weight lift off my shoulders and drift away over the housetops.

Danny rode up the city sidewalk and even though he was going dead slow, he skidded his back wheel sideways to a stop and dropped his bike.

"What's going on?" the woman asked. "Do I have to call the police?"

"What? No! Sorry," Danny said, stepping a bit closer. "My name's Danny and this is Brian. You're Grantree's daughter?"

"Sybil Grantree. And who are you?"

"I'm your dad's neighbour."

"Ooh," she said, setting down her book. "To the north? Are you the kid who broke his greenhouse?"

"Me? Yeah."

"He's kind of accident-prone," I threw in.

"That's putting it mildly." She smiled. "Who falls out of a tree into a greenhouse?"

"I figure greenhouses are asking for it," he said, chawing around his words. "All that glass is just waiting for a disaster. I kept seeing you in his house and nobody believed me."

"Oh, I've been back for a couple of weeks. I got a research position here. I was at UVic for almost ten years."

"Like, Inuvik up north?"

She blinked a couple of times at Danny. "No, University of Victoria. On the island?"

Danny took a couple of slow chaws on his gum, then stopped. "What island?"

"You've never been to BC? Oh my god, don't ask me what BC is. I might have to hit you with this book."

"Ha-ha. I thought maybe you were Gran—his nurse or something."

"Oh, for his hip. Hey, I offered to move back home and cook for him and everything. But he's so cranky!"

"Yeah, no kidding," I said.

"Cranky but kind," she added. "I can't complain. He's fixing up this bungalow for me."

"He owns this house too?" Danny asked.

"Yeah, kicked the renters out so I could move in. Had the whole place painted. And now this racket," she said, talking about the roofers.

"Wow."

"So, he's getting you guys to work for him, eh? I saw you out in his yard."

"Yeah. Sucks."

"I'm not a gardener," she said, wrinkling her nose to push up her glasses. "I'm not domestic at all. Besides, I'd rather buy books." The noise of the roofers stopped for a second, then started up with renewed fury. "Oh my god, I hope they're done soon. The sound in the kitchen is just incredible. So I guess I'll see you around?"

"Yeah," said Danny. "If I see you in your dad's house, I won't freak out again."

"He thought you were a ghost," I said.

She smiled. "Is that right? I stop by most days—Friday for sure."

"Why? What's Friday?"

"Oh, I gotta bring my dad for his big thing at the museum."

Danny swatted my arm. "What did you do that for?" I asked him.

"Museum?" he said, his eyebrows up. "Don't you remember what those plumbers said?"

"Uh…" I totally did not remember.

"What are you talking about?" the woman asked. "The plumbers at my dad's?"

"Yeah," said Danny. "They were talking about display cases at the museum."

"Ha! That's weird. Why would they care? So you've seen

116

them?"

"Yeah, totally," Danny said. "Scared the crap outa Brian here."

"Which one? Butt-Crack or Black-Eyes?"

"That's what you call them?" I laughed.

"The black-eyed guy is one thing. But the other one—wow. I think his name is Lyle. His back hair looks like it's pouring into his pants." She shivered. "God knows what it's doing once it's in there."

Danny pointed at her and said to me. "She's funny." Then he asked her, "So what about the museum? And they said something about stamps?"

"Yeah, that's on Friday," she told us. "Dad has this huge collection. Mom used to *hate* how much space it took up. Before his surgery he got all worried he'd die. Now he's getting it organized and selling bits and pieces. And yeah, he's donating some to the museum."

I could hear a beeping—like a microwave beeping—coming from in the house.

"Oh, shoot!" she said. "I gotta go. Nice talking to you. Don't let my dad work you too hard. He loves bossing people around." And she zipped inside.

Danny and I walked back to the city sidewalk. When we were out of earshot, Danny said, "Can you believe that? Freaking Grantree reproduced. Unreal."

"I don't know how she got to be so nice."

"Probably from her mom's side." He pumped his fists and made a weird face. "I get cash! Fifty freakin' bucks!"

I was going to ask him about getting a cut, like a finder's fee. But I realized I totally owed him, after abandoning him. Instead, seeing how happy he was, I said, "So, uh... Sorry about missing Grantree's. How'd it go?"

He looked blankly at me for a second. "Gran—oh! Whatever. It's the weekend. I didn't even bother. Don't we get a break? Besides, my dad sent me to check on my auntie. I was

117

there like, the whole morning!"

"Is she all right?"

"Dude, she's the opposite of all right. They wanted me to go this morning, and I'm like, *no!* I can't take it. The smell just sticks to you."

We picked up our bikes and walked in silence for a bit. Then I remembered something. "So I guess the stamps aren't counterfeit."

Danny looked at me wide-eyed. "What? How do you know? She just said her dad owns other houses and has this like, giant collection. He's a stamp expert guy. He'd totally know how to counterfeit."

I just looked at him. "Whatever. It's too dumb. She just said he was donating some of them to the museum. You can't get much more legit."

"Then why were they talking about 'real' stamps? What does that mean?"

I stopped on the sidewalk. "You want me to go back and ask her?"

He sighed and rolled his eyes. "We don't know anything about these people. They could be like—what are you doing?"

I had pulled out my phone. "I'm gonna call them."

"Who?"

"The museum."

Danny took two big chaws of his gum. "What are you gonna say?"

"I don't know yet."

It took a second to find the number for the museum, I didn't call the main number. I used my brain and called the office. Danny stood there chewing, impressed by my initiative.

"You have reached the Royal Alberta Museum. Our administrative offices are now closed." *Crap,* I realized, *it's Sunday.* "If you know the extension of the person, *blah-blah-blah.* Otherwise stay on the line to leave a message. We will get back to you as soon as we can."

When the line beeped, I said, "Hi," and immediately felt my heart pounding like crazy. I had never done anything like this before. "Uh... I heard there is going to be a new display case at the—"

"Exhibit," Danny butted in.

"What?"

"*Ask of they're setting up a new exhibit!*" he hissed at me.

I gave him an eye roll and asked, "I'm wondering if there's going to be a new exhibit coming up?" My question sounded incredibly lame.

"*For stamps!*" Danny prompted.

"For stamps," I said into the phone. "Oh, my name's Brian McSpadden." And I gave them my number.

I had barely clicked to end the call when Danny slapped me on the arm. "What's that for?"

"Ha! Well, that was awesome."

"Oh, whatever. We don't actually know anything yet."

"Meh." He shrugged and jumped on his bike. "I gotta go. I'll text you later. And if the museum gets back to you, freaking call me!" He sped off.

I stood there for a second just watching him. What the heck had just happened? Were things back to normal? I felt like somebody who'd been bruised and beaten for like, two days straight and no one even noticed. Ugh. I gave my head a shake and climbed onto my bike. If this kept up, I was going to get whiplash.

Chapter 11

When I got home, Mom gave me heck about being out so long. "Don't you have to get ready for this evening?"

"No, I'm good," I told her. "I just have to shower."

"Oh, really?" she said. "Look at your runners. I just washed them."

There was some gunge on them from my trip down to that ravine. "Okay..."

"Your lunch is on the counter there. You've got to shower and scrub those fingernails."

"Yeah, I know."

"And I made an appointment with Shelley for two o'clock."

"Really?" Shelley lived in the apartment a couple of doors down. She was in cosmetology school and she always cut my hair.

"And you really should clean your room."

"Huh? Why?"

"Oh, come on, Brian. On such a big day, do you really want to come home to a mess?"

I was already completely overwhelmed by what was happening that afternoon, so I just gave in to Mom's schedule. I did the Brian lunge down the stairs. This time, I reached super-far down the wall and the handrail, and managed to land on the very last step. Progress!

In my bedroom, I shoved a few things around so it didn't look too bad. Then I got the bit of gunge off my runners at the laundry sink by the washer. By then, my stomach was growling. I brought my runners upstairs and put them on the back step to dry. The boys had already eaten and were getting their baby-bird cleaning in the bathroom. So I sat there by myself, eating my sandwich in silence, still feeling shell-shocked after the events of the last couple of days.

I suppose I should have been having a big think about my life and the importance of the day. But the truth was, I just sat there with my mind a blank and my stomach doing cartwheels. When I was done eating, I couldn't even remember if I'd eaten or not. I looked down at my empty plate and thought, *Huh! that's weird.*

When I went outside to check on my runners, I spotted Shelley waving at me to come over. Their place was on the second floor of the only apartment building on our block. It was kind of creepy sometimes to see her and her mother sitting on their balcony, trying to get tans. It seemed like they were in the guard tower for our little grassy prison yard. It was only one thirty, but I had nothing else to do, so I went over.

Shelley's mom was at work, so she had her girly music blasting on the stereo when I arrived. "Hey, kiddo!" she had to yell at me.

"Can you turn the music down?" I asked her.

"What? You don't like it?"

"No, no," I said. "I want to tell you something. It's like, important."

"Are you sick?" She looked at me with huge eyes. "You haven't got cancer or something, have you?"

"Wha…? No! Can we just—"

"Yeah, yeah. Just a sec!" She disappeared into the living room and spun the volume down on their stereo.

Shelley was like, six feet tall and thin as a pencil. Everybody thought she was bulimic or whatever, but the truth was, she never stopped eating and I never saw her barf it up. I think she was about seventeen, but I could have been wrong. She always wore the freakiest clothes she could find—mostly her mother's stuff, which she adapted, like pajama pants rolled up to her knees and a lacy bra on the outside of her shirt. And she never wore matching socks. Like, never. And if people thought her clothes were bizarre, well, they never looked at her hair. She was her own crazy science experiment. Her hair wasn't just a different color or style every day. Sometimes she'd have like, three different styles before lunch. Today she was wearing multicoloured leggings with black short shorts over them and a super-bright pink belly shirt. Her hair was black with green tips.

I climbed onto the bar stool she had set up in the narrow kitchen and she draped me with a professional barber's cloth, touching my hair here and there like, sixty times before she started.

"What about the sides? You gotta go short, you know. I can't even look at it the way I did it last time. And can I do a pattern? Like flames, maybe, at the back of your neck?"

"I already asked," I lied. "My mom said no." I wanted the most normal, but cool-looking hair possible for my birth mother. No weird stuff.

"How about we get some dreads going?"

"Uh…"

"Oh, I know! Can I do like, a vampire pointy front? That'd be so chill."

"Shelley, come on. Just do it the same as last time. I really need it to be like, tame. I have an important thing today."

"Oh! You're such a disappointment. Fine. Tame. So what's your big event?"

I had never told anyone I was adopted. No friends knew and I certainly wouldn't tell anyone at school. But Shelley was different. It was sort of her job to keep people's secrets. "Well," I started, "today I'm going to meet my—"

"Wait, wait," she said, whirling off into the living room. "This is my favorite song." After cranking the volume again, she danced back to me and began spritzing my hair with water from a squeeze bottle and pushing it straight up. And then over. And then back the other way. Halfway through the blaring song she began cutting and I almost gave up on trying to tell her my news. But as soon as the song was done, she walked back into the living room and brought the volume down to non-deafening.

"Don't mind me," she said as she returned. "I live for that song. So what's this big thing you were going to tell me?"

"Oh, nothing. It's no big deal."

"Of course it is! Come on! Tell me! The suspense is killing me!"

"Seriously?" She was behind me and I turned to see her expression.

Her face came around from the back, reeking of makeup. "Seriously."

I thought, *Screw it. I gotta get used to telling people sooner or later.* "So…I'm adopted and I'm going to meet my birth mother today."

All cutting, combing and touching of my hair came to sudden stop. Shelley stepped around the other side of me and, hands on nonexistent hips, said, "You're not joking me, are you? For real?"

"For real. This is the first time I'm gonna meet her—well, since I was a baby."

I watched Shelley's face for a reaction. Slowly, like it was taking a very long time for it to sink in, Shelley face began to crumble. Her chin sank and her eyes squinted to keep the tears back. "My little Brian! He's going to meet his mum for the first time! Aww!" She flung her arms around my neck and sobbed onto the top of my head. "Little Brian! Why didn't you ever tell me? I've been cutting your hair for how long?"

"Like, I don't know, years."

"Aww! Little kiddo! That's so awesome! So you just found her? How did it happen? Were you searching for her? Tell me everything. I promise I won't cry on you anymore."

So I started from the beginning. How I always sort of knew I was adopted.

"Of course you were," she remarked. "You don't look anything like your little brothers."

I told her how I'd always wondered and planned to search for her but never really knew where to start.

"Oh," she said, "I would have been walking the city, banging on every door."

"Then some agency called like, last week, saying she had been searching for me."

"Of course she was."

"That's kind of it."

"Oh my god, that's so great. So you haven't talked to her or anything yet?"

"Just on the phone."

"That's huge!" Shelley exploded, flinging her arms out and scraping the kitchen cupboard with the point of her scissors. "What did she sound like?"

"I dunno, like normal."

"Is she young? Old? What?"

"Sort of young—like, compared to my parents. I don't

think she's thirty yet."

"Oh, Brian, I'm so happy for you. I want to tell everybody. Can I tell my friends and mom and everyone?"

"Well…"

"Okay, I know it's like, private. Just my mom. And I won't say your name when I tell my friends. I'll be like, 'One of my clients has just found his birth mother.' Is that okay?"

"I dunno. I guess."

"Tell me more. When are you meeting her? Today?"

"Yeah," I said, feeling my chest puff out with a calm happiness. "I'm going over there for dinner tonight."

"No way!"

Shelley's enthusiasm somehow dragged me out of my own idiot head and put the whole thing in perspective. I ended up blabbing to her for the next half hour about adoption. I got to say stuff I could never say to anyone else. By the time she finished with my hair, Shelley was in a state of giddy happiness for me. She couldn't keep her hand off my shoulder, telling me she was *soo jealous. Soo happy* for me. *Soo totally glad* I shared with her.

As I left, I felt I finally had my head on straight about this day. *That's* how people should react, I thought. Jumping for joy. All my anxiety was gone. My heart was full and my stomach butterflies were throwing a party. Plus, I did the perfect lunge down the stairs of her apartment building. Maybe it was the stairs or the railings; I don't know. But for the first time, it totally worked.

The afternoon of my big day rocketed by. Before I knew it, it was three thirty and I hadn't even had a shower yet. Shelley had gotten me into such a hyped state, my guts wouldn't stop jiggling. And I wore the stupidest grin you ever saw.

The boys didn't like my haircut.

"It looks just the same as last time!"

"That's what I wanted."

Apparently, that did not register. "Why?"

This was coming from a kid who looked like a 1950s minister's son.

"Whatever." I was too floaty-brained to let them get to me. I just walked away.

After my shower I got dressed and sat on my bed for like, ten minutes, just staring at my dresser, freaking out. I was meeting my birth mother in like, forty-five minutes. How was a person supposed to act in this situation? It was like I had forgotten how to be me. I couldn't face my birth mother like this. I was just some sort of puppet boy with a hollow head and way over-excited guts.

I was jolted out of my brain freeze-up by Dad calling down the stairs, "Brine!" The way he said my name was never Bri-an. It was always short and sharp so it came out like "Bri!" or "Brine!"

There was only one response and it was always instant: "Yeah!" I jumped up and opened my door as fast as I could.

"Are you ready to go?"

This time I hesitated. "Are you driving me?"

"Is that all right?"

"Yeah, totally," I lied. I couldn't believe he was going to drive me. Was he going to do some stupid heart-to-heart on the way? I cast a quick glance around my room, wondering if I was forgetting anything. I had a quick thought—that I would never see this room the same way again—then I hurried up the stairs.

Dad was sitting on the landing doing up his shoes. It was Sunday, so no hat hair. Just white quack grass.

Kyle was behind him holding his stomach, doing a weird little dance. "Can I come?"

"No!" The word was out of my mouth before I realized it.

Dad didn't look at me, but I saw him flinch. He glanced back at Kyle. "Not this time. And why are you jumping around?"

"I gotta poop."

"Well, go on and do it. And tell your mother we're leaving."

But there was no need to tell her. As Kyle raced away, she appeared behind Dad with what looked like a little book in her hands. A fake smile was pressing her lips flat. It took her a second to realize she was in a bit of a trance, then she blinked herself back to reality. "Are you excited?" she asked me. Her eyebrows were not sure what to do. Up, down, sad, happy, it was all in there.

"Yeah, for sure," I answered.

There was a silence in which Dad finished tying up his shoes, stood up and headed out the door. "I'll see you at the car," he said as he left.

Mom put her arms out for a hug. I went up the stairs and gave her a lame hug back. "Oh, Brian," she said. "I'm so proud of you."

"Proud? What did I do?"

"Nothing. Just you. You just be you, and you'll do fine." Her face crinkled into the beginnings of a sob. "Here," she said, showing me the book she'd been holding. "I made a little album for you to show her." She flipped it open and I saw it was full of pictures of me. There were maybe twenty of them, from when I was a baby up to my track meet photo from this spring. Most of them were school pictures, all of them hideous. "You can give this to her, if you like."

I took the album and stepped away from any more hugs. "Okay, thanks. Dad's waiting."

She stood there like I was going off to war and she might never see me again. "Good luck, Brian," she said as I hurried out the door.

And all I could think was, *Yeah, no kidding, Mom. I will not be the same person when I get home.*

Chapter 12

Dad had the car out of the garage already. One the worst things in my world was to be in the front seat of a car with my dad. Usually the boys and I sat in the back. I'd stare out the window while Mom, half turned around, disciplined the boys, and everybody ignored me. Now sitting beside Dad was both an honour and a dreaded thing.

We swung out onto 111th Avenue without comment or incident. He wiped his face and settled his butt in the seat better, but that was it. I wanted to check my phone sooo badly, but I knew he hated that. He always said, "What's in there that's more important than this? See this? Reality?" So I sat there digging a thumbnail into the edge of the photo album, watching the houses zip by.

Then suddenly, out of nowhere, he cleared his throat a couple of times and said, "I, uh…I never wanted anything to do with my parents. My birth parents."

I sat there without saying anything for a bit. Then I realized my silence was making things awkward. So I turned my head and said, "No, eh?"

"Never," he mumble-whispered. "I don't really remember much. The people who got me, they, uh…they told me I wasn't even thirty pounds, at five years old. Ribs sticking out, the whole deal. Foster parents weren't much better. Anyway…" His voice drifted into silence.

I felt I should say something. But I let a long time pass before I said, "Wow," in this like, noncommittal voice. I did not want to encourage him.

But he had one last thing to add. "You? Well, we got you because I wanted to do it right. You ain't no thirty pounds. You got your phone, a nice warm bed. I hope we're doing okay." He pressed his lips together in a weird way and blinked a couple of times at the mirror out the driver's side window.

All I could think to say was, "Yeah."

We drove the rest of the way in silence. Well, except for the radio. He jabbed it on and I sat there, morphing every single word of the song lyrics into something to do with me. Ugh. Before I knew it, we were turning off the avenue onto *her* street. My pits started raining sweat. I didn't want to stick my hand in there to wipe it off onto my pants, because then everything would stink. So I just squished my arms tight to my sides, hoping to hold it in.

I had Googled her address and seen the house on Street View, so I knew exactly how far down the block it was. As we approached, I tried to calm myself. I let my shoulders drop and stopped digging my thumbnail into the side of the photo album. The street was packed with cars and there was nowhere to park, so Dad just stopped in the middle of the street.

"You all right?" For the first time in like, forever, he seemed genuinely concerned.

"Yeah," I said, my voice cracking. "I'm good."

"You be a gentleman, now. You call when you're done."

"Okay." I opened the door and realized my legs might not be strong enough to keep me upright. They were total jelly.

As I stepped up to the curb, Dad pulled away. I stopped for a second to look at the house. It was a big two-storey thing with a wooden screen door and a weird little window in the attic. The ancient cedar siding was painted gray and the trim was dirty white. There wasn't much of a front yard. It was maybe ten feet of grass between the porch and the city sidewalk. But the place had this old homey feel, as if generations of kids had been born here and played on this street.

I crossed the boulevard and the city sidewalk and all of a sudden this blast of flower smell hit me. There were no flowers at the front of the house, so I wondered where it was coming from. Did somebody spill a tanker truck of fabric softener? Then I realized it was this huge bush off to the side. It had these big white tufts of flowers all over it and the smell was ridiculous—fresh and powerful and clean-smelling, like some kind of heaven for your nostrils.

I got two steps up to the porch, with the photo album starting to slip out of my sweaty hand, when a woman appeared behind the screen of the front door and opened it.

"Hey…Brian?"

She was so young-looking I was not sure at first if she was my mother. She was wearing this pale blue fuzzy sweater and jeans. I was a bad judge of ages, but she looked about twenty or so, her shoulder-length hair pinned back above her ears.

"Hey," I said and as I got closer, I saw she was a bit older than I thought. "Are you—?"

The minute I said this, her face crumpled into tears. She didn't cry, but she had to hold her eyes really far open and blink to see me. She stepped onto the porch, letting the door bang closed behind her.

"Come here," she said and I stepped up onto the porch and into her arms.

It was so freakishly like what I had always hoped for, I thought for a second I was dreaming. The scent of that flowery shrub was one thing. But the warmth of her and the smell of her hair and clothes felt strangely familiar. Tears leaped out of my eyes like monkeys jumping off a branch.

"It's so great to meet you," she said, and then she held me at arm's length. "Oh my god, you look exactly like my brother when he was a kid."

I wiped my eyes. I swear, I had the biggest smile on my face I had ever had in my entire life.

"You call me Alicia, okay? I know it's weird. We gotta work all this out. It's so great to see you!"

I thought I saw someone peeking through the blinds in the window behind her. But the blinds snapped back as I noticed them. She reached for the door without taking her eyes off me and let me go in first. The house smelled like a combination of that flower shrub, dark old wood, and fresh baby barf. The moment we were inside, three people came crowding out of the room to the left and stood in a row like it was a surprise birthday party. They were all grinning like champions. One of them was holding a little girl in a pale green dress.

"Brian," my mother said, "this is Cassie, my sister."

A tall woman with grey hair at her temples held out her hand. "I'm the oldest," she said, squeezing my hand like she was Iron Man or something. "Alicia is the baby of the family."

"Cassie was on the Olympic rowing team," my mother added.

"Oh," said Cassie, "he doesn't care about that right now. Finish introducing everybody."

The girl was being held by a scrawny guy with a little chin beard. My mom rubbed the girl's bare arm. "This is my daughter Madeleine," she said. "I guess she's your half-sister, eh?"

I took the little girl's hand. "Hey, cutie," I said, but she pulled away and buried her face in the shoulder of the guy holding her.

"I'm Jake," said the chin-beard guy. "I'm Cassie's hubby. Awesome to meet you."

"Yeah, same," I mumbled.

Jake used his free arm to point a thumb at the woman beside him. "And this is my sister Jill. Jill was so excited, I couldn't stop her coming. I think she's more pumped than any of us."

The woman named Jill was the only one of them wearing glasses. She was so overcome with excitement, her feet were doing a little dance on the floor under her. Her face was a mess of tears. "Hi, I'm Jill. I know we're not related. But can I hug you?" she asked.

"Um...okay."

The woman literally leapt across the floor and attacked me with her arms. If Jake hadn't stopped her, she would have choked me to death out of pure joy. "Omigod, omigod, I'm so happy for you." When Jake pulled her off me, she went and gave my mother a hug and said, "Oh my god, he's so handsome. You're so lucky."

My mother took it all with good humour. "All right now," she said, prying Jill's arms off her. "We're good, we're good. Doesn't he look like James? He's your uncle," she added for my benefit. "Just the nose and the eyebrows?"

Jill was using her fingers to wipe tears from behind her glasses. "Oh, completely. He's exactly the same."

The little girl was starting to squirm, and Jake gave her a bounce as he said, "Jill and Alicia were best friends growing up. That's how I met Cassie."

"Oh, cool," I muttered, not quite remembering who was who.

"All right," said my mother. "Come on in. We'll visit in

the living room for now."

Behind everybody, I kicked off my shoes, really, really hoping my socks didn't stink.

The living room seemed tiny and cozy for such a big old house. There were two loveseats opposite each other. One was an ancient-looking pink thing. The other was on some sort of cheap wooden frame. Both looked ratty and beat up. In the middle of the room, serving as a coffee table, was a wooden crate that was either a valuable antique or some crap found in an alley in like, 1962.

My mother sat beside me and Jill and Cassie sat opposite us. The guy, Jake, disappeared with the little girl for a second and returned with a flimsy metal kitchen chair. He sat down and plunked the little girl on his knee. Jill could not stop vibrating. She had her glasses off, wiping them with the hem of her shirt as tears continued to stream down her face. Cassie put a hand on her shoulder. "Oh my god, you gotta get it together, Jill. Seriously."

"I can't help it!" she said, knocking her knees together out of pure excitement. "I've never been to anything like this. I'm so happy for you, Alicia."

My mother and I were perched on the edge of the pink couch like birds. She tapped me on the side of the knee and gave me a smile. It was a cool little moment, like we were old pals who shared a secret. Then she gave her head a shake and rose. "What am I thinking? We've got tea. Do you drink tea, Brian?"

"Sometimes," I told her, but the truth was, I'd only ever just tasted it. I'd never had a cup to myself.

Before I knew it, she was striding across what was plainly the dining room, but which they were using as a play area for the little girl. I shocked myself, watching my mother leave. She was hot! And then I had to give my head a shake, thinking, *Dude, she's your mother! Stop that!*

"So tell us a bit about yourself, Brian." Cassie was clearly in older sister mode. I was being checked out to make sure I was made out of acceptable son material. "Do you like sports?"

I remembered she was the Olympic athlete. "Sure, yeah."

"Team?"

"Huh? Pardon?"

"A team sport? Hockey? Football?" Her questions were quick and aggressive.

"No, just whatever we do in gym class."

This took a moment to register, like she'd never heard of my kind of human before. "Oh." She sounded disappointed. "So what do you do for fun?"

"I don't know. Watch TV, play games." This sounded incredibly lame, so I added, "I goof around with plasticine a bit."

"So you're a sculptor?"

I shrugged. "I guess."

"What kind? Figurative?"

Her questions were so rapid-fire, Jake felt the need to stop her. "Cassie, whoa, slow down. Wait till Alicia's back. She'll want to hear this."

The room fell silent for a second. The little girl had buried her head in Jake's chest, sucking a thumb and staring at me like I was a TV.

Jill suddenly jumped up. "I better help Alicia. Don't talk about anything important till I get back!"

Jake stared at Cassie, as if his gaze were stopping her from being weird. "So, uh, Brian, eh?" he finally said to me. "You live just down the avenue."

"Yeah," I replied. "Couple miles."

I was expecting this to be an opener to a conversation, but he let it drop and nodded in the silence. "Cool."

All of a sudden I had this gut wrench. Who were these people? Why did I have to talk to them? Where was my mother?

Finally, I'm sure just to break the silence, Cassie cracked her knuckles and spoke up. "He really does look like James, doesn't he?"

"Yeah," said Jake, pulling on his little tuft of beard. "Totally. Somebody should find a picture of him. Brian, you really wouldn't believe it."

I nodded. "Oh, yeah…"

"Same eyebrows for sure." Then out of nowhere he said, "Do you like chocolate?"

With a shrug, thinking what a weird conversation this was, I said, "Yup. Doesn't everybody?"

"Oh, no," offered Cassie. "Not everyone. This lady at work just *hates* it. But the Kellys have a special love for it."

"What was that?" said my mother, coming back from the kitchen with a bunch of mismatched coffee mugs hooked on her fingers.

"Chocolate," said Cassie.

My mother clunked and clinked the mugs down on the wooden crate. "Absolutely."

Jill followed her in with a huge teapot and this little cream and sugar set in a wire rack. "Don't even."

My mother said, "Cassie brought me back this massive chocolate bar from Las Vegas. I swear, I ate it all in two days."

As Jill set a mug in front of each of us, I began to freak out that nothing important was being said. Were we going to talk about sports and chocolate the whole time? And I thought I was here for dinner.

Just then the front door banged open and a medium-sized man poked his head around the corner.

"Hey, hon," said my mother, stopping where she stood for a second. Then she came back to sit beside me. "How was everything?"

"Same old," he said, kicking off a pair of grubby runners. The guy had super-pale red hair and dark freckles, like all the colors were in the wrong place. The bottom of his pants looked as if they'd been sprayed with mud. "Tough day. Who's this?"

My mother looked at me and gave me a weak smile. "Don't you remember?" His face remained blank. "This is... Brian?"

"Oh," he said, somewhat interested. "Cool." And with that, he scuffed his muddy pants into the kitchen. A moment later, I heard the *Kuk! Pss* of a beer can being opened. He came out of the kitchen and scuffed up the stairs.

"That's Keith," my mother sighed, disappointed. "He's had a long day."

"What does he do?" I thought maybe he had been doing some tough physical job. But no.

"Oh, nothing right now. He was trucking up at the oil sands. But he lost his licence and they had to let him go. Obviously, that doesn't stop him quadding with his buddies."

"Oh, yeah..." I felt like I had been saying that a lot—oh, yeah, oh yeah. It usually meant "Oh yes, isn't that interesting." But in this case, it meant *I-can't-say-it-but...what-a-freak!* The guy didn't even say hello to his daughter. At least I thought she was his daughter. "So he's...your—?"

"We're just common-law right now. He doesn't believe in marriage."

"Oh, yeah..."

Cassie jumped in. "And he doesn't believe in looking for work, either."

My mother gave her a sharp glance. "Oh, come on. It's Sunday."

I finally got my brain into gear to say something other than oh yeah. "So you were saying you work at a cabinet place?" I asked my mother.

"Yeah, Sundance Cabinets. I totally lucked out with that one. I just love the smell of it. If I go shopping after work, the tellers ask me if I'm a carpenter or something. I guess it just lingers."

"Oh, come on, Alicia," threw in Cassie. "It's not that great." Then she told me, "She's way too nice. They totally take advantage of her there."

"Cassie!" My mom gave her sister a what-the-hell look.

Everyone smiled uncomfortably. I tried to save things. "So...you bring Madeleine to work with you?"

Before she could answer, Jill jumped in. "I don't know why. Breathing all that dust. I keep offering to watch her. I'm home with my boys, anyway. They're seven and eleven."

"Like the store," I joked. But no one thought it was funny.

"Maddy's just a prize," Jill continued. "Such a sweetie. Aren't you Maddy?" The girl squirmed closer into Jake's chest, keeping her thumb ready in case of an emergency. "You have siblings, right?"

"Me? Yeah. Two little brothers. They're like, four and five."

Cassie, who was checking to see if the tea was ready, asked, "Were they adopted too?"

"No."

"Isn't that the way it always is?" Jill laughed. "You think you can't have kids so you adopt one. Then bam! The hormones kick in and all of a sudden you have a brood."

"Are they in kindergarten or anything yet?"

"No. This fall, the older one starts." *If they can figure out how stop his honker from leaking,* I thought.

"No playschool?"

I rubbed my sweaty upper lip. "No, my mom's kind of... protective. She didn't want them to start too early."

Cassie rolled her eyes. "Typical."

Whatever that means, I thought.

Once the tea was steeped to Cassie's satisfaction, she poured a cup for each of us. The giant teapot made her arm muscles pop. She didn't seem to have big arms. But she was like, wow, cut.

I had tried black tea only once before and had no idea

how to drink it. Jill poured about a pound of sugar into hers. Jake took his black. Cassie just sat there with it on her lap as if the mug were a hand warmer. I saw my mother put milk in it, so I did the same. It tasted awful and I burned my tongue.

Then Cassie threw out, "Brian was telling me he's into sculpting."

My mom leaned back and looked at me. "Is that right?"

"Well, not really. It's plasticine. I'm just learning."

"I used to love working with clay in art class, in high school," she said. "So what do you make?"

"Just like...people's heads."

"Oh," Alicia said, as if it was now all clear to her. "You sculpt busts." The look on my face must have told her I didn't know what she meant, so she added, "Like, down to the shoulders. So they don't fall over."

This simple thing had never occurred to me. I had a flash of my little blue duck head guy lying on his ear. All I could think to say was, "Uh, yeah."

That killed that topic real quick. We started talking about favourite TV shows, for some reason. As far as I was concerned, I didn't care what we talked about. I was sitting beside my birth mother! I could smell whatever soap she used and when she tucked her hair back, the smell of that was incredible. It was strange and familiar at the same time. I kept glancing at her hands, trying not to get caught being weird. But her hands fascinated me. They were exactly the same shape and size as mine. The same fingernails, the same amount of tan. She even grabbed her tea mug off the wooden crate the same way I did.

Cassie piped up again, getting my attention by wagging a spoon at me. "Did you ask her about your father?"

"Like, my birth father? No."

Alicia rolled her eyes. "Oh, come on, Cass. Does it have to be right now?"

Cassie gave me a look and went all serious. "He was very

handsome and your mother was very young and stupid."

My mother shook her head. "Not as stupid as him. Killed himself rock climbing. No rope, or whatever they call it."

"Free-climbing," Jake put in.

"He was up in the Rockies with his buddies." Alicia glanced around. "What was that place?"

Jake knew that too. "Beauty Creek. Sunwapta Falls."

Again my mom rolled her eyes. "They were climbing ice. It wasn't even high or difficult or anything. Too much beer, too much weed, not enough sleep. He was nineteen. He wasn't even a sportsy kind of guy. Just showing off with his friends."

"Please don't say 'sportsy,'" said Cassie, but everyone ignored her.

"Were you guys like, a couple, or…?"

Again with the eye roll. "No, no. We, uh…we met at a party. It's just sad you couldn't meet him."

Jill cupped her hand to whisper loudly at me, "He was *hot.*"

"How do you even know that?" my mom asked.

"I saw pictures. You and him all lovey-dovey."

My mom stood up to whack her with the back of her hand. "Oh, come on. He doesn't need to hear that."

Cassie took a sip of her tea and said, "I wanted to adopt you so bad."

"Really?"

"Oh, that's right!" my mom said.

"It was completely impractical," Cassie continued. "I was in school, for goodness sake. I was going to run away with you and do like they do in Russia."

"How do you mean?"

"You know, start training when you're six months old? You would have been a total athletic mutant. But you know, famous."

"Okay…"

Keith interrupted the flow of chit-chat by thundering down the stairs for another beer. He was talking loudly on his phone the whole time and thundered back up the stairs, stomping two at a time, a few seconds later. I could tell my mother was embarrassed by him.

When he was finally out of earshot, my mother asked, "What's this?" I had tucked the photo album in between us on the couch. She lifted it out.

"Just some pictures my mom put together."

"Omigod, I want to see!" Jill leapt up and came to sit on the wobbly arm of the couch beside my mother.

She turned the pages one at a time, very slowly, with one hand covering her mouth. All she kept saying was, "Oh my god…oh my god…" Once she asked, "How old are you here?"

"Six, maybe."

"Oh my god…" She turned another page. "Oh, look at you here. Is that your dad? You like fishing?"

The picture showed me holding up a little perch, the first fish I ever caught. "I don't know. It was the only time we ever went." I did not want to tell her I cried because my dad threw the fish back.

She kept turning pages and resumed with the oh my gods again. "Is this for me? Can I keep this?"

"Yeah, totally."

When Jill returned to her seat, my mother brought out her phone and started showing me pictures of her family. I was really interested at first, but then it got to be too much. It was literally fifteen minutes of "and this is your maternal great uncle blah-blah. And this was him when I was four." My eyes started to glaze over. I wanted to steer the conversation back to something I cared about, like "What was giving birth to me like?" or "When's dinner?"

But then everything suddenly crashed and burned.

Keith came downstairs in his boxers, towelling his hair.

"You be ready soon?"

My mother looked at him wide-eyed, surprised. "What? I thought you were going out later."

"Change of plans," he said.

She got up and squeezed by me to go to him. They talked in whispers around the corner by the door for a few seconds while Jill and Cassie exchanged disapproving looks. I could hear my mom's voice pleading and explaining. She eventually followed him for a ways as he headed for the kitchen carrying his muddy runners. Then she came back to her seat.

"What's up?" asked Jake.

"Same old," my mom said. "I'm so sorry, Brian. I have to go in a couple of minutes to drive Keith. Do you want to stay? Or—"

This was all too bizarre for me. I did not come here to talk to these other people. At least, not until I got to know them better. "No, it's cool. You do what you gotta do. We got lots of time."

Jill got a little choked up at this. "Your whole lives, really."

I got up and went into the dining room to call home for a ride. The line was busy and I stood there, blankly listening to the busy signal way longer than I needed to. I could see the women in the living room all talking in hushed tones and throwing glances toward me. For sure they were comparing me again to Uncle James.

After that, I spent the next five minutes explaining what my parents' house was like. How many rooms, where my bedroom was, what sort of things my mom cooked. Keith came flying down the stairs and stopped long enough to say to me, "Nice meeting you," before heading out the front door. I couldn't tell if he was being sarcastic.

My mother followed him. "You'll be all right with Madeleine?" she asked Jill.

"Of course," Jill replied. Then, after checking to make sure Keith was out of earshot, she added, "This is not cool.

That's your son in there! You gotta grow a pair."

"Come on, don't start."

The rest of us stood when it was obvious my mother was leaving. She and I had a moment at the door with the rest of them standing around. She put a hand on my shoulder and looked me in the eyes for a second. "You're a cool kid. You're coming over ASAP, right?"

"Anytime."

"Okay; this week. Maybe we can meet somewhere?" She sounded desperate for it to be away from here, desperate for this not to happen again.

"Sure."

She gave me a long look. "I can't believe how awesome you are. Oh, I almost forgot!" She hurried back into the living room and returned with a flat gift-wrapped package topped with a bow. "I didn't know what to get you for your birthday. So…"

"Should I open it now? Aren't you in a hurry?"

"Yes! Quick!"

I tore at the paper and pulled a framed photograph out of the wrapping. It was her as a teenager, standing in a park, hugely pregnant.

"No way…"

"I hope it's not too weird."

"It is weird," said Jill, starting to blink away tears again.

"No," I told her. "It's like…awesome. Thank you."

I stood there like a goof as she went through a quick little ritual with Madeleine, smoothing her hair, rubbing noses, and coaching her to say, "Bye-bye, bye-bye," before heading out the door.

Jill took the little girl into kitchen. "Time for some num-nums, eh?" Over her shoulder she said to me, "It was so nice meeting you!"

I was left getting my runners on with Jake and Cassie standing over me. I did not want to wait inside.

"She's really a great mother," said Cassie. "It's just…that idiot has control of her. I swear, the moment she dumps him, her life will change forever."

I didn't know what to say to this. Luckily, Jake picked up the conversation. "I give their relationship two months."

Cassie snorted. "That's what you said two years ago. Are you sure you don't want to stay for dinner?" she asked me.

"Oh, no, it's fine," I said. I wasn't sure how to say goodbye to them. Shake hands? Tell them to have a good day?

Cassie took the cue. She stepped forward and gripped me in some kind of insane squeeze that was supposed to be a hug. I swear, you could hear the bones popping in my back.

When she finally let go of me, Jake put a hand on my shoulder. "I'll walk you out. You mind if I wait with you?"

"No, that's cool." I pushed open the door, suddenly wanting a big breath of fresh air. The second I was through, the smell of that flowering shrub from next door hit me like a cement truck.

I called home again and this time, Mom answered. "That was a quick visit! Your dad's gone to the park with the boys," she told me. "They were feeling left out. He should be back pretty soon. I'll come and get you." Mom almost never drove. But I was glad not to have to talk to Dad.

When I stuffed my phone back into my pocket, I had the most unreal sinking feeling. I couldn't explain it, but I was like, crushed.

Jake had followed me to the city sidewalk and I put on a brave face. The two of us stood there with our hands in our pockets. "I'm really bugged for you," he said. And when I looked at him to explain further, he went on. "I don't think that went well at all. I can't believe she left like that! But who am I to say. It's not my place. I just feel bad for Maddy."

He took a deep breath and changed the subject. We ended up talking about comics for a while. It turned out he had been collecting them since he was a kid. He ran some sort of fan website for all the different versions of Batman. It was a good distraction.

Finally I saw Mom driving up, slow as molasses, stopping at each house in turn, trying to read the numbers. I guess she couldn't see me standing there through all the cars parked on the street.

Jake gave me a sweaty handshake and offered, "Awesome meeting you," before I stepped out to the car. Mom waved to him.

When I was in, she asked, "How'd it go? Who was that?"

The car reeked of our family's old familiar smells. I sank into the seat and dug into my pocket for my phone. "He's, uh...my mother's...uh..."

"Brian, put the phone down."

I let my hands drop into my lap. "He's like, her brother-in-law."

"Did you have dinner?"

That was the one question I did not want her to ask. "Yeah," I lied.

She made a noise with her cheeks. "Well, that was quick," she said again. "You were only there an hour or so. What's that?"

She was talking about the photograph of Alicia, which I had face down on my lap. Awkward as it was, I couldn't not show her.

All she said was, "Oh." She swallowed hard and looked back at the road. A few seconds later, she asked, "So what's she like?"

I sat there, sunk in the seat, feeling like I wanted to have a great big honking cry. "Can I tell you later?"

"Of course, of course. Are you all right?"

"Yeah," I said. "Yeah, I'm fine."

Chapter 13

That night I had the blackest, most dreamless sleep of my life. I don't know what I was expecting from meeting my birth mother, but it turned out to be a thousand times better and a thousand times worse.

All my years of fantasy about her were a total waste of time. She was not a super-genius or a bazillionaire. She was not a psycho or a lunatic. She was just a normal person. If she was normal, then I was normal, whatever that meant. And that morning, it meant I just wanted to wrap my blankets around me and never get out of bed again.

I kept thinking about that stupid polar bear card. 'Cause what he looked like, that's how I felt. It was like yesterday I was let out of my cage for five minutes to meet my mother and now I was locked back in, forever. She was Maddy's mother and I was just a visitor. Just the fact that she was there and I was here…yeah, I might as well be in China. And don't get me wrong. I was only a little bit sad for me. Hey, I was all grown up and didn't really give a crap. I just kept thinking about little baby me, who, at some point, must have lain there in some pale green hospital room, wondering where the heck his mother was.

Yeah, now I knew. And it didn't help.

The call of my bladder and the thought of breakfast got me out of bed around seven thirty. I was totally starving after missing dinner the night before. I put on an old dressing gown I hadn't worn in years and dragged my butt upstairs. The place reeked of black tea and buttered toast. My dad was long gone off to work and the boys were sprawled on the living room floor. They were playing with toy cars, cartoons jabbering in the background. I didn't know where Mom was, but I wasn't keen on talking to her. So after a long pee, I went and stood in the doorway to the living room for a second.

The boys looked like they were having fun. They were deep in car-land, making *brrr* noises and telling each other stories about what the cars were doing and why they had to crash and cartwheel. The front door was open and through the screen I saw Mom out on the front sidewalk with a broom, gabbing with the neighbour.

When my eyes returned to the boys, Kyle snarked at me. "What are you looking at?"

I left in favour of some breakfast. With Mom outside, I figured I could sneak two bowls of cereal without her knowing. But it was not to be. I got like, two bites into me before she came inside.

"Morning," was all she said, going to the closet to put the broom away.

"Morning. I thought you were going to the…thing today…the specialist for Kyle."

"Huh?" she said, distracted. "Oh, don't remind me. It's not till this afternoon. Right in the middle of Jayden's naptime."

"Hmm."

I ate slowly, hoping she would leave the kitchen so I could eat more. But she hung around and hung around. All I could do was text Danny, praying for a morning of snacks and gaming—in that order.

sup today

The answer came almost immediately: *you cracked? grantrees dude*

Oh crap, I thought. We still had to do that?

b there soon

I zipped down to my room and dressed as fast as I could. I had put the photograph of pregnant Alicia on my dresser. Every time I looked at it, I got this little thrill of choked up joy. But the thought of Mom coming into my room and seeing it made me lay it face down before I left. Then, not caring that I was early, I tromped upstairs and pulled my runners on.

"Mom! Bye! I'm going to Danny's!"

"Will you be back for lunch?"

"Yeah, probably!" I figured, even if I ate at Danny's, I could totally come home and eat again.

When I got outside, I tried to figure out which would require less energy, walking or taking my bike. I decided on riding, thinking I could stay cooler that way.

It was one of those mornings where the sun was hammering down like a heat lamp. The world seemed like it was still half asleep, barely moving, and I was speeding along, wide awake. It had rained during the night and I was so distracted, I ended up going through a puddle and gave myself a wet tail going up my back. Of course I had to be wearing a white shirt.

It was quarter to nine when I got to the Cheevers' house. When I went in, I still felt a bit gun-shy, afraid Danny had maybe reconsidered the whole Ordry and Morgan thing and I was walking into a trap. But I calmed down when I got into the living room and was ignored.

Danny was playing War Demons with Randy. This was not going to end well. I thought *I* was too young to play that game. But Randy? I just rolled my eyes. Danny took chances as if he *wanted* disasters to happen. And sure enough, it took no time for things to go sideways.

"No! Come on!" Randy yelled. He had no lives, no points, and nothing left. "I wanna play again! I'll tell Mom if you don't let me!"

There was a saucer with three little Goldfish crackers on the coffee table. I got up and reached for one while they argued.

"What? I let you play and now you're going to betray me?"

"Just one more game. Please…? I won't tell if you let me."

"I have to go to Grantree's!"

"Just gimme five minutes."

Danny lifted his phone from the couch beside him to see the time. Then he looked at me. "Sorry, dude."

I grabbed another cracker. "Go for it," I said.

"Pig," said Randy to me as he took the last little Goldfish.

Danny whacked him with the back of his hand. "Shut up and play already. Last game."

"Don't be mean."

"Then don't be such a twerp."

I sat there sucking the flavour out of the cracker, turning it into pablum. *Wow,* I realized out of the blue, *I would never have a brother.* Somewhere in the back of my brain I had always wondered if my birth mom had had other kids; like, from the same father. Now I knew. Nope. I was it. Period.

That got me thinking about her situation. What did her sister say? They totally take advantage of her. The guys where she works, that creature Keith. As I watched the blood splatter on the giant screen, I kept thinking about killing off the boyfriend. I could save my mother from a whole world of annoyance and embarrassment. I would be the hero, great defender! Ugh. I gave my head a shake and realized Randy was watching me out of the corner of his eye.

"What's wrong with you?"

I gave my neck a stretch. "Nothing. Just slept weird."

"You look weird."

Danny's eyes did not leave the screen. "Zip it, 'toid."

Finally, they were done. Danny ejected the game disc and grabbed the metal case for it.

"How do you know we're supposed to be at Grantree's?" I asked, following him into the kitchen.

He put the disc away and snapped the case closed. "Oh, my dad called him. I was so ticked. I thought maybe everybody'd forget."

"Did you get your fifty bucks?"

"What? No, that's not happening."

"What do you mean? Why?"

"Well, I told my dad all about it. He even asked Grantree about his daughter and said I totally won."

"So...you don't get your money?"

"Uh...nope. My mom found out. Has to pay for me busting the TV."

"No way."

"At least I don't have to mow the lawn."

"Thuh!" The noise burst out of me. I couldn't help myself. All that big deal of me finding Sybil, just so he wouldn't have to mow the lawn. I just shook my head.

"What's with you?"

"Sorry, nothing."

Checking to make sure Randy wasn't looking, he slipped the case on top of the fridge and we headed outside.

"I hope he gets us to pick his raspberries," I said as we walked up the sidewalk from Grantree's secret gate.

"Yeah, no doubt."

I could see the old guy watching us through his kitchen

window. He met us at the door. For the first time, I was actually looking forward to working in the garden. I was like, dying of hunger and couldn't stop thinking about those raspberries. But it was not to be. Grantree held the door open for us. "You're working inside today."

"What?" Danny snarked at him.

"You heard me. I got stuff in here I ain't supposed to lift. On account of my hip."

Then Danny asked, "You aren't a pedophile, are you?"

I just about choked.

The big man lowered his brow and tipped his head to one side. "You try that crap on me and I'll tear your little head off."

"Oooh," Danny said, waving both hands. "Scare-y." And he stepped in past his neighbour's big barrel chest.

"Straight downstairs," Grantree said as I squeezed past him.

The house smelled super clean, like his garage, except more like food—which made my stomach start talking to me. The design of the house, I noticed, was almost identical to mine, which was creepy. I followed Danny down the tiled steps to the basement.

Unlike my place, the whole basement was carpeted and finished. It felt homey, in a fake, wood-panelling kind of way. The right side of the basement was a family room with a couch, an old tube TV and crappy pictures on the wall. To the left was the furnace and stuff, and a couple of little rooms, their doors closed. In the middle was a big office, cluttered with a ton of plumbing supply boxes and rolls of tubing and, behind it all, a huge desk. On it were all these little file trays labelled with the names of different countries. As soon as I saw that, I thought, *Bingo. Grantree's stamp collection!*

There was also, I noticed, a huge black antique printing press. Danny was standing there, staring at me, pointing at it with his whole arm.

I just raised my hands as if to say, *Okay, who knows?*

Grantree slowly made his way down the stairs behind us, one step at a time. He was using a metal cane that kept banging against the wall.

"See all them supplies?" He pointed to the office area. "I'm putting all that in the garage. The copper, the pex, the fittings, all that. I don't want my guys coming down here anymore."

He showed us the stacks of boxes he wanted removed. There were a lot. The guy obviously bought in bulk for his plumbing company. He gave Danny the key to his garage, told us where he wanted everything, and left us alone. I swear, some of the boxes were filled with lead. By the time we got everything out, there was a twelve-foot gap around the desk, where the carpet was crushed flat. It was only around ten o'clock, so he called us upstairs.

The similarities between Grantree's house and mine continued to creep me out. The biggest difference was the wall between the kitchen and living room in my house. At Grantree's, it was all open, with his dining room table right where the wall should be. Grantree's kitchen was crammed with gadgets. Expensive coffee maker, fancy red blender. And his fridge was twice the size of ours.

"There," he said, pointing to a couple of glasses of water on the counter. "I figured you'd need some hydration."

Danny and I went for the glasses. "You're not trying to poison us, are you?" asked Danny. He was smiling this time, like Grantree was in on the joke.

"If I were," Grantree grumped, "you'd be dead already."

When we finished downing our water, he showed us what would have been my little brothers' room in my house. It was another office, but like, super organized for more of his stamps. There were poster-size pictures of stamps on the wall and shelf after shelf of little boxes and big binders.

"How come you've got two collections?" Danny asked.

"One downstairs and one up here?"

"Ah," Grantree said, annoyed. "I started out downstairs, years ago. But after the wife moved out, meh, I got lazy. This room here was more convenient. So all the new stuff is up here. That old collection—I wanna sell most of it. But I gotta go through it all."

"So we have to move it?" I asked.

"Yeah. Some stuff, like what's in the bedroom closet here, that's going downstairs. Then all them little trays with the countries' names on them? You bring 'em up here."

The whole thing felt dumb and too complicated. But the old guy had his reasons. Danny made a lot of noise carrying boxes downstairs. Especially when we passed Grantree, who had parked himself at the dining room table beside a row of pill bottles.

"It ain't that heavy," Grantree said to him. "I ain't torturing you."

Danny whined, "What?"

Grantree just shook his head. "Is he always this annoying?"

I just sort of smiled. I didn't want Grantree to drive a wedge between Danny and me.

We were there until way after eleven. When we were done, he told us we could start late the next day. Doing what, I had no idea.

Just before we left, Danny decided to be friendly to him. "We met your daughter yesterday."

Grantree was still at the table. He squinted in pain as he shifted his weight. "My daughter? Sibby? Where?"

"At her house. I thought you said there was no woman in here, that day I asked."

Grantree grabbed his whole mouth with his big hand and squeezed away his annoyance. "She's my girl. You got some problem with that?"

"Your girl is like, thirty. I think that's a woman."

Grantree waved him away as if he was saying, *Toddle along*. "Tomorrow. And you leave Sibby alone. She's got stuff to do."

On the way back to Danny's, I said, "Think he's got enough stamps?"

"Yeah, really. The museum guys call you back?"

I shook my head. "Not yet. You see the printing press in the basement?"

"Oh, yeah. See, I was right about that too! He's totally counterfeiting down there!"

"Yeah, well, not recently. Everything's covered in dust!"

"Then what did those plumbers mean about the real stamps?"

"Who cares?" I said. "How many more days do we have to work for him?"

"I don't know. For sure this week. That's all I know."

When we got back to Danny's, Randy ran into the kitchen when he heard the back door bang. "Dad says we have to go to the store with him."

"What store?"

"Groceries, I think. We gotta help carry stuff."

Danny looked exhausted. "When?"

"Like, half an hour."

"What about lunch?"

"I guess he's gonna buy us some."

Danny had nothing to say to this. Randy went tearing back around into the living room. Danny said to me, "You wanna come?"

I was too hungry to take the chance that Mr. Cheevers's lunch would be late. And besides, I did not want my face burned off with Jamaican food again. "Naw, I'm gonna bounce," I said.

"What? No! Don't leave me with rheumatoid in there!"

"Hey, he's your brother. I'm gonna take off."

"You want to do something later?" Danny asked.

"Yeah, for sure. Message me when you get back."

When I got outside, I realized the day was really heating up. My bike had been lying in the sun and I almost burned my hand on the handlebars. I rode home, but I didn't even want to be there. Lunch was pure annoyance. I was still super-hungry from missing dinner the night before and I could have eaten four sandwiches. But all I got was one thin peanut butter sandwich with no jam or bananas or anything. I ended up eating the gross mangled pieces the boys left on their plates. Even then, it was *so* not enough.

Halfway through lunch, I got a text from Danny: *i am a dinkus*

That made me laugh. Five seconds later came a second message: *no i am half a dinkus*

I just stared at this one, not knowing what was going on.

Then the explanation arrived: *ignore prev msg randy stole my phone gonna pound his head in*

After lunch, I couldn't stand being in the house. I took a handful of comics outside and sat at our picnic table, trying to read in the blazing sun. There was a hot breeze trying to flip the pages on me and I ended up thinking about meeting my mom the day before instead of reading. I went over every detail about sixty times, as if I was in a huge hurry to have it all change me. It was weird.

I ended up with a sunburn on my forehead, so I went inside and down to the cool of my room. As soon as I saw my duck head guy, my comics got put aside. I took a minute to warm the plasticine enough to shape it. It didn't take long to squeeze the duck bill into a neck and shoulders and reshape the chin. As soon I did that, the whole thing looked about ten times more professional. And it stood up on my dresser, just like Alicia said it would. It still looked like a rock monster, but I squished the mouth down and the eyebrows up so that it looked proud to be a rock monster.

Alicia's sister Cassie's rapid-fire questions kind of bothered me—as if everybody in the world was driven, just like her. It was weird that my goofing around with plasticine had suddenly turned into me being a sculptor. But looking at my little blue head, I thought, *Maybe it's a good thing.* If I kept doing this, maybe Alicia would think I was awesome, and not just some lazy, TV-watching dummy.

An hour later, I got a message from Danny: *dropping off randy so I dont murderize him*

I didn't really have a response to that before another message arrived: *dad wants help loading lumber says hell buy us icecream*

I jumped on my phone: *us? u and me?*

There was a long pause.

yeah u coming?

He didn't have to ask me twice. *b there in 5*

When I got to Danny's, Cindy was home, too. She was up to her elbows in flour and sugar in this huge metal mixing bowl at the table. I thought I knew her well enough to make a comment.

"Kind of hot for baking, isn't it?"

She barely turned her head and gave me half a raised lip. "And who are you again?"

Well, that's crushing, I thought. Danny was in the bathroom and his dad was in his office quickly checking his messages. I had to stand there awkwardly in the kitchen while Cindy ignored me.

When Danny finally emerged, he led me outside. "So what's going on?" I asked. He was leading me toward the jeep, which had the top off and all the windows rolled down.

"Dad wants to fix up Auntie's porch. So we're gonna pick up some wood and stuff."

"Is he like, building it today?"

"No, no. Just dropping it off."

"Cool."

His dad was right behind us, shoving his phone into a pocket. The guy was wearing saggy track pants and a dress shirt, untucked. He obviously didn't care what he looked like. "Dan, you seen the hitch?"

"Should be in the back, right?"

Danny jogged to the jeep and, balancing on the tallest edge of a hardened mud rut, he dug around behind the back seat.

"What's the hitch for?"

"Huh? Oh, my dad doesn't want to scratch the jeep with the lumber. So we're renting a trailer."

"Nice."

It was weird, driving with Danny and his dad. I sat in the back seat by myself while the two gabbed like old buddies up front, half yelling to be heard over the wind and traffic noise. It was like Mr. Cheevers had never stopped being a kid. And he drove like it was a race, changing lanes and taking corners, almost screeching.

At the store, which was part of Westmount Mall a few blocks away, he left us to load the lumber on a cart while he got in line to rent a trailer. After we'd filled the cart, we waited and waited, watching a dozen people buy their stuff and leave while we had to stand there. After eighteen hours of no-where-near-enough food, I had only one thing on my mind.

"Where we getting ice cream?"

Danny was on his phone. "Uh…dunno. Why?"

"No reason."

"Well," he said, a little annoyed. "You sound like a greedy-guts."

Chapter 14

Half an hour later, with the lumber loaded onto the trailer behind us and soft ice cream melting down our cones, Mr. Cheevers steered his jeep back into their alley.

"I thought we were going to your auntie's to drop off the wood."

"We are," Danny said. "We're just picking up this *thing* Cindy made."

That made his dad chuckle. "Thing? I believe it's a zucchini cake."

Danny half turned to explain to me, "It's zucchini from Grantree. It's been sitting on our basement floor for like, two weeks."

"Mmm, yum." Then I thought I'd be bold. "Say, Mr. Cheevers, you know anything about Grantree's company?

Like, his plumbing and stuff?"

He yawned, rubbing his bald head. "Oooh, not much. He's good, though. I've been happy with the stuff he's done for us."

Danny offered, "Maybe that's 'cause he's our neighbour."

"Oh, no," said his dad. "He's got a good reputation. The man should think about retiring, though, especially after that hip operation. But I get why he keeps going."

"Why?"

"Well, he's by himself in that house. What's he gonna do? Sit around all day?"

"Huh," Danny said. "Maybe he should try gardening."

We pulled sideways into their yard and stopped with the trailer behind the garage. Danny wolfed the rest of his cone and ran into the house to collect the zucchini cake.

I decided to dig some more. "You know anything about Grantree's stamp collection?"

"Uh…nope," Mr. Cheevers said, glancing at me in the rearview mirror. "All we ever talk about is investing. Mutual funds, stocks, all that. Why?"

"Oh, nothing. We just had to move a ton of these little stamp boxes for him today."

"Hmm. Nice. Sorry," he said as his phone buzzed. "I gotta take this."

It was a business call. I got bored listening after five seconds and after I finished my cone, I dug out my own phone. A minute later, Danny was back, balancing a big metal cake pan on a dish towel, trying not to burn himself. When he got into the jeep, the smell of the warm cake was unbelievable.

Mr. Cheevers ended his call and dropped his phone into this holder on the dash. As we pulled away, he smelled deeply at the cake. "I could eat that whole thing right now."

Danny looked at his dad. "Why don't you?"

"Huh! Nah, your mother's got me on this no carb thing. It's killing me. And don't tell her about the ice cream, okay?"

"For twenty bucks, I will keep your secret safe."

Mr. Cheevers laughed. "How about I include you in my will? I was gonna let Cindy and Randy inherit everything. But hey, we can make a deal."

"Thanks, Dad. Nice to know you care."

It was after two by then and the sun was hammering the pavement. It didn't matter that we had the jeep's roof off and windows down. The heat blasted in like we were driving into a giant hair dryer. My sunburned forehead was glad to get into the shade of the spruce trees at his auntie's.

"Are we going in?" Danny asked. "Or are we just dumping this off?"

His dad lifted a shirt sleeve and wiped his brow. "I don't know. It's going to kill the afternoon if I get hooked in by your auntie. Oh, what the heck," he said, getting out. "I should check on her anyway. You said she was having chest pain?"

"Yeah."

"Fine. You guys unload. Just stack it on the sidewalk around the side. But keep the screws in the jeep."

Mr. Cheevers went up the short, overgrown sidewalk and then the steps, careful to avoid the holes in the crappy porch. He gave a quick rap-rap on the door and shouldered his way in. "He-llo!" he called in a sing-song voice. That was the last we'd see of him for the next twenty minutes.

Danny and I undid the straps holding down the lumber. He snarled them up and winged them into the backseat of the jeep, and the two of us began carrying the boards to the side of the house where there used to be a sidewalk. It was so overgrown, the first couple of boards kind of floated on top of the grass.

When we were done, Danny fetched the zucchini cake from the jeep and headed toward the front door. I was going to sit on the tipped steps and wait for him to do his thing. But he said, "You wanna come in?"

"And do what?"

159

"See inside. Come on. You won't believe your eyes."

I shrugged, thinking it would be an adventure. "Sure, why not."

But when we got up the steps, I began to have second thoughts. The smell was still lingering after Mr. Cheevers went inside. The storm door had a window high up and Danny stood on his tiptoes, shading his eyes to try to see in. Then he cranked the handle and gave the door a shove.

As soon as it opened, I saw Alvin standing right there, creepily staring out of his deep-set eyes. He was wearing the same clothes as before and they were not any cleaner.

"Hi, Danny. Your dad's here."

"Yeah, I know. We brought you some zucchini cake."

"To eat?"

"Uh, yeah. You met Brian before, right?"

Alvin just looked at me out of his sunken eyes. "Yes, I saw him before."

Right then, his mother's witchy voice came from upstairs. "Aaalviiin?"—*cough, cough*—"Is there someone else there?"

Before Alvin could answer, I heard the floor creak and saw Mr. Cheevers crossing the hall upstairs. "It's just Danny and me, Biddie. We brought you a cake from home. Hey, Alvin, what's with your toilet? How long has it been like that?"

There was not a flicker of a change in Alvin's expression. "Seven and a half months!" he called without turning his head away from us. "Oh!" he blurted, suddenly remembering something. "Come and see my new thing!" And he spun around and headed down the narrow hall.

"Aaalviiin?" came the voice again from upstairs. "Did he bring us something?"

"A cake!" Mr. Cheevers laughed, heading to her room.

In case she didn't hear, Alvin called out, "Yes!" and continued down the hall.

Danny was about to follow him. I leaned up close and whispered, "What happened to his old thing?" and I immedi-

160

ately got elbowed in the chest.

"I been practicing, Danny!" Alvin turned to explain.

"What did he bring?" his mother asked. But she began coughing again so violently she wouldn't have heard Mr. Cheevers's answer.

"Biddie! Biddie! Hey! It's a cake! You like cake?"

I was way more interested in the freaky house than in Alvin or the coughing auntie. The place was a disaster area and I kept my arms away from touching anything. The living room was so heaped with junk you couldn't see any furniture. Boxes of crappy clothes, dishes, a gross mattress—it looked like there'd been a flood and they'd piled half the house in there. And the dining room wasn't much better. The floor and table were covered in old newspapers, dirt and potted plants. I followed Danny and his cousin down the narrow hall. I wanted to ask why the place stank so much. The cigarette smoke smell was one thing. But I kept my trap shut, thinking it might be related to their toilet troubles—and I was happy not knowing anything about that.

"Wait'll I show you!"

We ended up in the kitchen, which made me grin with how freaky it was. Every surface—counters, sink, windowsills, floor—was covered in junk. Pieces of sink taps, this old mailbox full of pine cones, a full roll of toilet paper squashed under the window, scraggly vines everywhere.

For a second, peering into the kitchen, I did not know where Alvin had gone. The kitchen table was heaped in water-stained boxes and dead plants. Then we heard him.

"Look at me!"

We stepped forward.

Behind the table, Alvin was on his back on the floor with his ankles crossed behind his head, waving at us. He looked like a grasshopper that had been flipped over and gotten tangled in its own legs. Somehow, I was not shocked or surprised. The kid was so skinny, the freakish pose looked easy for him.

"Pretty good, eh?"

Danny was not even a tiny bit impressed. "Yeah, Alvin, we get it. You're bendy."

"And look what else I can do!" With no strain or effort, the kid unhooked his ankles and sat up and did the splits. But that wasn't the trick. He flung his rubbery arms behind him, clasped his hands and began lifting them up toward the ceiling.

"Ow," I commented. I could barely look at him.

"Wait! Wait!" he said. There was a gnarly crunching sound from his shoulders, and he brought his arms forward, all the way over his head.

"Okay!" said Danny. "We're done!"

Both of us were looking away, me quietly laughing to myself more out of shock than anything. "I have no idea how you do that," I told him.

Alvin was suddenly on his feet, giving himself a twist back into his proper shape. "You said he goes to school with you," he said. "I don't think he learns too much."

Yeah, I thought, *I'm the dummy here.* "Do you have a TV?" I asked, wanting to change the subject away from his pretzeling. I had realized there was no microwave and the stove was covered in dead plants.

Alvin looked up at Danny as if he had answered the question. "No; do you?"

Danny rolled his eyes. "Anyway, we brought you a zucchini cake."

"Okay," said Alvin. "Did you make it?"

"What? No. Cindy made it."

"I like Cindy," said Alvin, and the three of us stood around nodding for a second, as if Cindy was a really important subject we were discussing.

Danny went over to the round-shouldered fridge. "I'll put it in here," he said. "I don't want the flies to get it." When he opened the fridge, I caught a glimpse of filthy plant pots stacked in columns. But no food. Danny had to use his whole body to close the fridge door, which made a hard *clack!* sound.

The whole time we were in the kitchen, I could hear the auntie calling from upstairs. God only knew what she wanted. I assumed Mr. Cheevers was right there. But her calling and shouting was becoming more insistent and her coughing more extreme. She was now shrieking her son's name like it was a curse. "Aaalvin!"—*cough*—"Aaalvin!"—*cough, cough*—"Answer me, Aaalvin!" *Cough, cough.*

I was like, *What the heck is Mr. Cheevers doing to her?*

"All right!" Alvin yelled back. "I'm coming, already. Jeez!"

The kid started stomping toward the voice like an overly dramatic toddler. But he only got three steps down the hall when his mother yelled, "Get your uncle and me some cake!" *Cough, cough.*

The kid came back, found a dirty knife under some newspapers and pulled the cake out of the fridge. "Ow!" he said. "It's still hot!"

"Not really," said Danny. "You're just sensitive."

Hunched over like the cake weighed ten tons, Alvin made his way up the stairs.

"We should have bought ear plugs at the lumber store," I remarked.

"Huh," he said flatly. "No doubt. You could probably get lung cancer just looking in the windows of this place. See why Cindy makes 'em food?"

"No kidding. Why is there such a big secret about it? Don't your parents help?"

Danny leaned against the kitchen counter. "Oh, dude," he started. Then he realized there were creepy things moving through the dirt behind him and he jumped away and brushed off his pants. "It's a long story. You ever seen Randy's leg?"

"What do you mean?"

He leaned closer to me and kept his voice low. "He's got a scar like, all the way down one side."

163

"Is that something to do with his arthritis?"

"What? No. I mean, sort of. Alvin pushed him down the stairs there when he was little. Broke his leg in like, three places. He had to have all these surgeries and wear a cast and braces and do physio for like, years. And his leg is still not okay. I mean, obviously, with the arthritis." He paused for emphasis. "My mom hates Alvin. Like, *really hates* him. Even though they're my dad's relatives, she won't let us talk about him. And we totally can't come over here—even though Randy doesn't care. All he remembers is the teddy bears people brought him in the hospital."

"Doesn't your mom smell the lasagna and the cake and stuff when she gets home?"

"Oh, she thinks it's all for us and we pig out when she's at work. She doesn't say anything, anyway."

"Hey, you guys!" Alvin was at the top of the stairs. "Can you hear me?" His voice was kind of weirdly calm and pleading.

Danny strode out of the kitchen. "Hey, yeah. What's up?"

I followed, keeping my arms away from the walls. The front door was now wide open, blowing slightly cooler air in.

Alvin was leaning over the banister at the top. "Can you bring some water? I think something's wrong with my mom."

"What?" Danny said. "Isn't my dad there?"

Alvin shook his head. "No. He just went outside."

Danny nearly bashed me out of the way, returning to the kitchen for some water. There was swearing and the clink of dishes. Then he came back. "Your tap's not working!"

Alvin wagged his hands. "In the basement it works. On the post by the light!"

Danny swore again and disappeared.

I had no idea what to do. Alvin stood there flapping his hands like they were wet, watching his mother in the bedroom.

I didn't know where Mr. Cheevers had been. But he came

up the front steps and in through the door, clutching his phone. He seemed to be in a big rush. "Where's Danny?"

"Getting, uh…his aunt some water."

"Okay, good. Something's going on with her. I'm talking to Health Link."

"Yeah?"

I didn't even know if he heard me. Still with his phone to his ear, he went charging upstairs to the auntie's room. A second later, I could hear his voice, sounding low and panicky, ask, "Biddie? Can you hear me? Biddie? You all right?"

Danny suddenly came rushing down the hallway again with a really gungy-looking glass of water. He swung around the banister and hurried up the stairs. Then he and Alvin disappeared into the darkness.

I felt like somebody intruding on a family crisis. Should I even go up there? Alvin kind of included me when he said, "you guys." And I was curious, in a sort of demented way. So I headed up.

The farther up the stairs I went, the warmer it got. I thought at first it was just the summer heat rising. But as I reached the top, I realized there was a space heater in the open doorway to the right, blowing flaming hot air into the auntie's room. And the stink was unbelievable. The urine smell, the smoke smell, all cooking in the tropical blast of the space heater.

I could just see Alvin and Danny a couple feet through the doorway to the room. "Mom?" Alvin was asking. "Are you okay?"

Mr. Cheevers came into view. He still had his phone up to his ear, but he wasn't talking into it. "Biddie? Can you hear me? Can you try a sip of water?"

The room was almost dark. A full ashtray was sitting on the night table, with a lit cigarette burning away. I inched closer, trying to breathe shallowly. Several layers of frayed blankets were nailed up over the only window. The floor was littered with flimsy clothes, empty cigarette packs and dirty dishes. As my eyes adjusted to the darkness, I saw the auntie lying in the bed. She was just a small bump in the bedclothes and a thin face—so thin that it looked like a skull with nothing but wrinkled skin covering it. I could see her top teeth. They were just like Danny had said, small and black up near the roots.

"Mom?" Alvin asked again. When he didn't get an answer, he turned to Mr. Cheevers. "She's all right, isn't she? Can you do something?"

Mr. Cheevers tried to smile. "You just hang tough, Alvin. She'll be all right."

"But she's shaking so much! What's going on?"

"Hello?" Mr. Cheevers said into the phone. "Yeah, I'm here. No, she was already lying down. What? Say that again?"

In his panic, Alvin took hold of Danny's hand and began wringing it. Danny wriggled out of Alvin's grip. But maybe he didn't want to seem cold, because he put a hand on Alvin's back.

"Yes, she's breathing," said Mr. Cheevers. "But her heart's just racing… What? No, we're here. I can wait." He moved the phone away from his head. "I might have to call an ambulance."

"Whaat?" Alvin looked shocked. I stepped up beside the heater and tried to get a better look. Suddenly, the auntie began coughing wildly, swinging her arms out to the sides. Mr. Cheevers tried to grab the ashtray out of her way, but she knocked it off her little night table and it thunked to the floor, dumping cigarette butts in a heap.

"Dan," his father said. "Make sure there's nothing burning in there."

"Okay."

But Alvin was there first. He fished the lit cigarette out of the heap and as he was butting it in the ashtray, his mother's racking cough stopped, like a switch being turned off.

The room was as still as death. The auntie's back was arched like a bridge, her eyes and mouth wide open. She was frozen, as if a knife had come up and stabbed her from the bed beneath.

"Oh man, she's really sick," said Alvin.

Long seconds passed. Mr. Cheevers stood up straight, staring at her, not knowing what to do. The woman began quivering. This faint choking sound came from her throat. She let out a gurgling sigh and slowly her body flattened out on the bed.

"Hey! Hey!" Mr. Cheevers began barking into the phone. We all just stared at him. "Are you there? Oh, good god!" He pulled the phone away from his ear and swore. "I'm calling 911." He stepped past me out of the room and began hurriedly talking. "Hello? Yeah, I need an ambulance. Somebody just had a heart attack here!"

Alvin looked down at his mother. She wasn't moving except for one hand shaking and tapping the bed. He turned from Mr. Cheevers to Danny with a helpless expression on his face and then he looked at me, hoping I had some kind of other explanation.

Right then, from behind me, Mr. Cheevers blasted us. "You guys, get outa there! Get downstairs. There's nothing you can do. Keep Alvin busy. Go on!" And he gripped his phone and pressed it to his ear like he wanted to squish the circuits out of it.

Alvin barged past me, blinking away tears and knocking over the heater.

I stood the heater upright again and nearly burned my hand. The thing was dangerous, I thought, so I turned it off. Immediately, the room seemed ten degrees cooler.

Danny and I followed Alvin out the door. The last I saw of the auntie's room was Mr. Cheevers rushing around, mumbling into his phone, flinging clothes from the floor onto the bed. The three of us headed downstairs.

Alvin stopped by the front door and turned to us. He made this pathetic sound, sort of a high-pitched whimper. "Wha—?" he said. "Is my mom—" But he couldn't get the words out.

Danny gave him a pat on the back. "Just calm down, eh? She'll be all right. Oh god, I need some fresh air or I'm gonna die." Then he burst outside, jumped down the stairs and headed toward the city sidewalk.

I stood there with Alvin, who couldn't decide whether to go back to his mother or stay and watch Danny. I was about to say something consoling, like, "She'll be okay," or "Don't worry, she'll be fine," when Mr. Cheevers came flying down toward us. He rushed between Alvin and me and out the front door, where he read the house number into the phone. Then he came back in and went tearing up the stairs again. Before he disappeared into the room, the last thing I heard him say was, "No, she's not choking. She's just lying there shaking."

Danny was out of sight past the cinder block building next door.

I urged Alvin outside. "You okay? Come on. Want to get some air?"

But the kid just held onto the banister looking panic-stricken. I could see his knees quivering. It was so bad after a second, he had to sit down. I had no idea what to do or say, so I stepped back inside and dropped down beside him on the bottom steps.

After a while, with Danny still out of sight, the kid gave me a sort of half look, holding back a honking big cry. He sucked in his breath. "It's Brian, right?" he managed to say.

"Yeah."

He sucked in his breath again and sniffled, hard. "Thank you for bringing the zucchini cake." And with that, he totally let go with the biggest crying fit I'd ever seen.

Chapter 15

Twelve and a half minutes later, there was an EMS cube ambulance blinking in front of us at the curb. Alvin and I had wandered outside by then. Mr. Cheevers had given Danny the keys to the jeep and told him to move it forward. I couldn't believe he was trusting Danny with it. But hey, for a dumb Cheevers decision, it was pretty much average.

A man and a woman in dark blue short-sleeved shirts wheeled a stretcher up the sidewalk while a second man jogged up the steps and promptly fell through the rotten wooden porch. I didn't laugh. The other medics didn't laugh. But Alvin, with tears still dripping down his cheeks, blew a snotty guffaw across the boulevard and had to turn around so they didn't see him.

When the two stretcher medics hauled their buddy out

(with lots more porch boards cracking), they hurried inside and up the stairs.

Alvin stood there staring at the house, with me beside him. Danny got out of the jeep and stood by the ambulance talking to Cindy on the phone, head down, kicking the trunk of one of the giant spruce trees. I only caught bits and pieces of what he was saying. Stuff like, "No, Dad's still upstairs with Auntie. It could be bad if she's in the hospital for a while. What? No! Just text me if Mom comes home early, all right?"

A couple of minutes later, the EMS guys came out with the auntie on a stretcher. She looked unconscious, brown drool spilling onto the white cloth under her face. The two men wheeled her down the sidewalk and into the ambulance. The woman came outside with Mr. Cheevers, who handed her a grocery bag full of the auntie's clothes and stuff.

"He be all right, your nephew?"

"Oh, yeah, we got it."

"Okay, good. I left the house door open."

"Which hospital are you taking her to?"

"Just down the road. The Royal Alex."

The ambulance sat there for what seemed a really long time before driving off, siren blasting.

Mr. Cheevers checked his phone and shoved it back into his pocket. Alvin kept looking at him with big saucer eyes. "So what do I do?"

"Dunno yet. Is there anything you need from the house? You got your key?"

"I don't have a key. The front door doesn't lock."

"What about like, clothes, or—" He suddenly remembered something. "Is that heater still on upstairs?"

"I turned it off," I said.

"Good. You know you're coming with us, right?" he said to Alvin. "It could be days or...who knows? Before your mom gets home."

Alvin's eyebrows were up as high as they could go. "Can't I go see her?"

"Yeah, of course. Just not right now."

"When?"

"Look, Alvin, we gotta figure out a place for you to stay. That's the first priority."

"Yeah, but I want to see my mom."

This got Mr. Cheevers choked up. He put a hand on Alvin's shoulder and said, "Yeah, I know."

"Do I have to stay far away?"

"I don't know. Maybe."

"Should I bring my other pants?"

I gave Danny a look over Alvin's shoulder, like, this was the saddest friggin' kid I'd ever met.

Mr. Cheevers didn't bat an eye. "Yes. You guys want to go help him? No idea when he'll be back here."

The three of us trooped back into the house. Danny retrieved the zucchini cake from upstairs, carrying it sideways like a book. Alvin disappeared into a small room behind the front door. I followed him and stood in the doorway. The room was obviously Alvin's bedroom. There was junk about a foot deep on every square inch of the floor, and the bed—busted toys, more water-stained cardboard boxes, dresser drawers half-buried under garbage. Alvin picked up a pair of jeans that had hardened into a solid shape. He bent them and stuffed them into a plastic grocery bag. He gave a last look around the room. By then, Danny was back down the stairs.

"Is that it? Is that all you're bringing?"

Alvin looked at him like he was stupid. "Huh?"

"Never mind."

We all headed outside and Danny yanked the front door closed tight.

In the back of the jeep, sitting beside me, Alvin had a white-knuckle grip on his bag of hardened pants. When we got to Danny's, Cindy came running from the house as soon as we all climbed out. "Oh, Alvin! This is terrible! I hope your mom is all right. Are you okay? Do you want to come in? Here, let me carry that for you."

"No!" Alvin yanked his bag out of her reach.

Cindy jerked back. "Okay, fine, whatever," she said, throwing up her hands. "I just feel so bad for you."

"I'm fine."

I noticed with Cindy there, Danny was not carrying the zucchini cake sideways anymore. "Mom's not home yet, is she?"

Cindy just looked at him. "Hell, no. You think I'm crazy?"

She threw her arm around Alvin's shoulders and comforted him all the way to the house.

Alvin was hesitant to go in. As Cindy held the door for him, he looked up at the door jamb like it was the entrance to a place he might never get out of alive.

Danny slapped him on the back and squeezed past him. "Hey, don't worry. Our mom's at work. We're gonna figure everything out before she gets home."

Adjusting his grip on his grocery bag, Alvin gingerly stepped inside, followed by Mr. Cheevers.

Cindy kept holding the door for me and gave me an eye roll as I passed. "Family," she said.

It was the first time Cindy had said anything like, normal to me. Hey, if it took a disaster for her to not ignore me, no problem, I'd take it.

As I crossed the kitchen I saw that Danny had left the zucchini cake on the kitchen table. Mr. Cheevers was bellowing in the hallway, "Randy! To your room." Randy began to whine. "Now. And don't come out till I tell you to."

"Yeah, but—"

"Now!"

They pointed Alvin to a cushy chair near the big window in the living room. He perched like a bird on the edge of it, his fists around the neck of his plastic bag.

Randy was at the top of the stairs, hanging over the railing. "Hey, Alvin."

"Hey, Randy."

The two had a weird little moment before Randy disappeared up the last few steps.

"You ever play games?" Danny asked him. "Like, video games?"

Alvin shook his head.

I sank into the couch and picked up one of the controllers. "We can show you," I offered.

Alvin shook his head again. He was trying to hear Mr. Cheevers, who was in his office next door on speaker phone. His own voice was chipper and all nicey-nicey. The tinny voices on the other end were all like, "Hey! Long time no talk to!" at first. Then they lowered into a serious *hmm-hmm* when they found out why he was calling.

Danny fired up a saved game and he and I played with the sound low while Alvin watched. Cindy poked her head into the living room and then her dad's office; just looking, saying nothing. Twice she did that. The third time, she came in with zucchini cake for everyone piled on a dinner plate. Danny and Alvin ignored it. I just sat there staring at it, not wanting to look like an unfeeling pig by taking the first piece.

An hour went by. Mr. Cheevers came out of his office long enough to refill his coffee cup. He had his high-tech headset on, but wasn't talking. Another half hour passed, with Danny and I slouched on the couch, making perky noises at the game, trying to cheer Alvin up. The kid was super quiet and spent the whole time perched on the edge of his chair, like he was in a vet's office, waiting for his pet pants to get fixed.

Finally, Mr. Cheevers came in, looking at his watch. "We gotta go."

Danny looked up. "What? Where?"

"I'll tell you on the way. And we gotta get that trailer back after we're done. Brian, we'll see you later, okay?"

"What? No!" Danny objected. "Why can't he come?"

Mr. Cheevers sighed heavily. "Just…because. Look, Danny, come here."

Danny dropped his controller on the couch and I paused the game as the two went under the archway into the hall. I couldn't hear what his dad said to him, but I sure heard Danny's response. "You gotta be kidding me."

"*Shh.* That's it. That's all we can do right now."

"What about Uncle Simon? He's got like, a friggin' mansion!"

His father shook his head. "It's done. They're expecting him. Come on, hey, it's just temporary."

"Gimme a sec," he told his dad. Then he turned to me. "Can you help? Would your parents let you have a sleepover?"

Before I could answer, Mr. Cheevers grabbed Danny's shoulder and swung him back to face him. "Whoa, whoa. That's not happening. Alvin! It's time. Let's go."

"Daaad!" Danny pleaded in a yell.

His father ignored him, holding his arm out to welcome Alvin into it. "Is that all you brought?"

Alvin did not know what was going on and his face showed it. "Yeah?" he said uncertainly.

"Hey, that's good. Well done," said Mr. Cheevers, steering him into the kitchen. "Cindy, would you grab a toothbrush from the bathroom? There's a new one on the shelf. And a clean towel. I don't know if they have towels there."

I followed them all into the kitchen.

"Where's he going?" Cindy asked.

Mr. Cheevers was trying to be all jolly for Alvin's sake. "Just up the avenue. Family Services have got like a…shelter there for—"

"You can't take him there!" Cindy nearly screamed.

But Mr. Cheevers was having none of it. Behind Alvin, above his head, he made a lip zip motion to tell Cindy to shut it. "It'll be nice, Alvin. Just till we can find you something more permanent."

"But Daaad!"

He pointed at her. "One more peep."

"Oh my god!" she said, stomping out of the room.

"You coming, or what?" Danny said to me.

"Naw," I said, "I gotta get home."

"No, you don't."

"Whatever."

I followed them out to the backyard. In single file, the three paraded to the jeep, which was parked sideways behind the garage because of the rental trailer. Alvin walked like a robot with his grocery bag held tight to his chest. Before he got in, Danny shook his head at me, then looked at the sky for help. I watched them leave. Then I went around the front of the house and started home, not sure what to think of this crazy day full of crazy people.

When I got home, I couldn't wait to get downstairs. My clothes reeked of smoke and grossness. After I changed and stuffed my clothes in the hamper, I headed up to the living room and ended up watching TV till suppertime. Well, not even really watching it. Just staring while my mind wandered.

When Dad got home just before dinner, Mom had another meltdown about doctors. I guess that afternoon, the specialist found a great big bunch of nothing up Kyle's nose.

"So no polyps? What did he say it was?" Dad asked.

Mom shrugged, defeated. "We just have to watch him. Use the spray when it gets bad. It's mostly in the mornings anyway. He might be putting things up there. We have to wash all his clothes and bedding. Huh! Like I don't *do that* already."

"It was this long!" Kyle blurted, talking about the probe they used. "Right up my nose holes!"

"Were you brave?" Dad asked.

There was a pause. "Yes."

Jayden threw in, "He cried and cried!"

"You shut up!"

"Hey, hey, that's enough of that."

Later, when we were eating dinner, Kyle sat there blinking at his plate.

"What's wrong, kiddo?" Dad asked.

"My eyes hurt."

Mom looked at Dad. "They went up there pretty far."

"Into his eye sockets?"

Jayden again blurted, "And he cried and cried."

Kyle jabbed a savage elbow at his brother.

"Ow!"

My dad stopped the fight with, "All right, you two eat your supper now."

"I already ate everything!" said Kyle.

"No, you didn't. You had two bites."

"Can I go play now?"

"Only if you're quiet. We're still eating."

"Okay." And he slid off his chair and frumped to his room. He was soon joined by Jayden. Dad ended up eating the rest of their dinners before I could get to them.

After supper, I'd been down in my room for a minute when I felt my phone buzz in my pocket. It was a text from my birth mom.

sorry about no dinner can I make it up to you? can you come over wednesday?

As fast as I could, I typed her an answer: *Ill ask should b ok what time?*

five what do you like to eat?

I dunno pizza?

done were having pizza five oclock

I told her I'd let her know later for sure and stuffed my phone back in my pocket. Then I completely forgot to tell my mom about it. All that was in my brain was, *I get to see my birth mom again!*

I spent the evening in front of the TV, trying to get myself back to some sort of normal. I was so tired of other people, of strange situations, freaky houses, I just wanted to watch some crap sitcoms and go to bed—which I did, around nine o'clock.

The next morning, Mom woke me at 6:15 by rapping on my bedroom door. She was trying to be all gentle and quiet about it, waking me slowly. But she was pissed. After the third attempt to wake me, she opened the door a crack. "Brian?" For me, it felt like two in the morning. When I didn't answer, she called a little louder. "Brian?"

I flung the covers off. "What?"

The door swung open. I squinted at her in the bare-bulb light from the basement outside my room. She was holding some clothes. "What is this?" she asked.

"Huh?" I could barely see what she was talking about.

"Your shirt and pants from yesterday. They smell like smoke. Have you been smoking?"

I had not told my parents anything about what happened at Alvin's the day before. I rolled over on my side with a groan. "Ugh. No. That's not me."

"Then who was it? Has that Danny been smoking?"

"No. It's from his aunt's place. We were over there yesterday."

There was a long silence. I could feel her standing there calculating whether I was telling the truth or not. "What aunt?"

"On 127th Street. Mr. Cheevers drove us over. Cindy made them a zucchini cake."

"Who is Cindy?"

"Danny's older sister. We were bringing boards for their porch. Everything stank of smoke because of the aunt."

There was a shorter silence. "Oh. All right. Thank god. Go back to sleep now." And she left, closing the door behind her.

Ten seconds later, I heard her shuffling up the stairs. She

stopped at the landing. I thought I heard her say, "It's not him."

Then came the rumble of my dad's voice. He was probably putting his shoes on for work while they discussed me and my smoking.

Great, I thought. *How am I going to get back to sleep now?* But with the pillow over my head, I drifted off a while later. I ended up having a weird dream where Alvin's house and my birth mom's house were all shmooshed together. My mom was dying and when I went to help her, I realized I had no arms, which freaked me the heck out. I woke up, huffing and puffing, suddenly super-awake—like, noon-awake. Why couldn't I have dreams about bunnies and stuff? What the heck?

At the breakfast table, I got a text from Danny: *when u gonna be ready?*

I checked the time and typed as I ate: *its only 815 b there b4 9*

well, came the answer, *speed it up im waiting outside*

Okay, I thought. *That's weird.* I picked up my bowl and went to the window. Yup, there he was, in the morning sun, sitting on the picnic table with his feet on the bench, staring at his phone. I shovelled the rest of my cereal into my mouth and dropped my bowl in the sink.

Before I got two steps away, Mom called from the living room, "Brian! Rinse it out and put it in the dishwasher! You're always forgetting!"

Ugh. I went back, gave the bowl a swish under the tap, and jammed it into the dishwasher.

"Did you do it?" she called.

"Yes!" I yelled back, probably too loudly, and blasted down to the landing and outside.

Danny looked up. "Hey."

"What's up?" I asked him.

He slipped off the picnic table and glanced at the house. "Can they hear us?"

178

"What? I don't know. Why? Let's go down the alley. You all right?"

"Yeah, well, not really. I had a big fight with my dad last night. I just had to get away from him for a while."

"We still got Grantree's today?"

"For sure."

When we got out the gate to the alley, I asked, "Is this about Alvin?"

"Ooh, yeah."

"So what happened?"

"Well, you saw. He put him in a freaking Family Services home. Who does that? He's his own cousin!"

"Alvin is your dad's cousin?"

"Yeah, I told you. My auntie's my great aunt. So Alvin's my second cousin."

"That's bizarre. So your dad couldn't find any other place for him?"

"He barely tried!" Danny yelled. "All this time, I thought he was like, the awesomest dad. And now—"

"What?"

"It's like finding out he murders puppies for a job."

"Ha! I don't think it's that terrible."

"He's not your dad, is he? What else doesn't he care about?"

I had to change the subject or Danny was going to melt down completely. "So how's your auntie?"

"Pfft," he said, kicking a round rock down the paved alley. It skipped and began bouncing and knocked against someone's plastic garbage can with a thunk. "Dude, she's on life support. Even if she makes it, they think she's gonna be like, drooling hospital jello the rest of her life."

"That sucks."

"Alvin ain't going home. That's for sure."

"Well," I said, trying to cheer him up, "it wasn't exactly Buckingham Palace."

"What's that supposed to mean?"

"Nothin'."

"So I have to hang out with you today. Great. You don't have a game box or anything, do you?"

"Don't you think you're being a little jerky?"

Danny gave me a sour look. "That's how you're gonna be? What am I supposed to do? Everybody's out to friggin' get me today." And he strode ahead, flicking his hand like he was waving away a mosquito. "Go home. I don't need you."

I was left there in the alley, shaking my head, thinking, *Wow, this guy is losing it.* I turned and headed back home. I got like, ten steps away when I heard him call me.

"Brian!"

I spun around. "What?"

"Sorry! I'll see you at Grantree's, okay? Nine thirty?"

I gave him a thumbs up and continued on my way home.

Chapter 16

At Grantree's that morning, Danny was still in his strange mood. It was sort of no mood, a total flat-line, like you couldn't get a reaction out of him. We got to pick Grantree's raspberries, though. I ate like, half of them, being super sneaky. I'd pop them into my mouth and let the juice trickle down my throat so the old guy couldn't see me chewing. Unfortunately, the mosquitoes were unreal, the worst yet. If we weren't getting stabbed by raspberry thorns, the mosquitoes all pitched in to make sure we were getting the right number of punctures.

About half an hour into our picking, a vehicle drove up and parked behind Grantree's back fence. Danny turned around and made a fake scared face at me. It was the first time that morning his expression changed.

When the plumbers came in the back gate, we couldn't

not look. The black-eyed guy was first, staring at us like we were the freaks. But nobody said anything. He was carrying the spool of cable and his friend, the big guy, followed him through the gate with the tool case. The guy's pants were so saggy, you could see hair above his belt.

Danny turned sideways and blocked the view with a hand. "*Ah! My eyes!*" he whispered.

Grantree was waiting for them at the back door. I couldn't hear what the plumbers said, only Grantree's barrel-chested voice. "No, you can leave it right there. Or you can put it in the garage."

There was a complaint from the black-eyed guy.

"I don't care," said Grantree. "All the supplies are in the garage now. You can put it in there, if you like."

The plumbers looked at each other for a second. Then the big guy stepped close and said something.

Grantree laughed. "Don't try that with me. There's washrooms like crazy over at the mall. You don't need to come in for nothin'. Now go on. It ain't like you ain't got calls to make. How'd it go at that walk-up?"

There was mumbled talk for the next two minutes. All I caught was, "You call the city? You gotta call the city." And the plumbers came back down the sidewalk carrying the spool and the case. The garage door was open and they went in, set everything down and checked out the boxes of supplies we'd stacked up. There was more mumbling and the two came out, eyed us like we were scum again, and went out the back gate. I swear, there was the tiniest bit of a tire squeal as they left. Somebody was ticked.

We finished up with the raspberries just after ten. Grantree was impressed. "Bumper crop, kids. I freeze these for winter. I hope you ate a bunch while you were picking. I ain't got much freezer space right now."

Great, I thought. *All that sneaking for nothing.*

Then he said, "What day is today? Tuesday, right? You

two are done tomorrow."

"For good?" Danny asked.

"Unless you got something else you want to bust around here, yeah. Sibby's coming over to help me ship stuff. Besides, between the two of you, you paid for what you broke."

I thought for sure Danny would be jumping for joy. But the flatline continued. I was not invited into the Cheevers' house after. It was like Danny was depressed or something and didn't care about me or anyone else.

I spent that afternoon on the couch, catching up on my TV shows. The boys and I were each allowed to record three shows automatically. I always let mine accumulate and since I had awesome taste, the boys kept trying to watch mine before I got to them. It was sort of a compliment, but I hated them having their fingers and their eyes all over my shows before I did.

When I told them to please stop, their reaction was unexpected.

"Sorry."

"Yeah, sorry."

I was like, what drugs are you on? Why no fighting back?

When Wednesday arrived, I woke up at four thirty in the morning and realized I'd messed up. I had not told Mom I was invited to pizza dinner. And I had not gotten back to my birth mom. Aaargh!

At breakfast, my thumbs burned up my messaging app.

im so sorry I completely forgot to get back to you

My birth mom was really nice: *hey dont worry you still coming at 5?*

I still have to ask

k

When I told Mom, she was only concerned about one thing. "But how are you going to get there? Your father can't drive you. He's at his meeting on Wednesdays."

"I can take the bus."

"By yourself? Not at night you won't."

"It's not at night. I gotta leave around four and I'll be back before like, eight."

She thought about this for a minute. "Fine. But hide your cell phone so no one steals it. And you call 911 if anything happens."

"Pick one, Mom. Hide it or use it?"

"You know what I mean."

I got back to my birth mom and everything was settled.

At Grantree's, he got us to work inside again. This time we were boxing up stamps and making labels for them to ship. I guess he'd sold a bunch and had to send them off. He had all these big flat boxes we had to put together with a tape gun. He was going to store the rest of his stamps in them. But we made too many boxes and had to pile them up near the stairs. Danny's mood was still flatline, and he moved like he had lead weights on his feet.

Grantree's daughter, Sybil, was there. I swear, she had no other clothes in her closet. She wore the same white shirt, same round-necked sweater. I didn't think she was poor, she just didn't care about what she wore. We had to carry all the boxes to her crappy car. She was going to mail them for her dad.

Danny tried to carry like, four of them at the same time and totally fumbled them all onto the front lawn. Sybil was at her car and said, "If you knew how much these are worth, you'd be a little more careful."

I thought for a second he was going to snark back at her, the same way he usually snarked at Grantree. But he said, "I'm an idiot. Don't mind me."

When we went back inside the house, I thought there was more to do, but Grantree called us up to the kitchen. He had a box of muffins open on the dining room table that his daughter had brought and a big two litre bottle of Coke. "Sit down, you guys. Have a muffin. Sibby, can you grab us some glasses?"

Grantree was in a jolly mood with his daughter there. I thought maybe Danny would refuse the snacks and drag me outside, but he was the first to sit down and start peeling the paper from his muffin. I pulled a chair out and joined him.

"Sibby's just starting her new job. I can't even pronounce what she's working on. Alls I know is, she finds some pretty nice arrowheads."

Sibby set four glasses on the table and plunked herself down opposite her dad. She flashed a quick smile and didn't say anything.

"So..." I said, trying to break the awkwardness. "Is it like, archaeology?"

"Yup," she said, shoving her giant glasses up her nose and pouring herself some pop. She handed Danny the bottle and he slobbed all over the table.

"Oh, don't worry about it," she said.

Her dad was looking at her. "That's it?" he said. "You don't want to tell him what you do?"

"Oh, sorry. It's geoarchaeology. It's, um...multi-disciplinary."

Danny stared at her for a second with his mouth full of muffin. That made me crack a smile.

"My granddad used to find arrowheads in his wheat field," said Grantree. "Big buffalo jump down by the river. Out west of here by Lake Wabamun. I inherited them when he died. I guess I caught the collecting bug."

"Yeah," said his daughter. "And I caught the research bug." She showed her front teeth, which I figured was some kind of laugh, then began picking the crumbs from her muffin paper, even before starting on her muffin.

"So what'll you be working on?" I asked her.

"Me? Oh. The Late Wisconsinan Glaciation."

"The what?" asked Danny.

"It's when the first people crossed over to North America

from Asia."

Danny nodded. "That's cool."

Grantree shook his head slowly. "Eight years of schooling and she still hasn't studied granddad's collection. Could have diamonds. Could have coal. No idea."

Sibby ate with her mouth mostly open, head tipped back like she was trying to stop her glasses from slipping down.

I'd never met anyone like Sybil before and wanted her to keep telling us cool stuff. "So, there used to be like, dinosaurs here, right?"

She smiled. "Well, long before there were arrowheads."

"Yeah, I know."

"It was tropical," she said. "This was all a big sea. And around the edge you had giant ferns, palm trees—"

"Palm trees?" Danny broke in. "Did the dinosaurs all have like, little umbrellas in their drinks?"

Grantree rolled his eyes.

"Yeah," I said. "But they couldn't reach their mouths 'cause of their tiny hands."

"Died of thirst," Sibby added.

Right then, my phone buzzed in my pocket. I pulled it halfway out just to see who it was. It was my birth mother, sending me a happy face. I sort of panicked and shoved the phone back into my pocket.

"Something important?" Grantree asked.

"Um…" I said, not really thinking clearly. "It's just my mother."

Danny was holding up a chunk of muffin, ready to pop it into his mouth. "Your mother?" he said. "Your mom doesn't even own a cell phone. How can she text you?"

I thought fast. Grantree was staring straight at me. At that moment, I don't why, I thought it was way more important not to lie than it was to keep pretending to Danny. So I spat it out. "Um…well, it's my birth mom." The moment I said it, my heart felt like it grew about seven sizes and was about to squeeze right out of my throat.

Grantree kept staring at me, his eyes a little squinty, like he was trying to figure me out.

Strangely, Danny kept eating his chunks of muffin. "I figured you were adopted. Nobody like you has parents like that."

"Like what?" Sybil asked.

Danny sat up straight and shrugged. "I don't know. My sister made mac and cheese once and forgot to put the cheese in. And Brian's like...half cheese. You can tell when he cuts it." He pretended to wave away a bad smell.

Sybil snorted. Grantree was not impressed. "Ha-ha. All right with that, kid." Then he turned to me. "So, you always known her? Your birth mom? What do they call 'em? Open adoptions?"

I could feel my whole system wanting to go into shut-down mode. But I forced myself to sound casual and confident. "Yeah, no. I only met her like, last week."

Sybil went, "Aw..." as if she'd just seen the cutest puppy in the world.

Grantree's expression did not change. "Well, aren't you the lucky one. How did it go?"

I tried not to look at Danny. "Good," I said. "Weird."

"Of course," Grantree said.

Sybil had this totally amused smile. "So did you like, hug and cry and everything?"

"Yeah," I admitted. "Totally."

"That's so great!" she exclaimed, trying to find more crumbs to pick off the paper from her muffin. "So you have two mothers, eh? Must be nice."

Before I had a chance to answer, Grantree jumped in. "That's ridiculous. How'd you like to spend your first decade in someone else's house? How's that nice?"

Sybil's face stiffened for a second. She did not like being chewed out by her father. "I meant, maybe he gets two

Christmases and whatnot."

"I know what you meant," said Grantree. "It ain't that simple."

She shrugged and started digging the raisins out of her muffin and eating them, one by one.

Grantree turned to me again. "What's she do, your mother?"

"Oh, um, she works at this place on 111 Avenue. Sundance Cabinets. She runs the office and does the bookkeeping."

"That sounds pretty good," Grantree said.

"I'll bet it was great meeting her," Sibby put in.

"Um...yeah."

"You don't sound very convincing."

"It was fine. It was just weird."

"What was weird about it?"

"Oh, nothing. Just...her boyfriend. He treats her like cra—like, badly."

"And you want to kill him," Sybil suddenly said. "Right?"

I just looked at her. "Kind of."

"Freud would have a heyday."

"All right with the college stuff," said Grantree. Then he turned to me. "Does he beat her?"

"I have no idea. But he's super lazy and orders her around. She does whatever he asks."

"Yeah, I been there," said Grantree. Danny sat up a little straighter and looked at the man like he was insane. "Took me a long time to get my act together." Then he shook his head. "By the time I figured it out," he said to Sibby, "your mother was already living somewheres else."

Sybil kind of hunched and nodded at her muffin.

Grantree suddenly sat forward with a grunt and leaned over the table toward me. "You take some advice?"

"Um...sure."

"Don't bring it up. She's gotta feel bad about it. Don't

make it worse."

What the hell, I thought. I was taking advice from Danny's neighbour about my birth mother. Why, I wondered, was I spreading my personal life all over the place? I must have somehow lost some gears out of my brain machine.

The next ten minutes were a total blur. Sybil started talking about some professor she met who did research on adoption reunions. But my mind was in a fog. I smiled at remarks I hadn't really heard. All I could think about was what Grantree had said. The guy sounded like he knew what he was talking about.

When Sybil said she had to leave, we took that as our cue. Danny practically raced to the back door. But Grantree stopped him.

"Whoa-whoa-whoa there, kid."

"What?" he said, turning.

Grantree tried to get up, then decided against it. "It's your last day, right? You guys did good. Thanks for all your work."

"Okay." Danny was still poised at the door, looking like he did not want to wait for any more speechifying.

But Grantree continued. "No, really. Thanks. It's too bad about my greenhouse. I mean, I wasn't using it this year anyway. But still. You did good. Not too much belly-aching."

Danny gave him a fake smile. "Not a pleasure doing business with you."

"Yeah, yeah," said Grantree. "Your business being, what? Demolition?"

We left Grantree shaking his head as we headed to the door and out into the late morning. Finally, I thought, I was finished doing all this stupid work! Ugh. I never should have been doing it to begin with! I have to admit, though, as we passed the garden, which was now pretty much weed-free, that I had little moment of *I did that!*

Back on Cheevers turf, Danny kept looking at me.

"What?" I asked.

"So, uh," he said, chucking his chin at me. "You're adopted, eh?"

"Yeah."

There was a long pause. "Cool."

At his back door, he stopped and began kicking the step, each of us expecting the other to say something more. Finally I told him, "I don't want the guys at school to know."

"No problem. Must have been weird, not knowing your real mother."

"Yeah. It's still weird. I guess it always will be."

"So how did you find her?"

"She was searching for me. Some agency called. We talked on the phone. Then last weekend I went over and met her for the first time."

"Does she look like you?"

I could feel a flush of pride stream up the sides of my neck. I couldn't help grinning. "Yeah, totally. Same kind of hair and I think we have the same eyes."

"Dude, that's so awesome. I'd trade you any day. It'd be great to find out I wasn't related to Randy or Cindy."

"What? Cindy's awesome!"

"Yeah, well, you don't have to live with her." He paused for second. Then he said, "I'm gonna head. I'll text you later."

So I trudged home, feeling like all my guts had been spilled out for strangers to poke and examine and crack jokes about. Ugh. Why couldn't I keep my stupid trap shut?

Chapter 17

All through lunch, the boys were super nice to me, offering me their sandwich crusts and fetching me the remote when we headed into the living room afterward. I didn't really care at first, but after Jayden brought me a jiggling glass of ice water, I had to ask what was up.

"Can we go for pizza with you?" came the answer from Kyle.

"No," I told them firmly. "Sorry."

"But we never get pizza!" I thought that was the end of it and he'd go away pouting, but his mental circuits went in a totally different direction. "When can I find out if I'm adopted?"

"Probably never."

"Does Mom hate us?"

"I don't think so."

"But how do we get pizza?"

"Try making little fists and stomping around the house."

"Ooh!" He batted the air, pushed Jayden ahead of him and walked away.

Around one thirty, my phone buzzed in my pocket. I looked at the name: *Royal Alberta Museum*, and rushed into the closest private place—the bathroom—to answer on the third ring. "Hello?"

"May I speak to Brian McSpadden, please?" said a man's warm voice on the other end.

"That's me."

"My name's Kiril Ostergaard. I'm with the Alberta Museum. You called about our new exhibits?"

"I did, yeah." For a second my brain froze. Grantree's stamps were a zillion miles away from the soap and toothpaste smell of my bathroom. I couldn't think what to ask.

"Well," said the man, "we have three major exhibits coming up in the fall. The railroads of western Canada, a brand new Albertosaurus exhibit—we finally acquired the bones from the Dry Island Buffalo Jump find. I don't know if you saw it in the news?"

"No, I—"

"And then the unveiling of the new Marian Forrest sculpture in the lobby. Is there one in particular you're interested in?"

"Um…yeah, I heard there were display cases getting set up for like, some stamps?"

"Stamps?" The man sounded a bit surprised. "Well, yes, as a matter of fact. Are you thinking of the real stamps? A prominent Edmonton collector is making a donation to the museum."

"Is his name Grantree?"

There was a pause. "How did you know that? Sorry, I can't reveal the name until he—until the donor okays it. Nothing has been made public yet. Do you know him?"

"Yeah, kind of. Can I ask one question?"

"Shoot."

"What do you mean, real stamps?"

The guy on the other end burst out laughing. "No, no, not real stamps. I'm talking about the Riel stamps. From Louis Riel. You maybe heard about him in school?"

"Uh…maybe. How do you spell that?"

"Ar, eye, ee, el. Look it up. Just google the Riel Issue. It's incredibly rare. I think they're making a formal announcement right away here. Sorry, it's not my project."

"Oh, cool." I couldn't think of anything else to say. "Um…thanks a lot for your help."

"Hey, any time. We have a student outreach program, by the way. If your class ever wants to book a visit, I can give you a behind-the-scenes tour."

"Nice. Thanks."

And that was it. After I hung up, I sat there on the toilet seat for like, ten seconds, stunned by my discovery. Grantree was donating stamps to the museum. For sure those plumbers knew about it and were trying to steal them before the stamps were put permanently behind museum security. When I got my head back in the game, I jumped on my phone and googled the Riel Issue. It led me to a zillion boring articles about Louis Riel and how he was hung for high treason in 1886. The guy wanted to stop the white guys from stealing any more First Nations land. He even tried to set up his own Métis government with its own post office. The Riel Issue was the stamps he made. Some guy on a stamp collector website had scanned these old magazine articles about how rare the stamps were. When I read *Only one other copy of this stamp is known to exist,* I looked up to the ceiling and laughed. "That stamp must be worth a fortune!"

Mom suddenly rapped on the bathroom door. "Brian, are you in there? Kyle really has to go."

"Okay, I'll be out in a second." I saved the google search. Then I couldn't click Danny's phone number fast enough and kept flubbing my phone.

"Dude!" I said when he answered. "You're not going to believe this. It's Riel. Not real. Like Louis Riel!"

"What are you talking about?"

"The stamps! Grantree's donating them to the museum."

"Okay." He didn't sound excited at all. In fact, he sounded completely bummed.

"What's going on?"

"Nothing. I can't really talk right now."

"Gimme a hint."

By the way his voice changed, I could tell he was cupping the phone to his mouth. "Somebody beat up Alvin and he took off from the home."

"What home?"

"The home…like, the Family Services friggin' shelter they put him in."

"That sucks. What happened?"

"He got beat up! Some other kid didn't like him."

"Wow. Is he okay?"

"I don't know. It wasn't that bad, but he's gone!"

"You don't know where he is?"

"No. If you see him…like, call me."

"Yeah, yeah, for sure. He wouldn't have gone to his house?"

"No, I checked. Anyway, I gotta go." And he hung up.

I stared at my phone for a second, thinking about Alvin. That kid was not equipped for the real world. His family hated him. No school friends. Where would a guy like that go?

"Brian," Mom said outside the bathroom. "Come on now. Get out of there."

I stood and winged the door open. It banged against the wall and bounced back at me, ruining my dramatic exit. Kyle rushed in past me and flung the door closed again.

"You ought to be more considerate," Mom said. She was on her way back to the kitchen, me following. "You know the boys have tummy troubles. What time are you leaving?"

As I passed through the kitchen on the way to my room, I looked at the clock above the fridge. It was just after four. "Few minutes. I just gotta change."

"Why don't you wear your new hoodie?"

I didn't want to think about it right then, so I said, "Maybe," as I zipped down to the landing.

I did my Brian lunge down the stairs to the basement. I have no idea what I did differently, but for the first time on these stairs, I totally nailed it. I was so shocked, I actually went up to the top again and repeated it. Shazam, baby. I did it again!

In my room, I changed into some half decent clothes—not formal, not old, but not too fancy. I wanted to make a good impression. But I sure didn't want to have to dress up every time I saw my birth mother. And I was not wearing my new hoodie. If I had to kill her boyfriend, I didn't want to get blood all over it.

When I got outside to the bus stop, I tried to focus on questions I wanted to ask Alicia. First was, what was my birth dad like? Tall, short, skinny, fat? I was craving details. Then I wanted to know about her pregnancy and my birth, which made me realize I had an even bigger question: what was it like for her to give me up? But I couldn't ask that. I did not want to find out it was easy for her. *Spittooee! Bye! Have a nice life!* Ugh. It was way better not to know.

Halfway down 111 Avenue, two teenagers got on the bus and came to the back where I was sitting. They were maybe fifteen, a guy and a girl. The guy had a deep voice for a kid. The girl had blonde dreadlocks and was wearing a jean jacket with patches all over it.

Before sitting down, she looked out the back window. "Wow, it's really smoking now!" she said.

The guy turned. "It's probably somebody just burning leaves."

"Not with that much smoke!" she said. "And you can smell it. That's not leaves."

I ignored them for a couple of blocks, trying to focus on the game on my phone.

Then out of the blue, the girl said, "Oh, no way..."

I heard a fire truck siren. As the bus continued along 111 Ave, it turned out to be three trucks, two of them blasting their horns as they went by. I half stood for second to see where they were headed and saw the black smoke in the distance.

"Sucks," said the girl. "I hope everybody's okay."

"Oh!" said the guy in a high voice. "Dinner's ruined!"

They both laughed. When the bus jerked forward, the smoke and everything was blocked by trees and trucks on the avenue and I sat back down, thinking about Cindy's melted mixing bowl, hoping it wasn't anybody I knew.

When I got off the bus, I was ten minutes early. I crossed 111 Ave, suddenly feeling extremely light. I was getting to visit my birth mom! But my happiness nose-dived and crashed when I started walking up her street.

A bright yellow extension cord snaked out of the front door of the house and down the walkway to the street, where booblehead boyfriend was vacuuming a crappy little grey car.

I thought I could get by him before he noticed me, but I couldn't. He backed out and shut off the vacuum just as I walked up. "Hey, you're Alicia's kid, eh?"

"Yeah." I wanted to keep walking, but thought I'd better not be rude. When I was in court for murdering this guy, the judge would probably ask.

"Coming by for a visit?"

If this guy creeped me out before, he was making me ill right now. I hated his pale hair. I hated each one of his giant freckles individually. And I really hated that his beer-breath voice was talking about my birth mom.

"Yeah, just for dinner."

"That's nice!" he said, and he reached out to pat my head. I totally flinched and moved my head away. "Hey now, kid. I'm not going to bite you. I guess I'm gonna be your new stepdad, eh?" As he talked, he dug a pack of cigarettes out of his side pants pocket.

"Why?" I said, "Are you getting married to her?"

He lit a cigarette with a plastic lighter and snorted some smoke like a bull. "No, of course not. Marriage is for idiots. I don't need no ball and chain." And he tried to tap me with his elbow, like we were both in on the joke.

"Okay," I said, being half nice, "I'll see you later."

With his cigarette hand, he pointed at me. "Later, alligator."

I got up the sidewalk and the steps, almost shaking. I hated that guy so much, I forgot to enjoy the smell of the flowering shrub next door.

"Go on in!" the guy shouted from the street. "She's just changing the baby!"

I ignored him and knocked on the wooden screen door. My mom's voice called from somewhere deep in the house, "Is that you Brian? Come on in! I'll just be a second!"

I stepped inside and started kicking off my shoes. There wasn't much room, since there was a mountain bike and a longboard right in the little hallway.

Right then, she came out of the bathroom in the hall with Maddy on her arm. "Hey! You can leave 'em on, if you like. And sorry about Keith's stuff. I told him to move it before you got here." She swung by me into the living room and set Maddy down on the couch. "Come in," she said, sitting down beside her daughter. Her hair was half-tucked behind her ears. I couldn't get over how young she looked. "So, how's it going?"

I shoved my heel back into my shoe and went to sit opposite her on the chair. "Good. okay. Weird, I guess."

"Really? Weird why?"

The past few days had been a whirlwind. Alvin, the freako auntie, the rare stamp thing. I wanted to tell her everything. But being here with her was like, so much greater, I couldn't really concentrate. I wanted to hear her voice, not mine. "Oh, nothin'. So, how long you been in this house?"

"Oh…about two years, I guess? I so lucked out. It's owned by an old gay couple. The rent is so cheap. A friend was moving out and asked if I wanted it. I was like, Uh…yes! By the way," she lowered her voice, "I'm so sorry about last time. I just want to make it up to you."

"Hey, no problem."

"Sometimes Keith can be such a…" I could have finished her sentence with about fifty different words. She made a noise in her throat and waved away the subject. "So tell me what was weird about your week. I want to hear everything."

So I told her all about Alvin and Danny's aunt. How gross their house was and how the aunt was taken away in an ambulance.

"Oh my god, is she all right?"

"I have no idea. I guess I'll hear later."

"Well, that's exciting, in a grim sort of way. Oh, before I forget." She reached over and picked up this small white paper bag from the old trunk coffee table. "This is for you."

"What is it?"

"Oh, nothing. It's for your art. I don't know if you have some already."

I reached into the bag and pulled out a bunch of weirdly shaped wooden sticks. "Are these for—?"

"For your plasticine."

"Cool! Thank you!"

"Hey, they were like, five bucks. I just thought maybe you could use them."

"Heck, yeah. These are awesome. You know I'm not like,

super-artist guy."

"Oh, you never know. Someday."

I stuffed them in my pocket, minus the bag. I couldn't wait to get home and start sculpting. I could feel my skills improving, just having the dang things in my pocket.

I remembered my plan to ask questions, so I steered the conversation back to stuff I wanted to know. "So where did you grow up?" I asked. "You were on the north side here, right?"

"Oh god, yeah—108th and 109th Ave. Not too far from the hospital."

"No way."

"Yeah, it's only a few minutes from where you live. Neat, eh? We used to play in the hospital parking lot and stuff, turning people's mirrors crooked, playing hide and seek."

She looked at her daughter, who was cruising around the coffee table, pushing fliers and mail onto my legs and feet. "Maddy, come on over here, sweetie. Brian just wants to sit."

She told me stories about dumb things she'd done as a kid. Breaking a tooth the first time she rode a two-wheeler. Winning ten bucks for never missing a day of school in grade three. Then blowing it on candy and barfing all over her sister's bed. And in grade five, falling off a horse when she tried to ride it standing up.

"You must have done stuff like that when you were young."

"Not really."

"Sounds like you live a pretty protected life."

"Yeah, I guess. My parents don't really like to do stuff. They watch TV. My mom goes to church sometimes."

"Hey, it's Canada," she said cheerfully. "People get used to hibernating."

Finally, the pizza arrived. I swear, I could smell it before the driver even got it up to the house.

"Let's go into the kitchen. I hate eating in here. I like a

proper table, you know?"

When we got settled at the table with Maddy in her high chair, I asked, "So what were your parents like?"

"Oh," she said, shaking her head, "intense; really strict. My dad was like, seriously religious. Owned the Catholic bookstore downtown."

I'd never heard of it, so I just said, "Yeah?"

"His whole life was that store and, well, church. Tried to turn us all into little robo-Catholics so his customers would buy more stuff. I couldn't take it. I ran away for like, two nights when I was fifteen and got pregnant. I was sixteen when you were born. He still doesn't know about you."

"Really?"

"Hey, don't feel bad. I had to tell him Keith and I were married in the church or he never would have accepted Maddy."

"Wow."

"And you, well…he would have died if he knew I had a baby with a heathen. Devon—your dad—was absolutely not a Catholic."

My head literally snapped back on my neck. "That's his name? Devon?"

"Oh, you didn't know?"

"No." I felt this black hole open up in my guts. I took some sneaky deep breaths to try to calm down.

She leaned forward and began scratching one thumbnail against another. "Yeah, he was pretty awesome. Tall…sweet. I never met his family. But I heard they were like, the opposite of religious." She seemed lost in thought for a second. "Not that it matters anymore. My dad's old. Sold the store long ago. He lives in Arizona now. He's all high up in the Legion of Mary and Knights of Columbus. I'm not going to burst his bubble."

"So where were you born?" I asked.

"Oh, here. In the Royal Alex."

"Yeah? Me, too!"

"Uh…" She laughed. "I know."

"Ha! Of course."

"I was a pain in the butt when I was a teenager. Went to stay with my aunt and uncle up north when I was pregnant. My dad was glad to have me out of his house. But still, if he knew I was 'with child,' he would have been like, violent for sure."

"Really?"

"Oh, yeah. He couldn't have faced the shame. He even said it to my face. 'You want me to put you in that hospital over there? Have sex before you leave this house.' He's mellowed now, but he's still a jerk."

"Didn't you say you had a brother?"

"Yeah, James. The one you look like. He's the same as my dad. Religion first, people second. We don't talk much."

I was halfway through my first slice of pizza when booblehead came in, dragging the vacuum. He made a racket in the hallway, smashing the vacuum against the wall and swearing. We stopped talking till he was finished.

"So you go to Westmount?" she asked.

"Yeah, in the fall. I just finished at Westglen. I'm lucky. In September, I get to wake up late and just walk across the street."

"Nice!" said the boyfriend, coming into the kitchen. I wasn't sure if he was talking to me or talking about the pizza. But he went straight for the cupboard and looked inside. "No plates?"

"They're in the sink," said my mom. "Except for our two. You used them all, remember?"

"Hey, no worries," he said, coming over to the box on the table. And without a word, he tore the lid off the box and began stacking pizza slices on to it.

"Hey, hey, come on! Leave some for us!" my mom said.

"Whatever. I vacuumed your stupid car. Don't I get to

eat?"

"Yeah. Somewhere else, please."

"Do I have to use a fork, too?"

"Keith, just—"

"Maybe hold my pinky out? Screw that." The freak lifted an arm and pretended to rub the pizza in his armpit. "Mmm, delicious!"

"Oh, gross. Come on!" said my mom. "We're trying to have a nice dinner here."

The freak gave me a creepy wink and strode back down the hall. I could feel my blood start to boil and it took me a minute to calm down. I could hear the TV go on in the living room. The show sounded like sports.

From then on, it was brain-picking time. I remembered a ton of my questions and my mom didn't mind answering them. Some of her answers were quick and short. Others lasted for like, ten minutes. "I'm not boring you, am I? It's not too much information?"

I was like, "Um, no. I never heard any of this, my entire life. This is awesome!"

"You stop me if it's too much."

"Okay."

I heard more about her hard-ass father, and how they could only keep Christmas and birthday gifts for a year. Then they had to be given to charity so the kids didn't get spoiled, having too many toys around. Her mother, my birth grandmother, had died about four years ago from breast cancer. "You would have loved her," Alicia said. "She was a courier driver till she had kids. Loved driving. That's how she met my dad. Big car accident; wrecked her left arm." I heard so much stuff about her and my birth family, I began to get scared I would forget it all. She even pulled out this hardcover book on the family history and showed me all these pictures of people from Nova Scotia who looked like me, which was freaky.

Then I asked about my birth father. "Is there like, a grave I can visit? Do you know where he's buried?"

That caught her off guard. "No. I've no idea." She stared at me for a long second. Then she said, "And I wouldn't go poking around. He didn't know about you. And his family certainly didn't."

"How come?"

She retucked her hair behind one ear. "I don't know. I guess I was kind of selfish."

"How do you mean?"

"Well, he died before I even knew I was pregnant. He went to the mountains with his older cousins, I heard. You know, Devon and me...I'm sorry, but like, it was just a fling. I obviously thought he was awesome. But it never would have worked out. His family was like, wild. I was all freaked out about my dad knowing. And then after I heard Devon died, well, you were like, the last thing left of him alive. If his family found out I gave you up for adoption...I don't know...I was afraid of what they'd say. I had enough people angry with me."

As soon as she said this, I got this huge jolt. She kept my birth a secret because she was afraid of what people would say. Wow, that sounded right out of my McSpadden mom's playbook. But I had to let it go. She hadn't noticed my reaction and I really wanted to hear what she was saying.

"I had the happiest time being pregnant. Hormones, I guess. I wanted to have like, ten kids after that. And the hospital. Oh my god, they were so nice. Anything I wanted, they were right there."

She went on about the ultrasound on her big belly and how nice the nurses were. It was hard to imagine I was there, back then, in that hospital. But it was cool getting the blank scenes of my life filled in. She was the only one who knew me before I was me. And I totally lapped it up.

"Oh my god, I haven't been able to say anything about this for years. My sister Cassie doesn't come over much." She leaned over to me and said in a low voice, "She hates Keith's guts. There's nobody else to tell, really. Who would care except you?"

By the time I had to go, I felt like my mom and I had a weird bond. With her talking about her parents, my birth dad, and her pregnancy, things were getting real. It was like there'd been this big explosion in her life with stuff flying off in all directions. And I was the bomb.

At the door she gave me a hug that felt like it was twelve years in the making. I didn't even notice I had tears in my eyes.

"Are you all right?"

"Yeah, yeah," I said, a bit embarrassed. "My friend calls me Cryin' Brian."

"Ha!" she laughed. "We have that in common. I need a whole box of kleenex to get through a movie sometimes."

"Yeah?"

"Don't get me started or you'll miss your bus."

When I got out onto the street, I sighed all the way to the bus stop. Yup, things were definitely getting real.

Chapter 18

I had turned my phone off before I got to my mother's. It wasn't till I was sitting at the bus stop to go home that I realized I probably had messages and flicked it back on. I had sixteen messages. All of them from Danny. The latest one said:

r u dead? did u lose ur phone?

I scanned the previous messages really fast, my eyes getting bigger and bigger.

fire at my aunties place.
dont know where Alvin is!!!
r u coming?
what the hell?!!!

The bus arrived as I was trying to answer him and I couldn't finish until I was on the bus. I ended up sitting beside this drunk old guy. I didn't know he was drunk till he breathed all over me. I turned sideways and hunched over my knees.

"Is that one of them new smart phones?" he asked.

"I think they're all smart these days," I said. And I thought, *Unlike you.*

"They're getting thin, eh?" he persisted.

"Yeah," I answered, trying to type. I told Danny where I was and asked if he'd seen Alvin anywhere.

i thought u were dead, dude, he answered. *no Alvin im freaking out u on the bus still?*

yeah

can u get off at 127 street?

yeah for sure

I waited for more news.

The drunk guy was trying to read off my phone. "Hey, no offense, kid," he said. "I was just tryna—" Thankfully, he realized I was ignoring him and shut up. His bad breath was still hanging in the air. You could have lit it with a match.

Finally, Danny sent me something: *they got the fire out no way could u live in that house again sucks*

All the way down 111 Avenue, he gave me updates, like a slow-mo play-by-play:

stinks I hate fire if Alvin is in there burnt up Im gonna lose it cops are asking us if we saw anything Cindys taking Randy home shows over news truck is leaving too ur bus is super slow are u like pushing it or what?

As soon as the bus stopped at 127 Street and I jumped off, the reek of the fire hit me: wet burnt old house. And it wasn't just charred wood. It was the smell of all the crap inside that got fried. The plastic bread bags, the dust and clothes and couch cushions. All of Alvin and the auntie's stuff, burnt up together and then peed on by a fire truck.

The street was blocked off at both ends with yellow caution tape tied between the streetlight poles and the trees. Three fire trucks were crammed into the middle of the street, with hoses everywhere. There were a couple dozen people scattered over the boulevards and sidewalks. I scanned for Danny and when I couldn't find him, I went all the way around and down the next street, to the other side of the barricade tape. Still no luck. So I texted him. As I waited for an answer, I paced back and forth, checking out what was left of Alvin's place.

From where I was, it looked like someone had punched in the front of the house and sprayed it with dull black paint. The porch was gone and the whole front wall had fallen backward into the cavity of the house and crumbled there. The spruce trees on the boulevard had gone up like candles. Weirdly, all the new boards we'd brought for the porch were still lying there, in perfect condition.

I didn't get a message back from Danny. Instead, he found me and came up behind and slapped me on the back. "*Dude! What the hell?*" he whispered. "*Took you long enough! Come on!*" As he walked away, he looked like he was in a hurry and didn't want anyone to know it.

"What?" I said. "Where we going?"

"*Shh,*" he hissed at me, and urged me on with a jerk of his head. "Just—come on."

He led me down 110 Avenue and we hung a left at the next alley. "Where we going?"

He stopped to let me catch up. "I got Alvin."

"Yeah?"

"He's hiding back here."

"Did he start the fire?"

"Quiet, dude. Just a sec." A couple of houses in, he looked back to see if anyone was watching. Then he zipped over to where two garages stood close together. There was a crappy low fence, maybe four feet wide, in between them. Behind the fence, the weeds were as high as my head. "*Alvin,*" Danny whispered. "*You there?*"

A small voice issued from the weeds. "Who's that with

you?"

"Dude, it's Brian."

The weeds parted low down and Alvin's narrow face appeared. "Hi, Brian."

"Hey, you all right?" I asked.

The kid just looked at me. "Not really." His face was blackened by soot, dirt and who knows what else. And there were trails down his face from crying.

"So, what happened with the fire?" I asked.

"I didn't do nothing," Alvin answered firmly.

Two people were walking by at the end of the alley. Danny spun around and leaned against the fence. I did the same, so we weren't drawing attention to Alvin. "What's-their-face," Danny said, "Ordry and Morgan were bumming smokes off him."

"Oh, no way. You smoke, Alvin?" I asked.

An annoyed, "Noo!" came out of the weeds behind us.

Danny continued. "They were getting him to steal his mom's cigarettes for them. I guess for like, months."

"They said they were gonna beat me up if I didn't give 'em smokes," Alvin put in.

"Nice," I said.

"After he took off from that Family Services place," Danny continued, "he went and hid in the basement."

"No, I didn't!" Alvin said. "I went to see my mom."

"You did?" Danny exclaimed. "How'd you even get there? Is she all right?"

"Noo!" came the answer. "I walked a long time! This man nurse showed me where she was. She was just lying there, staring. She didn't even see me. They said she might have to go to a special place to live—like, forever. She can't even feed herself or anything."

"And *then* you went home, right?"

There was a long pause. "The man nurse started asking me all these questions. I got scared and ran away."

208

Danny rolled his eyes. "Anyway, he ended up at his house. Stayed in the basement so no one would see any lights on."

"And Morgan walked right in!" Alvin shouted.

"Dude," Danny chided him, "shush already. Let me tell it. If somebody hears you, it's all over."

From the weeds came his timid, "Okay."

"So before this—like, the other day, they heard Alvin and Auntie were gone and broke in. They found that carton of cigarettes we brought and totally sold it to their friends. Then they came back to look around for more. They couldn't find any, but they did find Alvin."

"That sucks."

"They made him go upstairs and try to find if she had like, a secret stash somewhere."

"I kept telling them there was nothing!" Alvin put in.

"Dude," Danny warned.

"Okay," came the meek reply.

"I guess they were following him around the house, flicking matches at him. His shirt got burnt. It was really bad. When the curtains caught on fire, they just booked it. Alvin was stuck there, trying to put it out."

"And all my stuff got burnt up. Even my best pants!" Alvin added.

"Sucks," I said. "So now what?"

Danny sighed heavily. "I don't know. I'll think of something."

"Why don't you talk to your dad?"

Danny swore. "After he dumped Alvin at that place? He's the last person I'm going to ask."

"So...?"

"Alvin's gotta hide. The poor kid could be sent to like, juvie or something if they think he burned down his own house. Anyway, it's like, late now. I gotta get home."

"Yeah, same," I said. "So what are you going to do?"

"I dunno. I was thinking he could sleep in my garage."

"Ha! Wow…really? The door doesn't even close. It's got like, a dirt floor."

"It'll be like camping!"

I just rolled my eyes. "What is wrong with you, dude?"

Danny came right up to my face. "If you aren't going to help, just shut up. We're going, all right? Alvin," he said to the weeds behind me, "you stay here for a sec. We're gonna go check if the coast is clear."

His meek voice sounded like a verbal squirm. "Well… yeah…okay…but what if somebody sees me?"

"Dude, come on. Really. No one's going to see you."

There was a rustling in the weeds as Alvin settled down. Danny and I hurried back out into the middle of the alley, trying to seem all casual as we headed back to 110 Avenue. We were about twenty feet from it when Cindy burst out from the sidewalk.

"What are you doing back here?" Danny asked. "I thought you had stuff to do."

Completely out of breath. Cindy bent over for a second. "I just wanted to see…if you found Alvin."

"What if I did?"

Cindy stood up and squished a hand into a running cramp in her side. "Oh, my god…I can't believe you. Where is he?"

"Nowhere."

"Ugh!" She threw her hands up. "Brian, come on. Is he here somewhere? Did you find him?"

"Yeah," I said, noting that Cindy remembered my name. "We're gonna hide him."

"Why are you saying that?" Danny smacked me. "You idiot!"

"Oh my god," Cindy said, rolling her eyes. "I knew it. So what's your big plan?"

"I'm not telling you," Danny snapped at her. "The fewer people who know, the better. You're gonna be like, 'Oh, poor Alvin, I'll just bring him some milk and cookies!'"

210

"What?" Cindy said. "That's ridicu—oh, my god, you were going to do something really stupid. Wasn't he?" she asked me.

"No."

"Then what?"

Danny wiped the sweat from his top lip. "He was going to sleep over at Brian's."

I wasn't sure if I heard him correctly and blinked. "What?"

But Cindy jumped in again. "Really?" She seemed suddenly relieved. "That would be so awesome! Just until we figure out something better. Oh my god, you're the best!" And she stepped forward and gave me this huge hug. Having Cindy's cheek against mine and her boobs squished up against me made my whole face turn totally red. I completely lost the power of speech. "So where is he?" she continued. "He's hiding somewhere, right? Okay, I don't care. Just keep him safe, would you?"

Danny's eyes narrowed. "Yeah, yeah. We got it under control."

Cindy turned to leave and threw back at me, "Seriously, Brian. You're the best ever. We'll figure out everything in the morning. Thankyou-thankyou-thankyou." And she dug her phone out of a pocket and spun around, dialing a number. As she reached the street, we could hear her exclaiming to some friend or other, "Omigod, you won't believe this." She disappeared around the corner.

Danny continued on to the sidewalk. But I didn't move. "He's not really coming to my house, is he?"

He looked both ways to see who was on the street and turned back to me. "Huh?"

"You were just faking. He's still staying in your garage?"

"What? No! Of course he's going to your house. It's just for tonight."

I laughed and shook my head. "Ha! He can't come to my place. There's just no way. I've never had anybody sleep over.

I've never even had people over for a birthday party."

"There's always a first time."

"Not at my house. My dad would never allow it. And my mom would be like, *No!*"

"But why? That's so weird!"

"Not my fault, man. They're old. They like their routine. They're like robots that can't do anything different."

"But you'll try, right?"

"Oh my god…"

"Come on. The worst they can do is say no. But everything will be awesome if they say yes."

"They're never going to say yes."

"Wow, what a chicken. You're gonna make Alvin, whose house just burned down, sleep on a dirt floor with all the mosquitoes and the drunk bums coming in? Really? He can't have one decent night's sleep first 'cause you're too chicken to ask?"

My mind went blank for a second. All I could think about was Cindy's boobs against my chest. I realized I was not saying no to Danny. I was thinking about how Cindy might hug me again if things went well.

Two seconds passed. Three seconds passed.

Danny jumped into the gap. "Ha! You are the best. Just don't screw it up."

Chapter 19

Alvin did sleep over. I got him settled with a comic book, sleeping bag and pillow on the floor beside my bed. But I made a tiny little mistake that blew up right in my face.

I left Alvin in the alley behind my place for a minute and went up the walk. I was thinking that if I was all chill and acted like sleepovers were normal in our house, maybe I could trick my parents. I was going to say, "Hey, my friend's gonna hang out tonight."

And Mom would say, "Oh, there's an extra blanket in the cupboard."

And I'd be like, "Okay, thanks. Good night!"

But as I opened the screen door and stepped inside, my heart dropped like a rock into my guts. The house smelled like they'd had burgers for dinner. I could hear Mom putting the boys to bed, and mumbling from the TV in the living room. This was totally not going to work.

Then I realized that no one had heard me open the door. And I had an idea.

I snuck back outside and slipped through the back gate. Alvin was still waiting. "Hey, it's all cool!" I said to him. "Let's go!"

"Really?" he asked. "Your mom said it was okay?"

"Yeah, yeah," I told him. "But we gotta hurry."

Alvin pushed his hair to one side, thinking he was going to meet my family. "Do I look okay?"

I had tried getting him to clean his hands and face a bit using his shirt. That had just smeared the dirt and soot on his skin into streaks. We didn't have time for messing around right now. "Totally, yeah," I told him. "Let's go."

As he followed me up the sidewalk, I scanned the windows, looking for movement. When we got to the house, I eased the door open and said in a low voice, "My room's downstairs. Just be quiet, okay?"

"Smells like dinner," he said. "Should I take my shoes off?"

"*No!*" I said in his ear. "*Just leave 'em on. People are sleeping. We gotta be quiet.*"

"*Oh. Okay.*"

I watched him go down the stairs. He was like a little kid, creeping from step to step, his movements exaggerated.

I went up into the kitchen and made a racket, acting like I'd just come in. Then I peered around the corner into the living room. "Hey, I'm home."

Mom had finished putting the boys to bed and Dad was half asleep in his recliner, with two empty beer bottles beside him on the end table. Mom leaned forward to see me around the lamp beside her, her eyes sliding back to her show. "Oh, hi. Did you have a nice dinner?"

"Yeah, it was okay. We just had pizza and sat around."

"That's nice."

"Yeah." I wanted to say more, to make it seem that everything was okay. Then I realized I'd said all I usually said to them anyway. "Okay, so I'm pretty tired. I think I'll conk out."

"Really?" Mom looked at her watch. "It's only just after eight."

"I know. Sorry. Long day."

"All right. Brush your teeth."

"Yeah."

I went into the bathroom, closed the door and made a freak-out face at myself in the mirror. I brushed my teeth, being super quiet, listening for any noises from downstairs. Then I had a last pee and tried not to hurry past my parents in the hallway.

"Night," I said.

"Night," Mom replied.

Dad raised one hand, not even looking at me, and lowered it again without saying anything.

I was so terrified by my success, I had to hold onto counters and chairs for support as I crossed the kitchen. Then I headed right downstairs, seriously hating that my plan was working. And that was it.

I got a sleeping bag from under the stairs, found Alvin an old cushion he could use as a pillow and got it all arranged on the floor beside my bed. While I was getting everything ready for him, he quietly poked around my room.

"What's with your windows?"

It took me a second to figure out what he was talking about. Then I clued in. It was the fake frost stuff. "Oh, my mom did that. It's this stuff that comes in a can. She's weird."

By then, Alvin was at my dresser, where I'd set down my new modelling tools. He pointed at my blue head with its neck and shoulders. "Did you make that?"

"Yeah."

"You're good."

"Thanks."

"Are you gonna do armature and stuff?"

I looked at him. "What do you mean?"

"Like, you put wire inside to make the body."

The idea had never occurred to me. "Huh," I said. "Maybe." Why did everybody know more about sculpting than I did?

The kid would have talked all night. I started yawning and nodding instead of answering to make him shut up. And I was really glad he took the hint. When we finally lay down and I turned off the light, Alvin was like, the perfect guest. He didn't snore. He didn't cough. He even wished me the nicest good night ever, sounding like he was super happy for the first time in his life.

I just lay there under my covers, staring up at the ceiling, my heart racing. I was the biggest idiot that ever lived. Boobs had made me do this. What was I thinking?

It took me a long time to get to sleep. I don't even know how I did it, with my whole body churning with dread. As a distraction, I tried to figure out how I felt about my birth mom not telling anyone about her pregnancy or my birth. It was like the world didn't want me to have grandparents. All my McSpadden grandparents had died when I was little or before I was born. Alicia couldn't/wouldn't tell her father about me. And nobody on my birth dad's side even knew I existed. Ugh! I knew this was all important to think about. But my guts were in such a twist over Alvin, I couldn't concentrate. I just lay there freaking out, hour after hour. I have no idea how I got to sleep.

Come morning, things did not go as I'd expected.

I rolled over before it was light out and saw that it was only four o'clock. That was the last thing I remembered before like, six, when I was awakened by a huge noise from upstairs. People were running and stomping around. And there was some shouting and little shrieking screams. At first I was like, I wonder what's going on? And then I remembered Alvin and sat up so fast, I think I sprained my neck.

I looked down beside my bed. No Alvin.

I tell you, I could not get my covers off fast enough. I swung my legs over, jumped up and grabbed my old dressing gown from the bed post. Before I could get to the door, I heard someone in bare feet coming down the basement stairs. They reached my door before I could.

Bam-bam-bam! "Brian! Get up!" Kyle called. "There's somebody upstairs! He says he knows you!" I flung the door open. Kyle's face was white and he was wide-eyed. "Daddy's got him in the kitchen!"

As I rushed to the stairs, which I took two at a time, I heard Mom in the hallway shrieking, "But who is he? And how did he get in?" Hearing Mom freaking out like that scared the heck out of me. I think I got from the landing up to the kitchen in one leap.

And there was Alvin, sitting in Dad's chair with a cereal spoon in one hand, his arms held up like he was being robbed. With his dirt-streaked face, burnt shirt and his belly sticking out, he looked like one of those starving kids on TV. Dad was facing him with a weapon. At least I thought it was a weapon at first. But it turned out to be the dustpan brush, which he aimed at Alvin like a knife. Dad was in his t-shirt and boxers, his hairy white legs about six times scarier than any intruder.

"Who is this?" Dad barked at me. "He says he knows you. What is he doing in here?"

My heart was so far up my throat I could feel it throbbing at the back of my tongue. And for a second I couldn't get a word out.

"Boy!" Dad shouted at me. "Speak up!"

"Uh! This is Alvin. Leave him alone! He's okay. I invited him over for a sleepover!"

"What?" Dad's voice had turned into a girlish scream,

high and screechy. "What? You did what?"

Mom was at the end of the hall, hunched over, peering out of their bedroom with Jayden's head poking out around the side of her dressing gown. Kyle was still at the top of the landing behind me. I thought I heard a snicker from him. Poor freaking Alvin was like, bug-eyed, his chin squished down to his neck in the most pathetic kind of fear.

I suddenly got some courage and barged in between Alvin and Dad. "His name is Alvin! God, Dad, leave him alone. He's not going to hurt anybody. He had no place to sleep. His house burned down and everything."

"Oh my god," said my mother, putting a hand up to her mouth. "He's a homeless person?"

"No!" I desperately tried to explain. "Didn't you see the smoke yesterday by 127th Street? Didn't you hear the sirens?"

"We don't care about any of that!" said Dad, still aiming his dustpan brush. "Why didn't you ask? Why did you bring him here?"

They were acting like I had just brought a serial killer into their house. But in fact, I realized, I was just trying to do something nice. My attitude did a one-eighty and I found myself red-faced angry with them. "Are you kidding me? What is wrong with you?" I grabbed Alvin by the arm. "Alvin, come on. Let's get outa here."

As I pulled him up, he clumsily dropped his spoon back into his cereal bowl, which was half full of bran flakes. The spoon hit so hard, the bowl broke and spilled milk all over the table.

"Brian!" Mom screamed, seeing her precious bowl snapped in half. "Look what he did!"

Right then, hauling Alvin bodily past my dad, I think I might have swore. I can't remember. But Dad leapt out of the way in his creepy boxer shorts like Alvin was radioactive. "Just go!" he said. "Get him outa here. This is not how we do things in this house!"

With Kyle watching, his face full of shock and amusement, I dragged Alvin back downstairs. "Where are we going?" he asked. "How come we have to leave?"

Back in my room, I got dressed at lightning speed. "Just get your stuff," I told him. "We gotta go."

He stood there while I pulled on my clothes. "I don't have any stuff," he said, which didn't make me feel any better about my parents' reaction.

When I was ready, I brought him up to the landing and was in such a hurry I grabbed my shoes and shoved out the door. Mom was behind me, trying to stop me. "Brian? Brian!" Somehow I got my runners on and stormed down the back sidewalk, with Alvin behind me trying to keep up.

Even though it was only around quarter after six, it was already super light out. The sun was still below the houses and it was the coolest I'd felt the air in days. Still, I could tell it was going to be a hot one.

All the way down the alley south, Alvin was silent. Then I realized it was too early to go to Danny's—or anywhere else, for that matter. So I stopped and turned to him. His face was this twisting mess of confusion and fear. "Dude," I said. "I'm really sorry. I should have told them you were sleeping over."

Alvin looked like he was going to cry. I put a hand on his shoulder. He turned his head and looked at it there as if it was a glob of snot. "Seriously," I said. "I'm really sorry. I so screwed up. I didn't tell them because I knew they would be like that. I was just trying to be nice. You had nowhere else to go, right?"

The kid looked down at my feet. "Yeah," he said.

"Did you sleep okay?"

There was a pause. He wiped his nose with the back of his hand. "Yeah."

"Did you get some breakfast?"

He looked up at me with his weirdo eyes. "I thought your dad was gonna kill me."

All I could do was try to laugh it off. "Ha! With a dustpan brush? Come on. He just thought you were a home invader guy. He didn't know you were my friend."

"Yeah."

"Just let me text Danny," I said, digging my phone out of my pocket. "We'll wake him up and get you some more breakfast, okay?"

"Okay."

I stepped up beside him and we started walking again. "How are you doing?" I asked. "You gonna be all right?"

"Yeah," he said, warming up to me a bit. "Your dad really scared me."

"I know," I said. "We're good now. You don't have to go back there."

I wanted to tell him that everything was going to be fine. But I knew it was a lie. What the heck was going to happen to this kid? He needed food, clothes, shelter, school—all that normal stuff. Not just a dirt floor in somebody's garage.

It took a while for Danny to text me back. All I'd messaged him was: *u awake?*

His answer was: *I am now is r friend ok?*

My thumbs nearly stabbed right through my phone. *NO! we're walking 2 ur house*

While I waited for an answer, I brought Alvin down the alley behind Danny's. We hid in a giant hedge while a car passed, then I started typing another message. But Danny replied before I could send it: *b out in a minute where r u xactly?*

alley south

k

Ten minutes and two cars later, Danny came wandering down the alley in a shrunken t-shirt, pajama pants and rubber boots. He was apparently freezing in his dinky shirt. His arms were crossed tight over his chest.

"What are you wearing?" I exclaimed. "Aren't you going to take care of Alvin?"

He looked at me calmly, as if I was out of my mind. "What? What are you talking about? You got me outa bed. It's not even seven yet. Hey, Alvin."

"Hey," Alvin muttered under his breath.

"You sleep okay?"

Alvin looked at me, afraid to answer.

"Dude," I said to Danny, "it was horrible. My parents lost their minds. The boys were screaming and crying."

"Huh? Why?"

"Because I snuck Alvin in. I didn't tell them he was sleeping over."

"Well, duh."

"Come on," I said. "Can't you hurry up? What are we supposed to do here? Stand around forever?"

He turned to Alvin. "So, you okay?"

Alvin shrugged.

I moved toward Danny and began pushing him home. "Go get dressed. Go get some food for him to eat. Quit screwing around."

"All right, already, hands off! I'm going!" he said, turning around to walk backwards. Then he pointed at me. "You totally rock, you know."

"Yeah, yeah."

"The best. The bomb. The shiznit."

"The what?"

"Don't let anybody see Alvin. I'll be back real soon."

"Real soon" turned out to be forty-five minutes later. Alvin and I chilled in the giant hedge. I tried to get him to open up just to kill the time. "So how did you end up upstairs? Why didn't you stay in the bedroom?"

He gave his nose a wipe with a finger. "I didn't have anything to eat yesterday. I was hungry for breakfast."

"Oh." That shut me up for a second. "So you went up and got a bowl of cereal?"

Alvin nodded. "I was real quiet. But I only ate like, a

couple of bites of food and I had to poop. So I went and pooped. But I didn't want to wake anybody up flushing the toilet so I went back out to the kitchen real quiet and kept eating. That's when your little brother came out of his bedroom. I don't know if he saw me. Maybe he thought I was you or something. I said good morning and he looked at me and screamed really loud and ran back down the hall."

My eyes went wide. "You didn't flush the toilet?"

"What?"

"The toilet. You didn't flush it?"

Alvin looked down. "Um…sorry."

I rubbed my forehead. It was just too incredible. A bunch of Alvin's logs were floating in my parent's toilet at this moment, waiting to be discovered. *Huh,* I thought. *Great.* This morning just kept getting better and better.

Finally Danny came sauntering down the alley, choking a plastic grocery bag. He was wearing runners, finally, and normal clothes.

"Oh, thank god," I said when he reached us. "It's about time. Did you bring food?"

"Yeah. And Alvin, I brought you another shirt." He pulled a pink fundraiser t-shirt out of the bag. The slogan said *I'm Running for My Sisters* and there was a picture of a twisted ribbon below it. Alvin just stared at the shirt for a second, till Danny added, "My mom gave it to Cindy, but she never wears it."

That made Alvin reach out and grab it. He scrunched it up to his nose. "Oh," he said with a twinge of a smile, "it smells like Cindy." And right in the middle of the alley, he flung off his crappy burnt shirt and put on the pink one. It was too big for him, but that wasn't important. He stretched the front out to admire it. "Nice. I like Cindy. She's my cousin," he added for my benefit.

"Yeah, I know. Can we go now?"

"Where?" Danny asked.

I gaped at him. "What? How about not here in the stupid alley!"

"Oh," he said. "I thought you had a plan."

"Oh jeez…you're making me crazy."

"Oh, calm down," Danny said. "There's nothing even open at this time."

"The mall's open. And the pool over at Coronation. And maybe the rink, too."

"The rink's open in the summertime?"

I huffed. "Dude, just shut up. Can we go to the mall, at least?"

"Hells, yeah. Come on, Alvin."

Alvin had been sitting in the gap in the hedge, gently smoothing his new shirt. "Okay," he said, getting to his feet. "Can we get pancakes?"

"What?" I said.

"It always smells like pancakes at the mall."

"Dude, calm down. I brought you stuff. And you, too," Danny said to me.

"Yay. I'm starving."

He slapped the grocery bag against my chest. "Take it. Let's go."

As we started walking, I peered inside the bag. There was a Granny Smith apple, a handful of broken crackers, one chocolate-covered granola bar and a bare piece of cheese covered in crumbs from the crackers. I was so disappointed, I handed the bag to Alvin. "Here. Chow down."

Alvin held the bag like a dead chicken for a second. "Huh?" Then he peered inside. "Oh, I'm okay. Hey, Danny, I had cereal this morning."

Danny glanced at him. "Good for you."

"But I like cheese," Alvin said. He dug out the crumb-covered slab and ate half of it in one bite.

Danny was looking at me as we walked side by side. "Really?"

"What?"

"What are you now, like a martyr or something? Eat, already."

"Nah."

"Dude," he said, taking the bag from Alvin, "eat and shut up." He handed me the granola bar. "For the shiznit."

I gave in and took the granola bar from him. "Thanks. What does that mean, anyway?"

"It means like, you're the bomb. You know, the best."

"Right."

When we got to the mall, the only things open were the pancake place and a pastry kiosk in the food court that reeked of cinnamon buns and coffee. There were only two other people there, both of them seniors. We found a table and I slouched down in my chair with my phone and a couple of broken crackers. "So what's the big plan? What are we going to do with Alvin?"

Danny was already absorbed in whatever was on his phone. He shrugged. "I don't know. Beats me."

"Well, where's he going to sleep?"

"Uh…" Danny looked thoughtful for a second. "Maybe he could sleep in the river valley. There's bums; they've got like, whole camps down there."

"Really? You're going to fling him a blankie and hope the bums don't kill him? And what if it rains?"

Danny rubbed sleep out of one of his eyes and yawned. "I got a tarp he can use," he said.

"And how is that saving Alvin? You may as well get him a hunk of cardboard and let him start begging right now."

Danny looked up from his phone. "What's the cardboard for?"

"To make a sign! *Help! My Dink Cousin Has No Imagination!*"

"Shut up. We need a real plan."

"No kidding."

"Someplace safe he can go," Danny mused. "Alvin, you don't know anybody at all? Don't you have any like, friends or neighbours or…"

Alvin had been sitting up straight with his hands in his lap, watching us like we were a Ping-Pong game. Suddenly his face lit up. "I know Mrs. Kushnir across my alley. She likes me."

"Would she let you stay there?" I asked.

Alvin shrugged. "Maybe. She let me stay there when my mom had her operation. She even brings my mom to chemo and I help her make perogies. She's really nice. Oh, I just remembered! I can't stay there."

"Why not?"

"She's in Vegreville for her holidays."

Danny looked at me, his expression vacant like his brain was churning. Then he said, "Awesome! That's perfect! Could we sneak into her house somehow?"

Alvin made a face. "Oh, easy. But you gotta have the code."

"The what?"

"For her security thingy. Or the quiet alarm goes off and—"

Danny groaned loudly and spun around. "Urrrh! Come on. There's got to be someplace."

The conversation died and we sat staring at our phones for the next half hour. A scrawny security guard with nothing better to do kept hovering a few yards away. I was afraid he was going to kick us out.

"You got any money?" I asked Danny.

"Why?"

"So we can be like, customers and tell that security guard to screw off."

"I got no money."

I didn't either. I mean, I had my birthday cash, but no way was I going to blow it on junk just to keep a security guard happy. "Great," I said. "I'm bored. I'm going to go walk around."

"Me too!" said Alvin.

Danny groaned as he stood. "Fine!"

The three of us ended up walking the entire mall, up one side and back the other, bored out of our minds.

"Let's go outside," Danny said, and we followed him out the nearest doors.

Cars were starting to accumulate in the parking lot. Groat Road was thick with vehicles now. By the time we'd circled the whole mall and ended up on the west side, my legs were tired of walking.

"You want to go to the pool?" I asked, thinking I'd get to sit down there.

"And do what?"

"Not stand," I said.

Danny shrugged. "'Kay."

The public pool was on the other side of the high school, a great big building with a swoopy roof. When we got there, the early Lane Swim was going strong, with about ten people bobbing back and forth. The smell of the water and the echo of every little sound finally woke me up. Well, not as much as Alvin calling, "Hey. Hey. Hey," and listening to his own echo like, sixty times. It was embarrassing and I was afraid we'd get booted out. Danny was amused. As gently as I could, I told Alvin to shut up. We slouched against the bleachers and went straight into Phone Land again.

After two hours of sitting on the hard floor, leaning against the bleachers, I said, "I gotta do something." My back was killing me. I rose and walked around the pool for a while by myself, trying to figure out what to do with Alvin. *Somebody has to*, I kept thinking, *'cause Danny sure isn't doing it.*

When I got back to Danny and Alvin, I'd still had no big brainstorm. But I was getting antsy and annoyed. "I think I'd better go home."

"Huh?" said Danny. "Why? I thought you were going to help me."

"Well, you don't seem to be helping yourself very much. And Alvin not at all. Where's he going to sleep tonight?"

"Oh, come on. Calm down. I'll think of something."

"Yeah? When? It's like, ten o'clock. How many more hours are we going to drag our butts around like hobos?"

Danny set his phone on the bench, stood up and stretched. "Is that…ungh…what hobos do?"

"Oh my god," I said, frustrated with his casualness. "I gotta go home. My mom and everybody are probably still freaked out about this morning. And I'm gonna get killed when I get there. I just want to get it over with."

"Fine," said Danny, all calm. "Bye-bye." He waved like a two-year-old.

I was about to go, but I stopped myself. "Seriously," I asked, "what are you going to do about Alvin?"

Danny shoved his hands into his jeans pockets and tipped his head. "Why do you care? Why don't you just go home and—" His eyes suddenly lit up. I mean literally. I could see white for about ten miles above his pupils. He yanked his hands out of his pockets and held something up. It was a little brass key.

"What's that?"

Danny burst out laughing. "I'm an idiot!"

"Huh?"

"Dude! This is the key to Grantree's garage! I forgot to give it back!"

"So?" It took a second for it to sink in. "Oh, no. You're not going to put Alvin in Grantree's garage, are you? Really?"

"Why not? He can sleep in Grantree's big truck."

"Oh my god…" I groaned.

"What's wrong? It's a great idea!"

Alvin was looking up at us. "Who's Grantree?"

"His next door neighbour. Old guy. Hates Danny."

"Oh," said Alvin.

"Not as much as I hate him. But whatever. You'll be right next door! I can bring you stuff and it'll be awesome!"

"Yeah," I said, "but he's gotta sleep in a truck."

"What's wrong with that? Just don't fart too much or you'll suffocate. I learned that at scout camp. Small tent, too much musical fruit."

I groaned. "Just keep the truck door open."

The plan was for Alvin to hang out in the Cheevers' garage until it was dark. Then Danny would sneak out of the house and take Alvin over to Grantree's.

"What time does it get dark?" I asked.

"I don't know. After nine, I think. Why?"

"No reason."

"You think something's going to happen."

I just looked at him. "Maybe. You know your whole family is accident-prone, right?"

Danny wiped his mouth. "Yeah, well, whatever. I'm going to be up like, super early, and get Alvin out of there."

"You know what I'm gonna do?"

"What?"

"I'm gonna bring a lawn chair. This is gonna be better than you crashing through Grantree's greenhouse."

"Shut up."

I hung out with Danny till way after eleven, completely friggin' bored out of my tree. He had no plans for lunch and I was starving. But I totally put off going home. I really didn't want to face my mother after the disaster with Alvin that morning. Finally, though, my stomach won the war against my dread and I headed home, legs shaking, nearly barfing with fear over the trouble I'd be in once I got there.

Chapter 20

Strangely, Mom only had a limited-edition freak-out about our soot-faced intruder that morning. I'd already told her his house had burned down. I guess she hadn't heard, or maybe she forgot. All she remembered was, he was homeless.

"Where was he sleeping before? There could have been bedbugs!"

"No, Mom, I don't think there were bedbugs."

We were standing in the kitchen, Mom making lunch, the boys playing cars in the hallway, ten feet away.

Kyle piped up. "What's a bedbug?"

"You are, sweetie," she answered, then said to me, "But how do you know him?"

I had to lie. I was worried that if I told her who Alvin really was, she might phone Mrs. Cheevers. "Danny was walking down this alley and saw him. He texted me while I was on the bus home. This kid was going to sleep in these weeds beside a garage. I just felt sorry for him."

Mom thought about this for a second. She glanced at Kyle and Jayden, making car noises. "How old is this Alvin?"

"I dunno; maybe ten or eleven?"

She looked at the boys again. "And he had nowhere else to go?"

I just shrugged and shook my head.

"Well," she said firmly, "you should have asked if he could sleep over. He scared the wits out of us."

"Sorry."

"Just ask next time, would you?"

"Okay."

And that was it. I spent most of the day hiding out in my room, afraid she wasn't finished talking about it. But she left me totally alone. And hey, with my new modelling tools, I had lots to keep me busy. My rock monster's face quickly got smoothed and shaped better and started to look like an actual human. It was kind of embarrassing that my birth mom thought I was a sculptor of some kind. I knew how lazy I was. Heck, I could win prizes for lying around. But Alvin's compliment kept echoing in my head: *You're good. You're good.* Still, that wasn't enough. I wanted people like my birth mom and Cindy to say I was good. Then I had a weird moment, this rush of enthusiasm, thinking, *I don't want them to just say I'm good. I want to actually be good at it.*

When Dad got home from work, he didn't even bring up the Alvin disaster. He dropped two bags of green farmer potatoes on the kitchen floor and went straight to the fridge for his after-work beer. The boys piled onto his lap. When dinner was ready and I went into the kitchen, he just gave me a look like he was too exhausted to be disappointed in me. Whew! Bullet dodged.

I spent the evening in the corner of the couch, out of my

parents' line of sight to the TV, not saying a peep. The fan was circulating the day's hot air all around the living room. I kept thinking it was blowing my fear-sweat around so they could smell it. I watched all their crappy shows, still afraid one of them would suddenly jump up and start barking at me. Then I headed to bed early, thanking whatever puppies I'd saved in a past life.

The next morning, I was out of bed at like, six. I couldn't sleep anymore, wondering how Danny had made out with Alvin. Did he get him into Grantree's garage? Did Cindy bring him lasagna or something without Grantree spotting them? The whole thing was like a slow-motion car crash. I couldn't wait to see what happened.

The sun was barely up, shooting rays in a fan shape up from the horizon. Our house was still baking from the day before and all the windows were open, letting cool air blow in over the kitchen floor. I was standing at the window by the sink watching the sky show when Dad came in.

"Whoa," he said, seeing the pink and blue clouds and the sunlight spraying upwards. "Where's the baby Jesus?"

"Nice, eh?"

"It's going to be a good day," he said. Dad was a morning person. Sometimes you couldn't get five words out of him after work, but he gabbed my ear off over breakfast while Mom was downstairs, already doing laundry.

"So, that kid yesterday. He okay?"

"I think so."

"Don't do that again, all right?"

"All right."

Now that he had my ear, he decided to tell me stuff I really didn't care about. "You know how many crimes we got in this country? Home invasions and all that? Four a minute. *Four*," he said again. "Every minute. Enough to make a guy crazy."

He blithered on like this till I was ready to shoot myself.

I was totally glad he was not yelling at me. And it was kind of comforting, being talked to like a normal person. But he wouldn't shut up.

When Mom came up to say goodbye to Dad, I headed downstairs and texted Danny. It wasn't even seven yet. But I couldn't resist.

Is A ok?

I thought maybe he'd be annoyed with me texting him so early in the morning, but I shouldn't have worried. I didn't get an answer till nearly eight thirty—so maybe he'd turned his phone off.

dont know just got up u coming over?
now?
sure y not?
k see you n a bit

When I got up to the landing and started putting my shoes on, I yelled at Mom, "I'm going to Danny's!"

But she was right behind me. "How much longer are you working for that Mr. Graintree?"

"Huh? Oh, we're done. Wednesday was our last day. We're just going to hang out."

There was a pause. "Why don't you ever hang out over here?"

When she said that, a little bit of spit accidently went flying out of my mouth. This was the weirdest question Mom had ever asked me. "Uh...I don't know."

"Well, what do you do over there?"

I shrugged. "Play games and stuff."

"Couldn't he bring his games over here?"

"No. It's a game box, like...it's attached to his TV."

"Oh...I see." She sounded disappointed.

"Okay, bye!"

As I rushed out into the soon-to-be-flaming-hot morning, I had to resist shaking my head in case Mom was looking. *What the heck was that?* I wondered. *"Why don't you ever hang out over here?"* I swear, my Mom had been taken over by aliens.

When I got to Danny's, I saw the jeep was gone as I was parking my bike beside the house. I knocked at the back door and heard Mrs. Cheevers tell me to come in. Her voice was short and sharp and as soon as I got inside, I saw why. Mrs. Cheevers was in the kitchen avoiding Randy. She was dressed for work in this white skirt and green top. And Randy, in typical Cheevers mode, had bitten the top off an ink pen and had blue ink all over his mouth and hands.

"No. No. No!" Mrs. Cheevers was not amused by Randy's attempts to give her a hug goodbye.

The kid was only half joking. He actually seemed desperate to get some attention from his mom. "I'll just put my arms around you like this!" He did an air hug while she squirmed out of his way, purse and laptop held high.

"Cindy!" she called. "Randy, no. Stop, please; I have to go. Randy!" she screamed in desperation. "Not now!"

I thought for a second she was going to kick him. But she managed to charge around into the living room and out the front door without getting blue ink all over her. The kid went straight to the kitchen sink and began rinsing his hands under the water, getting blue ink all over the tap and not really getting much ink off. "Danny's upstairs," he grumped at me.

As I started toward the living room, I heard Cindy yell from down in the basement. "What did mom want?"

Randy barked back, "Nothing. She's just gonna be late again."

There was some muttering from Cindy, but all I caught was, "Great."

I hadn't even gotten to the living room when I heard a faint rumble from the stairs, as if someone was racing down from the second floor at top speed. Danny blasted around the corner, breathless.

"What's with you?" I asked.

He made a face and pointed in the direction of Grantree's

house. But as soon as Randy turned around, he dropped the face and tried to seem all casual.

I wandered over to the sink behind Randy and looked out the window over his head. I didn't see anything unusual.

Randy turned around. "What are you doing?"

"Nothin'."

As soon as Randy returned to washing his hands, I made a questioning face at Danny, wondering what he'd been pointing at.

Danny stood on tiptoe and looked outside. Immediately his eyes lit up and he pointed again. This time, he was actually freaking out.

I looked. And there, at the corner of Grantree's garage where the little people door was, stood the two plumbers, the big guy and Black-Eyes. Apparently the garage door was unlocked, because the two men went right inside.

Danny jumped over the steps straight to the landing and smashed into the opposite wall. He was in such a rush that he struggled with the door handle for a second, swearing. Then he put his shoulder to the door and bashed outside with me following him. Danny had always been a total track-star guy in our class. He got down the sidewalk and around to Grantree's gate before I even made it to the alley. By the time I reached the gate, he was up Grantree's sidewalk.

The plumbers had already found Alvin and were dragging him by his pink shirt to their boss's house. The big plumber had Alvin by the collar and the kid was turning and twisting so that his collar was tightening around his neck, choking him.

Danny charged through the garden, sending beet leaves flying, and stopped in front of them on the sidewalk, waving his arms. "Stop! Stop!"

"Da-h-nn-!" Alvin croaked out.

The big plumber was in front. "What's this now? Who are you?"

"I'm from next door," Danny yelled. "This is my cousin. Let go of him!" He tried to pry the big man's fingers off of Alvin's collar.

The plumber squinted at him for a second. "Really? What was he doing in there, messing with our stuff?" He plowed past Danny, hauling Alvin toward the house. "You're coming with me."

Danny stumbled off the sidewalk.

"Hey, you," said Black-Eyes to him, "back off." He stood on the sidewalk and held a hand up for Danny and one up for me, in case I came close.

Danny was like, screw you. He rushed forward and grabbed Alvin by the arm.

Black-Eyes reached out and pried the two arms apart like he was breaking a rope.

"Ow!" Danny yelled.

By then, Grantree was at the back door. "What's going on? What's all this?" He was wearing work pants, slippers and a pajama top, and his hair was all flat, as if he'd just gotten out of bed.

"This kid was in the garage. Your truck was open and everything."

"My truck?" Grantree barked, then he looked at Alvin. "Who the hell are you?"

"He's my cousin!" Danny said, stomping up onto the deck to stop beside the big plumber. "Can you let go of him, please?"

The big plumber looked at his boss, who was holding the screen door open, grimacing in pain from his hip.

"Just...quit choking him," Grantree said. "There's no need for that."

The big plumber adjusted his grip. He gathered a great big fist full of the back of Alvin's pink shirt and held it. The kid looked like his puppet.

On the other side of Grantree's house, some neighbour

lady had her door open. She was wearing a tank top and leggings and had obviously been working out. Sweat stuck her hair to her forehead. "Everything all right?" she called.

Grantree stepped out the door a bit to see her. "Yeah, we're good, Suz. Some kid broke into my garage."

The woman said, "You know the MacMillans had their car broken into on the weekend."

"'Zat right?"

"I don't think they took anything. Just made a mess."

"Well, we got this. We'll talk to you later."

"How's the hip?"

"Oh, better every day. You take care!"

The woman waved and closed her door halfway, still wanting to see what was going to happen.

"Let's take this inside," Grantree said.

"What?" Danny exclaimed. "No! Just let him go. He wasn't doing anything!"

"You," Grantree said in a lower voice, pointing at Danny. "Be quiet. Lyle, you let go of him. Kid, you're coming inside, nice and calm. Unless you want the police here in five minutes. You want that?"

Alvin shook his head, lips pressed tight. The big man let go of his shirt. With his lips still pressed together, Alvin pulled his shirt straight and looked at Danny for direction.

"It's okay," said Danny. "Don't worry, all right?"

Grantree headed inside and went slowly up the steps to his kitchen. Lyle held the door and gave Alvin a mean little shove ahead of him.

"Hey!" Danny complained. The big guy ignored him.

"After you," said Black-Eyes to me, performing a fake bow and sweeping his hand toward the door.

I followed Danny inside, and Black-Eyes came in behind me. The guy smelled weird—like, sort of cabbagey.

We all tromped up into Grantree's kitchen. Grantree spun a kitchen chair around and told Alvin, "You sit there."

236

Alvin perched himself on the edge of the chair seat, his head tucked into his neck.

"So what's going on here?" Grantree demanded.

Danny started blathering. "Nothing's going on! Can't you just let him—?"

"Hey!" Grantree shouted. "You shut up for a second. I didn't mean you."

Danny looked like he was going to explode. But he took a breath and gave his neck a twist like he had a kink in it.

Then Grantree asked Black-Eyes, "What were *you* doing in the garage?"

Black-Eyes gave him a weird look. "Me? Nothin'. We just come in the back gate. The garage door wasn't locked and I wanted to see why."

"And the kid was in there?"

"Right in yer truck with the door wide open. The kid sat up when I looked in."

"And you're his cousin?" Grantree asked Alvin, jabbing a thumb at Danny.

Alvin's chin wobbled and he nodded.

"What were you doing in my garage?"

Alvin's mouth started doing an in-and-out, fat-lip-skinny-lip dance. "Sleeping," he said to his hands, which he was gripping for dear life on his lap.

"How'd you get in there? Did he break the lock?" he asked the big plumber.

"Dunno. Don't think so."

"He didn't break anything," said Danny. "I still had your key." He pulled the garage key out of his pocket and laid it on the kitchen counter.

Grantree gave him a bulldog scowl.

Danny blurted, "I'm sorry! I forgot I had it. I was desperate. I had no place for Alvin to stay!"

Grantree snorted. "So you picked my garage? What's wrong with your place? And there's hotels from here to Chinal!"

Danny gave his head a rough scratch. "Sorry. Look, his house burned down. Maybe you saw the smoke yesterday."

Grantree blinked. "The one that was in the news? Over on 27 Street?"

"Yeah. That was his house."

"Where's your parents?" Grantree asked Alvin.

Alvin looked at Danny for permission to answer. Danny made big-eyes at him. So Alvin said, "My mom had a heart attack. She's in the hospital."

"Great," said Grantree. He took a huge breath and began shaking his head. The tension in the room began to calm.

Mr. Black-Eyes let out a laugh and pushed past me. "Now I heard everything," he said.

But Grantree tried to stop him. "Where you going?"

"I gotta take a leak. You mind if I—?"

Grantree made a noise and said, somewhat annoyed, "Yeah, go ahead. But use the downstairs one, eh?"

The black-eyed guy bumped past me going the other way, his cabbage stink trailing down the basement steps.

"It's still technically break and enter, even though he didn't break nothin'," said the big plumber. "Technically, he didn't have your permission. And this one stole your key. So…"

"All right," said Grantree, slowly lowering himself into his usual chair beside his row of pill bottles. "Gimme a sec to think." He did his weird mouth grabbing thing, like he was squishing away his annoyance.

Danny spoke up. "Look, I'm sorry I forgot to give your key back. It was an accident!"

"All right," Grantree calmed him. "And your cousin here needed a place to sleep. Why's that? Why wasn't he bunking at your house?"

Danny scratched his forehead. "'Cause my mom hates him. Look, it's a long story. Nobody else was helping him. My dad totally like, abandoned him. He's not bad. Alvin's not a

238

bad kid. If you're going to blame someone, blame me."

"Oh, you're getting blamed," said Grantree. "Too bad my garden ain't any bigger. You'd be weeding till you were forty."

Right then, I heard the back door swing open. Every turned their head. A woman's voice said, "Hey, Dad, it's just me."

Grantree leaned over a bit. "Hey, hon'."

His daughter, still in the same clothes as ever, stepped halfway up to the kitchen and saw everyone. "Oh, sorry," she said. "I'm just going to put your stuff downstairs." I heard the swish of plastic bags and she disappeared down the steps.

As soon as Grantree's attention returned to the room, Danny said, "Can we go now?"

Grantree snorted. "I don't even know where to begin. Where's this kid sleeping tonight?"

"I don't know," said Danny. "I'll figure it out." And he grabbed Alvin by his pink shirtsleeve, wanting him to get up. Alvin looked at Grantree and, seeing no objection, got slowly to his feet.

"Does your dad know what's going on?"

"No!" Danny blurted defensively. "And please don't tell him."

"Why not? You don't think he's in a better position to—"

"'Cause he started it," Danny cut in. "He put Alvin in this emergency group home place and he got beat up."

Grantree's gaze went up and down Alvin like he was searching for bruises.

"Look," said Danny. "It's complicated. I'm sorry I used your garage. If he made a mess or anything, I'll totally clean it up."

Grantree just sat there, rubbing his top lip. Then he said, "You know what your problem is?"

Danny gave Alvin a shove toward the door.

"You don't reco'nize any authority. Nobody knows nothin' but you. You're gonna get that kid into more trouble."

"Whatever," said Danny.

Afraid of being last in line to get out of the kitchen, I moved to get outside first. But something stopped us in our tracks.

From the basement came Grantree's daughter's raised voice. She was arguing with Black-Eyes, saying things like, "What are doing with that?" and "That's none of your business."

Black-Eyes kept saying, "You never mind. You get outa here. Go on!"

"Sibby!" Grantree called from his chair. "Everything all right?"

Instead of answering, she let out a yell. "Hey! Get your hands off me! No! Hey!"

We all froze. When I glanced back, Grantree was already on his feet. The second he took a step forward, the big plumber moved toward him and held up a hand to block his way. "You just wait a minute there, boss."

"Sibby?" Grantree called again.

From the basement came the sound of empty boxes falling over. Then his daughter's voice, "Dad! He's making a big mess of all the— Aah!"

"Danny! Kid!" Grantree suddenly barked. "Go see what's going on."

Danny looked at him like he was crazy. "Me?"

Grantree was bursting with frustration and tried to shove past the big plumber. "Lyle, you get the hell outa my way."

But the huge man just put an arm across his boss's shoulders and moved him without any effort. Grantree basically stumbled backward onto his chair. "Sibby?" he called out.

Danny looked at Grantree, then at me. "Oh, what... ever," he said, totally frustrated. "Alvin, just stay here for a sec." And he skipped down to the landing, looked to see what was going on below, then charged down the rest of the stairs to the basement.

All I heard was the black-eyed guy saying, "You, kid, stay right there."

And Danny saying, "Really? I think you better let go of her."

When Grantree heard this, he tried to get up again. But he only got an inch off the chair before the big guy shoved him back down, hard. Grantree really looked like he was in pain now.

All of a sudden the guy in the basement yelled out, "Lyle! Hey! Ow! Get down here!"

The big plumber edged toward the stairs and yelled back, "What? No! Just forget it! Let's get outa here!"

Then came the sound of more boxes falling—or being crashed into.

"Lyle! Ah! What the hell? Gimme a hand, would you?"

The big guy turned around and gave Alvin and me a look. I held up my hands and backed off. I did not want to get involved in any of this. All I could think about was getting the heck outside. The Lyle guy strode past Alvin and I and stomped down the stairs.

"You! Go see what's going on," Grantree said to me, obviously in major pain. His hand was pressing into his side like the big guy really injured him. "And don't go down there! Just look and come tell me, all right?" He reached for a crappy flip-phone on the table on the other side of his pills. "Go on!" he barked at me. "I'm calling the cops."

As soon as he said this, I got a huge jolting wake-up call. Whatever was going on, this was serious. "You be okay?" I said to Alvin. "You can go outside, you know."

Alvin looked confused and like, traumatized. All he said was, "Yeah." He kept standing there, frozen.

I rumbled down to the landing. When I got around the corner and peered down the long stretch of stairs, the first thing I saw was the big man. He was right at the bottom of the stairs, stopping Grantree's daughter from getting past, pushing her away like she was bothersome fly. God knows what Danny and the black-eyed guy were doing, but I could hear a lot of grunting and swearing.

Sibby shouted, "Why are you doing this?" and rushed right back and tried to shoulder her way past the big guy. But he grabbed hold of her wrist and held her, twisting her arm down so she couldn't move. "Ow—ow!"

"What's going on?" Grantree yelled at me from the kitchen.

I don't know why, because it wasn't true, but I yelled back. "It's okay!"

I couldn't not do something. I was just hunched there like an idiot while somebody was being hurt. Then I had an idea. I had the perfect way to knock the big plumber flying so Sibby could escape: the Brian lunge. My special trick for getting down a flight of stairs without touching a single step. I could totally clobber the big guy. Lay him out flat. The stairs were exactly like the ones at my house. But they had a railing on each side, which was even better.

Trying to be super quiet, I reached as far down the railings as I could. I took a very big, very silent breath and launched myself off the top step, feeling like a total badass hero.

The trouble was, there was an overhang at Grantree's that I didn't have at my house. It stuck out about three-quarters of the way down the stairs and I totally did not see it. Going full speed, I cracked my forehead on it so hard, my feet went flying out in front of me. I landed at the bottom, flat on my back and curled into a busted heap.

Chapter 21

Okay, so you know you've really injured yourself when even the bad guys drop everything and come rushing over to help you. I heard their voices long before I could move.

"Kid, you all right?"

"He was trying to kick you down, Lyle. Boy, did that ever not work."

I was lying there in a fetal ball, a pulverized mess at the bottom of the stairs. The big man was going all doctorish on me. "Don't touch him! You're not supposed to touch an accident victim. He mighta broken his neck, the stupid kid. You all right? Can you talk at all?"

All I could do was let out this horrible squeak. I'd totally knocked the wind out of myself. I could feel exactly where I'd smacked my forehead on the overhang and exactly where the back of my head had cracked into the corner of one of the bottom steps. The rest of me was concentrated on getting air into my lungs, which seemed impossible to do. Why couldn't I breathe?

"Jimmy, should we call an ambulance? He might have a concussion or—"

"What are you talking about? There ain't gonna be no ambulance. He's all right. And if he ain't, they can call one later, after we're gone."

"Fine," said the big guy. "Let's get upstairs. There ain't nothing down here."

Black-Eyes leaned close. "You stay put, kid. Don't try and move or anything. You might make it worse."

Next thing I knew, the two of them were walking over me and stomping up the stairs.

Finally, I was getting little puffs of air into my lungs.

"Oh, dude," said Danny, leaning over me, hand rubbing his own forehead. "That was terrible. You knocked the wind out, eh? You gonna live?"

The truth was, I was more embarrassed than I was hurt. I was just glad they weren't laughing. Still lying in a ball of pain, I tried moving my head, still trying to get a decent breath. "Ow. Gimme a sec."

Danny stood there shaking his head while I slowly recovered my lung power. "There you go. You all right?"

"I'm okay," I managed to squeeze out, staying on my side. "I really…bashed my elbow. It's still like…numb."

"Oh, you poor guy," said Sybil. She knelt down beside me and shook her head. "You're a stupid kid, you know."

"Yeah…I know."

"Good." She stared down at me for a good five seconds. Her lips were tight. "Anyway, thanks for…whatever that was. At least he let go of me."

"Yeah." I wanted to get off my sore elbow and she tried to help by grabbing my other arm.

"You want to sit up?"

"I don't know," said Danny. "Like that guy said, you're not supposed to move somebody with an injury."

"It's not…that bad," I told him. "I'm just sore."

Danny shook his head. "And stupid, apparently."

I could hear the plumbers knocking things over upstairs, and Grantree yelling at them. It sounded like they were in Grantree's office.

Sybil continued to help me up. She got me into a sitting position and I felt good enough to try to stand. Danny helped by supporting me by my numb arm. I stood, head pounding, my back singing from every vertebra.

"You're not going to fall over?" Sybil asked.

"No, I'm good."

Danny suddenly got all stressed and blurted, like it was one big word, "I-gotta-go-see-if-Alvin's-all-right." He rushed up the stairs behind me.

"Check on my dad, okay?" Sybil told him.

"Yeah."

Sybil hadn't let go of my arm. "You want to sit for a minute? There's a chair right there."

"I'm okay," I said. "I just gotta hang onto something."

We could hear Grantree barking at the two men, who sounded like they were moving furniture in the office.

Danny came blasting halfway down the stairs. "You gonna chill here? Or—?"

Sybil didn't seem to know why he had returned. "What are you—? Ugh," she said, letting go of me. "I want to make sure they're not hurting my dad." She barged past him up the stairs.

I started making my way up toward Danny, moving quite a bit slower than Sybil. "What's going on up there? Are they like, violent?"

"No, they're just tipping everything over."

"Looking for the stamps?"

"No doubt," he said. "Grantree's just sitting there."

When we got up to the kitchen, the first person we saw was Alvin, leaning back against the kitchen counter, biting his hand—like, nervously, right into the meat of his thumb. Sybil was on the far side of the dining room table, as if she was guarding Grantree. The old guy was still on the phone, a fist pressed into his side. He was either listening or on hold, keeping an eye on what was going on down the hall.

Alvin looked relieved to see us. He took his hand out of his mouth long enough to point at the back door and say, "Can we go now? Danny? Can we go?"

"Just a sec." Danny moved carefully past the stove and peeked down the hall. Then he said to Grantree, "Should we try to stop them?"

Grantree just shook his head. "No, you leave all that to the police."

"They're on their way?"

Grantree nodded. "Yup." He was surprisingly calm. Then he saw me and chucked his chin to get my attention. "Are you all right? I heard what happened. How's your head?"

"Dented."

"Huh!" said Grantree, glancing at Danny. "That makes two of you."

Sybil was pacing in the living room, chewing on the side of her lip. We all stood around listening to the chaos in the office. Boxes were being tossed, filing cabinet drawers were slamming open and closed. And there was a ton of swearing.

"What if they ain't in here?" asked the big plumber.

"What?" came the annoyed answer. "I don't know. Don't ask me. Go look somewhere else!"

Two seconds later, it sounded like the big man was much nearer. "You want to just tell us where them stamps are?"

Grantree looked up. "Not really."

I was still at the top of the stairs when the big man came into the dining room. Alvin and Danny backed away from him toward me.

"We know they're here," said the big man. "We know about the museum today—you giving 'em your big donation."

Grantree sat up straight, blinking away the pain it caused him. "How do you know they're not in a safety deposit box somewhere? How do you even know what you're looking for?"

"Oh, I did my research," said the big man. "When we were working on your rental, we asked Sibby all about 'em."

Grantree's head spun toward his daughter.

She held up her hands. "Sorry, Dad, they just asked. I didn't know they were going to—"

Grantree shifted his phone back to his mouth. "Yeah, I'm still here," he said. Then he listened for a second. "No, they're still ransacking the place. We're just watching." There was another pause. "All right." He moved the phone away from his mouth again and asked the big plumber, "So, Lyle, let's say you find them. What the hell you gonna do with 'em? It's not like you can sell 'em at the local pawn shop."

"Oh, we got a buyer." But the guy did not sound particularly convincing. "That's what the internet is for."

Grantree chuckled. "You don't think they can trace that stuff? Some dumbass trying to sell a rare stamp on the internet? You don't think I already know half the serious collectors in the world? I've been doing this since I was a teenager."

"Oh, just shut up," said the big man. He gripped the back of a dining room chair while he scanned the kitchen cupboards and counter.

But Grantree persisted. "And with the cops coming, you're just going to drive off in my van?" Grantree turned to us and jabbed a thumb toward the big plumber. "I think somebody's a few peas short of a casserole."

The big plumber slammed the chair viciously against the table.

"Dad!" Sybil said. "Come on. You're just taunting them."

Grantree lodged his fist in his side again and sat back. "I'm just gonna sit here and watch The Stupid unfold before me. Yeah, I'm still here," he said into his phone. "No, same. They ain't hurting no one. Just making a mess."

"Jimmy," the big man barked. "What are you doing?"

The black-eyed guy's voice snapped back, "What? There's ten million little boxes in here. What are *you* doing? Look around, would you? What the hell?"

Grantree turned to the big man. "Better speed it up, there, Lyle. You have about two seconds to get out of here. The police are on their way right now."

The big guy snorted and began looking around. He flung open the door to the hall cupboard and looked at the contents, eyes scanning up and down. Then he strode into the living room and glanced around there. He found a pile of mail on the TV stand, flipped through it, then tossed it on the floor.

Sybil marched toward him, her arms crossed, then stopped and stared him down.

"You find anything?" called Black-Eyes.

"What?" Lyle answered, annoyed. "Not yet." He tried to move. Sybil stepped in his way, and began matching his every move. "All right with that," he said, and gave her a little push so he could get back to the hall.

"Hey!" she shouted at the top of her lungs.

The big man just ignored her and barged into Grantree's bedroom. He wasn't in there two seconds before he said, "Hey, Jimmy, I think we got something here."

Sybil looked at her father. He raised his free hand and closed his eyes, as if to say *It's out of my hands.*

I moved farther into the kitchen so I could see.

Black-Eyes stepped out of the office. "Whatcha find?"

Lyle came out of the bedroom with a little folded cloth in the palm of his hand. He started to unwrap it with his other hand. "Ha!" he said, looking at Black-Eyes. "There we go,

Jimmy. Don't ever say I didn't do nothing for you."

"Where was it?"

"Just on the dresser there."

"You sure that's it?"

The big guy spread out the cloth and showed him. "Yeah. Look."

Sybil took a step forward and looked at Grantree. "Dad!" she complained.

Grantree just sat there. "More shame on you, Lyle, Jimmy. You take that out of this house, you'll pay for the rest of your lives."

Black-Eyes burst into a weird cackle. "Oh, there'll be payment," he said. "Except we'll be the ones getting paid—in cash. Look at that, Lyle. Not bad, eh? For a day's work?"

Everyone was trying to see what Lyle had found in the bedroom. Even Alvin had stopped biting his hand and stepped forward. I couldn't see exactly what it was, but Sybil was the closest and she seemed shocked by the contents of the cloth. "Dad! Really? Come on! You're just going to let them—?"

"You never mind, girl. Mr. Ottis, you put that back where you found it."

But Black-Eyes's cackle just continued while Lyle rolled up the cloth again and began to tie it.

Sybil looked around at us as if we were brain-dead. "What is wrong with you all? Oh my god!" She rushed forward. Before Lyle could stop her, she snatched the cloth out of his hand and spun around to get away.

I just about let out a cheer.

But Sybil got absolutely nowhere with the folded cloth. As she tried to spin out of the way, Lyle just reached out and grabbed her in between her neck and shoulder.

"Aah!" she screamed in pain.

I was too messed up to do anything. Not Danny. He suddenly flew across the kitchen and bashed into the big man like he was trying to knock down a door. That made Lyle let go of Sybil and she dropped the packet of stamps on the floor.

Danny leapt at it. "I got it!"

Sybil, afraid of being caught again, scrambled to her feet and got well into the living room before turning around. Alvin and I crowded near Grantree so we could see.

Once again, the big plumber's long arm reached out. He grabbed Danny by his shirtsleeve and spun him around as if he was a toy. "Gimme that!" he shouted, trying to take the stamps.

Danny hugged the packet of stamps to his chest and tried to squirm away.

The big guy was not in a mood for fooling around. He began rapping Danny in the head with his knuckles, trying to get him to drop the packet. It must have really hurt, because Danny started yelling, "Ow! Ow! No! Ow!"

The next thing I knew, there was a person running at the big man—from right behind me in the kitchen. I was like, what? Who the heck is that?

It was Alvin. Running full speed. He bashed past the table and literally launched himself off the floor at the big guy. I thought for a second the kid had springs on his feet. It was like levitation. He flew through the air and landed like an alien octopus on the big man's head and shoulders, wrapping him in arms and legs and biting teeth. The big man grunted out a scream and tried to stand up straight. But Alvin didn't stop. His fingernails dug into the man's face and neck, and his teeth bit into his balding head like it was a giant apple. The guy swung Alvin left and right and up and down, trying to get him off. For a second, I actually felt sorry for the man. Alvin looked like he was going to kill him.

Danny had rolled away from the big man and leapt to his feet. "Alvin, whoa! Alvin, get offa him! I got the thing! Let him go!"

By then, there were scratch marks on the big man's face

and neck. Alvin was in some kind of psycho violent trance and kept digging at him. While the big man spun, Danny pried Alvin off the man's back. As soon as Alvin's feet hit the floor, Danny held the squirming kid in place with both arms.

The big man had his back to them. He dabbed his face and his hand came away dotted with blood. "Why you freakin' little—" Out of the corner of his eye, he saw Alvin behind him and with one quick move, he jabbed at the kid with his big elbow. The elbow cracked Alvin between the eyes and the kid suddenly stopped struggling.

Danny let go of him.

The big guy reached out and ripped the cloth packet of stamps out of Danny's hand.

We all held our breath. The big plumber looked from one person to another, breathing hard, planning his next move.

Right then, Alvin broke the silence with the most horrible, blubbering cry I've ever heard in my life. "*Muuuuaaaaah!*" His hands were at his nose, and blood dripped out from the bottom of them, while tears shot out from the top.

As soon as Sybil saw Alvin burst into tears, her expression morphed from panic to anger. By the time she started moving, her face was like some kind of banshee, twisted and gnarly, her eyes bugging out of her head. She knocked Black-Eyes out of the way and went straight for the big man, who stepped back, horrified at this geeky woman coming for him.

"What did you do?" Sybil screamed at him. "You hurt this child. What kind of a monster are you? You beast! You sick man! You sick man!"

The packet of stamps dropped from the man's hand and plopped to the floor. Black-Eyes was right there and scooped it up. The big man backed away from Sybil, hands up in surrender, until he banged into the hall closet door. The woman shook her fist in his face, spitting and threatening. "You hurt a child? I'll hurt you! I'll hurt you! You sick man!"

The guy backed toward the office until he realized he had

nowhere to go. He threw his arms up to block his face from Sybil and stumbled into the middle of the living room. By then, Black-Eyes was near the front door and grabbed him by the shirt. "Come on! That's it! We're outa here! Let's go!"

Danny looked like he was going to block their way, but Grantree got halfway to his feet and called him back. "Kid, no! No! Let 'em out!"

The two men struggled with the deadbolt for a second and then burst out the front door, nearly breaking it off its hinges in their rush to escape.

Breathing hard, Sybil headed for the door.

Danny stood there, outraged. "They got everything!"

Grantree sat back down. "Don't you dare go out there!" he said to them. "Let 'em go, I said!"

"But they're getting away! You can't just let them—"

"Hush! Get back in here, you two. Let the police take care of them. That's their job."

Danny stomped back to Alvin, who was sitting on the floor in a pathetic heap. "You okay?"

Alvin's mouth went completely oval. It barely moved as he cry-talked. "No-I-think-he-broge-my-dose-it-hurts-so-bad! Aah!"

Grantree started wagging his hands at me. "You, kid, get the boy some ice for his nose. Come on now."

I grabbed a dishtowel. It took me a second to figure out the ice maker on the front of the fridge. I picked up the chunks that landed on the floor and wrapped them in the towel and took it over to Alvin.

Sybil came into the kitchen. She looked like she was going to look out the kitchen window for the plumbers, but her father stopped her. "Get me my pills there, girl," he said. Somewhere in the all the action, Grantree's neat row of pills had gone flying off the table. And his phone was lying in front of him, open. He picked up the phone and listened for second. "No, not the heart pills," he said to Sybil. "I hate those things.

The clear bottle there." He clapped his phone closed. "That's it. And can you get me something to drink?"

Even before she had the pill bottle open, Sybil was back with a glass of water for him.

I watched through the window over the sink as the plumbers, leaving the back gate wide open, climbed into the van and drove off. I couldn't believe no one was talking about it. After all that fuss and violence, the bad guys were just driving away with the treasure. I just stood there and, painful as it was, shook my head.

"They gone?" asked Grantree.

"Yeah."

"That's awright, kid," Grantree said to me. "They got a few slips of paper. You calm yourself down."

"What about the museum?" Sybil complained. "You've got nothing to give them now!"

"They'll live," her father said calmly.

His daughter turned around to face us. She leaned against the counter and crossed her arms. She stared at the floor for a minute, but her eyes were going back and forth like she was thinking.

"You kids better get going," said Grantree. "The cops are going to be here in a minute. I'm pretty sure you don't want to get mixed up in all this."

"Yeah, no kidding," said Danny. "Especially not with Alvin. They might be looking for him."

"Why's that?"

Danny and Alvin exchanged looks. "Well," said Danny, "they might blame him for his house burning down. And Family Services are probably looking for him."

"What about his nose there?" Grantree asked. "He should probably get to a medi-clinic. Have that checked out."

Danny stared at Alvin again. This time he looked sort of defeated.

"Sibby," said Grantree. "When the cops leave, you be nice

and drive this kid over? Get his nose looked at?"

Sybil did not answer. Instead she tipped her head at her father and narrowed her eyes in a weird squint, like she felt sorry for him. "The cops aren't coming, are they?" she asked.

My eyes flicked over to Grantree. All the wrinkles of his face suddenly sagged, like they were melting. He rubbed his mouth with the back of his hand. "What?"

Sybil stood there and crossed her arms, staring at him. "Just get real, Dad."

"Sibby, now, come on. Why would you think that?"

"Because it's true. Where are they? They should have been here ages ago. And there's nothing."

Grantree rubbed his mouth again, looking extremely uncomfortable. "I don't know! They're taking their time. I don't have no control over how they—"

"Dad."

Grantree looked all around the room—at the stove, the floor, the table—avoiding her gaze. Finally he gave his mouth one last, aggressive swipe. "Fine," he said. "You got me."

Chapter 22

"Okay, what?" said Danny.

Grantree ignored him. His daughter stood there at the counter shaking her head for a second, staring at Grantree. She looked too wound up to speak. Then she let out a breath, shoved off the counter and grabbed the kettle off the stove. She filled it with water, set it back on the stove and came to sit at the table across from her father. "So what did they get?" she asked him.

Grantree squinted at her.

"What did they get away with?" Sybil persisted. "Was it the Riel stamps?"

I stood there trying to keep my mouth from flopping open. What in heck was going on?

"Yeah," said Grantree. "Kind of. But come on—hey. I gotta get ready for the museum. We can talk about this later."

"What? No," said Sybil firmly. "I don't even know what you're talking about. Either the stamps are gone or they're not."

"Oh, come on, Sib," Grantree pleaded. "These kids don't need to hear—"

"Dad?" She paused. "Dad!" she said louder. "Look at these boys. You know what they did for you? I think maybe you owe them an explanation. And me!" She grabbed her upper arm and squished the muscle toward her so she could see the back of it. "I'm going to have bruises where that man grabbed me. What did those plumbers get? If it was the Riel stamps, why are you talking about still going to the museum?"

Alvin gave a huge sobby sniffle right then. He was still sitting on the floor with his dishtowel full of ice up against his face. Grantree waved an arm toward him, annoyed. "Can somebody get that kid a chair?"

Danny helped Alvin into a chair, then sat down beside him. Left standing there, I slipped into the chair nearest me.

Grantree shoved his fist into his side, hard, and sat back. "They got something," he said. "Not much. But they'll get a few bucks out of it."

"So…"

"You," Grantree said to me. "You saw my guys drive off, right?"

"Uh, yeah."

"Danny, kid. Get up and get into that narrow cupboard by the stove."

"What?"

Grantree repeated it slowly for him. "You deaf? The cupboard, to the right of the stove."

Danny launched himself out of his chair. He went to the cupboard and flung the door open so hard, it banged against the drawers behind it.

"Careful now," Grantree scolded him. Then to Sybil he said, "The stamps those plumbers took? Well, they just ain't real."

"Huh?"

"Get in there, kid. There are a couple of things mixed in with the muffin tins and cookie sheets that don't belong."

Danny dug around for a second. "What am I looking for? Oh, no way!" Out from between the cookie sheets he pulled two heavy old metal plates. Grinning from ear to ear, he carried them to the table and set them down gently before Grantree.

"Don't scratch my table!"

"Sorry."

"You know what these are?"

Danny grimaced.

"Is that what you make the stamps with?" I offered.

"You're smarter than Cheevers here looks," said Grantree. "These are Riel's original plates. These are what I'm donating to the museum. The stamps those plumbers stole are just 'essays.' The museum had them printed from these plates for their exhibit. They made a few for me as a keepsake."

"Can't you make your own?" I asked. "You got like, a printing press downstairs."

Grantree just looked at me. "That old thing don't work. It was my grandfather's. And I'm sure as heck not spending any money on it, only to find out it wrecked these plates."

"So they must be worth tons, eh?"

Sybil had an elbow on the table. She was chewing a thumbnail.

Grantree turned slowly and gave me a serious look. "Oh, yeah. Quite a bit."

"Yeah, I bet," Danny remarked, running his fingertips over the metal plates. Alvin reached out and did the same.

"It's tough to read backwards," Grantree told them. "It says *Republic Canadienne*. Made for Louis Riel's rebel government."

"So," I asked, "what did you mean, like 'essays'?"

"When you're just testing the plates, the stamps you make are called essays. There's a woman in Quebec who owns the real essays, from way back when. Only two or three exist. She's got them all. They're worth a chunk of change."

"Yeah?"

"The ones my guys stole, who knows what they're worth? Something, anyway. If they can find a gullible buyer." Grantree took a couple of quick breaths, as if his hip was killing him. "Even the real stamps, nobody ever used them. If they did, they'd be worth a lot. Riel's republic fell before they went into circulation."

"But what about these plate things?" Danny asked. "Like, how much are they worth?"

Grantree grunted as he leaned forward and rested his elbows on the table. "Well, kid, to Canadian history, they're pretty much priceless."

One of Alvin's ice cubes slipped out of his towel and clattered to the floor. Sybil scooped it up and threw it across the room into the sink.

I had gotten up to look closer at the plates. Each rectangle was about an inch long. In the middle of each stamp was a woman's head surrounded by words. "Is that the queen?"

Grantree choked for a second and coughed. "*Pff-kha!* No, son, it's Lady Liberty. Riel had a lot to fight for. The Métis were screwed out of their inheritance, left completely out of the Indian Act. They weren't European and they weren't First Nations, even though they were both. The Métis were the lost people, stuck between two worlds. It was just sad."

Sybil raised her eyebrows and stared at her father. "I'm still waiting."

Grantree snorted. "Kids these days. Too smart for their own good. What do you want to hear?"

"The truth! Is this some kind of insurance scam? What is going on? Why did you let those men ransack your house and then just drive away? I don't get it."

"We all got our secrets, kiddo."

"Yeah," she said, "and some of us got bruises and bashed heads and bloody noses. Come on, Dad—seriously."

Grantree looked at her for a long time. His expression was like, pure regret. Like he now had to tell her she was the milkman's kid. "So," he started, laying both hands flat on the table in front of him. "The, uh…company ain't doing so good."

"How's that?" Sybil asked. "You're a tradesman. You work, you get some more money. What's the problem?"

"The problem, my dear, is that I promised my guys, Lyle and Jimmy, a pension. We're all getting on. We all been paying into it for twenty/thirty years. I collected the money from their paycheques every month. It came to quite a bit. But I thought I'd try to make a bit more. You know, get some interest on it."

Sybil covered her dad's hand with her own. "Oh, no… you didn't."

"Hey, sorry, kid. I didn't know the stock market too good. I just got some bad advice." He paused, then he lifted a finger toward Danny. "It was your dad talked it all up."

"My dad?" Danny asked.

"Sounded like a sure thing. Oh well. I shoulda just stuck to what I know."

Sybil closed her eyes for a second. Then she opened them with a sympathetic look. "So how much do you owe these men?"

Grantree shook his head. "Oh, a lot. Wages and everything. At first I just gave them the van and the tools and signed over most of the company to them. The past year, *I* pretty much been working for *them*. And then my hip went and that went out the window. They'll get a few bucks from what they took. But they'll be back. I messed up. I don't mind paying for it."

"So that's why you've been selling things."

Her father nodded.

"What about the house I'm in?"

Grantree looked pleadingly at her. "Sorry, girl, that's gotta go too. Probably in the next couple months."

"And this one?"

"This house? Well, that'll be my pension. That's all I got."

"So that's why you've been fixing my place up? So you can sell it?"

Grantree pressed his lips together. "Yeah, well, half and half. For you, of course. But yeah, it's gotta go."

"Oh, Dad," she said gently.

"Sorry, girl."

"Oh, whatever," she said. "I have no attachment to that house. But if you need money, why are you donating these priceless plates to the museum? I don't get it."

Grantree still had his hands on the table. He dragged them back toward him and laid them on his lap. "Well, that's a story. Not many people even know these things exist. I didn't exactly get 'em through normal channels. People owed me favors. You know your mother's Métis, right? I kind of got 'em for her when we were separated, trying to win her back. But she got *real* ticked at me."

Sybil snorted. "I'll bet she did."

I didn't get it, so I asked, "Why?"

Grantree shrugged slowly. "Having all this history for our own. She said it wasn't right. Made me promise not to let 'em go back into private hands. They belong to the whole country."

"No kidding," said Sybil.

"Anyways, I hung onto them. I shouldn't have. But I did. So now I need the money and I had to stop myself. A promise is a promise, even though your mother still hates me. So I phoned up the Métis Nation people."

"Not the museum?" Sybil asked.

"The Elders got a deal with the museum, you know, to

protect their historical stuff. It all worked out. Temperature controlled rooms and humidity and everything. Anyway, it's all good now. But I sure coulda used that money."

Sybil stretched an arm toward her father again. "Oh, Dad. I'm so sorry."

"Huh! Well, things happen."

I felt like I was intruding on a family crisis. I just sat there, not really knowing what to do.

But Danny had a question. "So why didn't you just give the stamps to those guys? Why did you let us try to stop them?"

"Well…" Grantree snorted at the irony. "I'm kind of a private guy. I didn't want anybody knowing my business."

"You mean," put in Sybil, "you didn't want me knowing your business was going under."

"Yeah, well…there's that. Anyway, I sure didn't want Lyle and Jimmy knowing about the plates. I wanted them to get out of the picture till I could make it to the museum today."

"O…kay…" said Danny. "Tell that to Alvin. He didn't do nothing to deserve getting bashed in the beak."

"Yup, yup," said Grantree. "You're right. I owe you guys. And I'll start by helping out your cousin here."

Danny sat back, crossed his arms and looked at Grantree. "You? You're gonna help him? No, we're good. I'll figure something out."

Grantree started to blink and splutter like he wanted to reach across the table and choke Danny. But Sybil broke in. "All right, all right. Just calm down for a second. So what's the deal with him? What's your name? Alvin?"

The kid nodded.

Grantree butted in. "These two had him sleeping in my garage last night."

Sybil looked at Danny and me, her eyebrows raised. "Oh, really? How'd that happen?"

Danny sighed, all dramatic. "His mom's in the hospital,

like, maybe permanently. My mom has this grudge against him so he can't be at our house."

"Okay…"

"So my dad like, put him in this Family Services place. There were all these violent kids. He got beat up and ran away. Now, like…I'm trying to figure out what to do."

Sybil put on a no-nonsense face. "So what makes you think you're the best one to help him?"

Danny was taken aback. "Well…there's like, nobody else."

Sybil's expression did not change a bit. "Okay. Just to let you know, the world is full of people who know how to help."

Danny made a kind of snarly face at the table.

Sybil continued. "So did this all just happen? Alvin, where were you sleeping before last night?"

Alvin looked at Danny as if he needed his permission to speak. He pointed at me. "At his house."

Sybil looked at me. "And your parents are fine with this?"

I cracked a smile. "Uh…no. We had kind of a disaster yesterday morning."

"What does that mean?"

I made a face. "Well, they kind of didn't know he was sleeping over. Scared the wits out of my parents and my little brothers."

"So what's your big plan now?" she asked Danny and me.

Danny shrugged. I didn't say anything.

"You know," said Sybil, "my dad has like, ridiculous connections." She looked at him. "Weren't you on the board of some youth place?"

"Me?" said Grantree. "Oh, yeah. Uncles at Large. Christmas Bureau. All that. We did the renos for the Hope Mission, too."

"See?" said Sybil. "He can help."

Danny was not convinced. "So he's gonna get put in another Family Services home? Yeah, no."

"Fine," said Grantree. "We'll put that aside for two seconds. Sibby, you got a spare bedroom for a couple of days?" He didn't give her time to answer and continued. "Danny, let me prove something to you." He laughed. "Ha! Listen to me, talking to the kid who busted my greenhouse and broke into my garage." He gave his head a shake. "Look, maybe I can get you to trust me. How be I find out whoever hurt Alvin, get 'em charged with assault. And whoever let it happen, I'll get 'em fired. How'd that be?"

Danny stared at the table, trying to keep a straight face. But he couldn't. "Okay," he said, cracking a grin.

"Fine. Sibby?"

Her eyebrows were raised like she couldn't believe what was happening. "All right. I only have a foamy in the spare bedroom. Maybe I can borrow some blankets and whatnot."

"You betcha," said Grantree.

"You're not selling the place right away, are you?"

"No, no. Couple months, at least."

Sybil turned to Alvin. "So what do you like, Alvin? What do you do?"

Alvin still had the dishtowel with the ice up to his face. With his one visible eye, he searched the table for a second. Then he remembered something and said, "I can do tricks."

"Tricks? Like what?"

"Like…" Alvin's one visible eye lit up. "I'll show you!"

The kid suddenly dropped the dishtowel on the table and leapt off his chair. Two seconds later, he was lying on his back on the floor, flipping his feet back behind his head.

"Okay…" said Sybil, her eyes big.

"I can do other ones, too!" Alvin proceeded to demonstrate his entire repertoire of bendy poses. None of them looked difficult for him. Grantree and his daughter clapped and commented on each one. It soon became clear the kid was never going to stop unless someone stopped him.

"All right, that's good," said Grantree. "We get the idea."

"Yeah, but—"

"Hey, hey, we're good, kid. Really."

Alvin sat back down with his dishtowel full of ice. This time, he was beaming out from behind his bloody nose.

Grantree sat forward again. "So what time does the medi-clinic open? Sibby? You got time before we gotta go, eh? We ain't gotta be downtown before eleven thirty. You can get him all checked out?"

His daughter nodded. "Sure."

"How are you, kid?" Grantree asked me. "You want to go, too? How's your head?"

I rubbed the dent in my forehead and shrugged. "Oh, it's okay. I'm all right."

We all started to get up. Alvin remained seated, kind of hunched, with Danny hanging onto his arm.

"Can I ask you something?" Danny said to Grantree.

"Shoot."

"About that one guy. His black eyes; they're—"

Grantree began nodding. "Jimmy? Farming accident when he was a boy—a fertilizer or pesticide. Of course, he scares the wits out of everybody he meets. He's been to forty, fifty doctors since he was a child and they all say the same thing: 'There's nothing we can do. Your vision's fine, so don't bother yourself over it.' He's a good guy. I get comments all the time."

While her father was talking, Sybil came around the table and fetched a plastic container of raspberries from the fridge. For sure, they were the ones we'd picked. She pulled the lid off and put the container down in front of Alvin. Alvin just looked at her. She gestured for him to dig in. Gingerly, he picked one out and popped it into his mouth.

Danny decided he wanted to go home to change, if he was going with Sybil and Alvin to the medi-clinic.

Me, I couldn't wait to get out of there. I did not want to spend the day with sickos waiting for a doctor. "I think I'm going to head home," I told Danny.

"Huh? Yeah, okay. I'll come out with you."

"Kid?" said Grantree to me. "You sure you're all right?"

"Yeah."

Grantree continued. "I just want to thank you for trying to help out. You and Danny here, you're, uh…I hope you keep this to yourselves. Like I said, I'm kind of a private guy and—"

"Don't worry," said Danny. "I like secrets. Especially yours. I can use the leverage if I mess up again."

"What?"

"I'm joking!" said Danny. "I don't care what you do."

"You're killing me, kid," Grantree said, shaking his head slowly. "One bit at a time."

I turned to Alvin. He had placed raspberries in a row in front of him, and was eating them one after another. "I guess I'll be seeing you."

Alvin was looking pretty happy. "Yeah."

"Danny's got my number," I said. "You can call me anytime."

But Alvin was so distracted that he just nodded and said loudly, "Okay, bye!" even though we were still standing there.

"That's all you gotta say? After all this?"

But all I received from Alvin was a dumb, "Huh?"

Danny snorted. "Whatever." He turned and gave me a push, "Let's go, dude."

As I followed Danny outside, I felt completely disoriented. The sun was blazing down, so hot it felt like a weight on my shoulders, but it seemed like a different day altogether. The back gate and the garage door were still open. And so was the door of Grantree's fancy SUV, which was now making a dinging sound. We went into the garage, slammed the door and made sure the garage door was locked behind us.

"Maybe we can do something later," Danny said when we got out to the alley. Then he suddenly became animated. "You see that guy's face when Alvin jumped him? He was like, '*Aah!* There's a monkey on my back and he's gonna tear my face off!'"

I laughed. "Alvin totally rocked it."

"Cindy's not going to believe this."

"Does she even know—like, about Alvin in Grantree's garage?"

"Naw, she still thinks he's sleeping at your place. Should I tell her?"

I just shrugged. "I don't care. Your call."

"I can't believe this all worked out. I thought Grantree was going to lose his mind when they caught Alvin. And of course, it had to be my fault. I'm like his arch-nemesis."

You and your father, I thought, but I didn't say it.

Riding home, the bathwater-warm air blasting my face and my elbow still feeling goofy, I couldn't help grinning the whole way, thinking what a wild morning it had been.

When I got in the door, Mom didn't even say hello. "What happened to your forehead?"

"Huh?" I had to think fast. "Frisbee."

The boys came rushing over to gawk. "Ew! What happened?"

"Did Danny do that?" Mom asked.

"What?"

"He must have thrown it pretty hard. What do you two do over there?"

I chuckled to myself all the way down the stairs—which I descended like a normal person. For the first time, I was totally enjoying being injured. Somehow, I was being let into the wild man club that the whole Cheevers family seemed to belong to. Right now, though, I needed some calm and quiet to lick my wounds.

Chapter 23

That night, I found myself watching the local news to see if there was anything about our little adventure. I kept thinking Grantree had called the police when, of course, he hadn't. So I sat there watching a stupid segment about how the mosquitoes were bad now because of all the rain the week before.

I grabbed my phone, thinking I'd check out concussions. The front of my head felt really dented and there was a line there, as if I'd been wearing a tight hat. But something came on the TV just then that made me sit up so fast, I literally yelped.

"What's wrong with you?" Dad asked from his easy chair.

"Nothing."

On the screen, a young male reporter was interviewing a curator guy from the museum. As he talked about the history of Louis Riel, they cut to Grantree shaking the curator's hand while Sybil held up one of the heavy stamp plates. Then they cut to a short interview with some Métis Elders—a very serious man and a jolly woman—about how important the plates were to their history. There was a shot of a glass display case with the plates mounted all nice inside.

The segment was only like, a minute long. I chuckled when Grantree lifted his cane and accidently bashed the TV guy's microphone. Sybil didn't even notice. But they showed a kid off to the side who covered his laughter with a flat hand. It was Alvin—with a bandage across his nose. After the medi-clinic, they'd obviously got him a better shirt and combed his hair. The kid looked like the sort of geek you'd expect at a stamp collector event.

My dad didn't even notice the name—Grantree—as belonging to the guy I'd been working for all last week. I was glad I didn't have to talk about it. It was just weird, how out-of-the-loop my dad was.

I didn't hear much from Danny for weeks after that. There was no real reason. I know he had to return the War Demons game when Tyler Lupul got back from holidays. But maybe Danny and I had just hit the peak of our friendship. We texted a bit, but I got no more invites to go over. I totally missed seeing Cindy and I totally missed the constant excitement. Because the truth was, both of my parents' houses, the McSpaddens and Alicia's, were pretty boring. They were homey and everything, but because nothing ever happened there, both places were quiet and kind of lonely.

Thanks to freaking Alvin, I clued in to the world of armature. There'd been no point in doing plasticine arms and legs before—they just fell apart. But when I found some old electrical wire in a corner of the basement, a whole world of possibilities opened up for me. Not only could I do bodies, I could do poses. I started doing these skinny guys dancing or flying or bending over to fart. I was on a roll. And even though I didn't have much plasticine to work with, I made a ton of different things. Thanks, Alvin!

And I wasn't the only one he'd had an effect on. I soon realized that me bringing that weirdo kid home had broken something in our house. The boys had never had a real birthday party with like, relatives and friends. But when Kyle's birthday came at the beginning of September, he wanted to invite the kid from across the street and half the munchkins from his grade one class. I couldn't believe Mom gave in. She bought an ice cream cake and balloons and everything. She cleared my birthday cards from the mantel and left them in my room. Not wanting to be reminded about that super-sad-looking polar bear, I stuffed them in a drawer without even looking at them.

When all the kids arrived, it felt like explorers were entering the mummy's tomb for the first time. Weird running shoes appeared near our front door. Strange voices echoed in our kitchen. Cake crumbs from alien mouths landed on our carpet. Kyle thought he was the luckiest kid on the planet because he got freezer pizza. The kid entertained everyone by walking around with twists of kleenex up his nose. From then on, the boys had friends over constantly, which was incredibly annoying for me. But hey, I figured that was the price of normal.

Somewhere in mid-November, Danny and I ended up hanging out during gym class. When our teacher was called away on some emergency, the librarian came and stared at her phone while some of the class took shots at the baskets. The rest of us chilled on the benches around the sides of the gym.

I hadn't really talked to him for weeks, so I asked, "How's it going with your auntie?"

He was leaning over his knees, spinning a basketball between his fingers. "Oh, they put her in a long-term care facility."

"They ever figure out what happened that day? Was it a

269

heart attack?"

"Stroke, they think. She was in a coma for a couple months. Now she's like, brain-dead. Just lies there grinding her teeth."

"That sucks. And Alvin?"

He decided to bounce the basketball and slammed it down harder than he'd intended. The ball went flying up and he had to jump up and grab it out of the air. When he sat back down, he said, "I don't really want to talk about Alvin."

"Because…?"

"He's still at what's-her-face's. Sybil's. You see the *For Sale* sign on her lawn?"

"No, I haven't been over there."

He began spinning the ball again. "Well, she's gone all day. Alvin's home alone, watching contortion videos on You-Tube. The kid can do all of it, easy."

"That doesn't sound so bad. Is she gonna like, adopt him or foster him or whatever?"

Danny went "*Pfft*," and shook his head. "No. I thought, oh, she's a geek, he's a geek. It'll totally work out. But I saw Grantree outside like, last week or so. I guess he got the Family Services guy fired. The guy who was supposed to be watching Alvin?"

"That's good."

"The kid who punched Alvin, though—who knows? They're giving Grantree the run-around. Probably nothing's going to happen there."

"So…?"

"So I asked Grantree what the deal was with Sybil. He says she's got him registered for foster care. They're just waiting for someone to pick him. And I was like, 'What? Why can't she be the foster parent?' And he like, laughs. 'I hate to break it to you, kid. She ain't got a maternal bone in her body. She likes her books. That's her thing.'"

"Great."

"Yeah, no kidding, eh? I was so ticked. He looks totally different, though. He's got a phone now and like, normal clothes. They're moving to a high-rise right away."

"Yeah?"

"Alvin's stoked. They have a weight room and everything."

"Alvin's stoked about the weight room?"

"Yeah." Danny chuckled. "I said to him, 'Hey, Alvin, you gonna get all buff for the chicks?' He just looks at me with this fat lip. I just laughed." He bounced the ball a couple of times. On the last bounce, he tried stopping it with his foot and had to chase it across the floor. When he got back, he said, "My mom met Alvin, though."

"No way."

"Yeah. She didn't know it was him. She thought it was Sybil's kid. Out in front of Grantree's. They were going to Sybil's car."

"So what happened?"

"Nothing." Danny shrugged. The basketball was firmly under one foot. "She hadn't seen him in maybe, seven years? Cindy and I were like, freaking out, trying to get to the front step so we could hear what was going on. But all we heard was my mom saying, 'What a nice young man.' I just about crapped myself."

"No doubt."

"They said it could be like, years before someone fosters him. Everybody wants babies and little kids. Nobody wants teenagers or like, freako rubber boys." He pointed at a hoop that had just freed up. "You wanna go play?"

"Yeah, sure."

We goofed around, shooting baskets for the next ten minutes. Underhand, overhand, backwards, through our legs. Almost nothing went in. But we were laughing our heads off while all the serious jocks were having the most boring time ever. That's one thing Danny and I knew how to do: have dumb fun.

Then he stopped and said, "Oh, I forgot to tell you."

"What?"

He threw a basket normally, and totally missed. I grabbed the ball after the first bounce and we went to sit down again.

"Remember those plumber guys? Guess how much they got for those fake stamps?"

"The 'essays' or whatever?"

"Yeah, yeah. *Twenty grand.*"

"That's all?"

"What are you talking about? They aren't even real. It's *twenty grand*," he said again. "Grantree couldn't believe it. And you know what he's gonna do? He's gonna pay me to weed his garden next year. Says I should save to go to trade school."

"Ha! Are you guys like, best buds now?"

"Shut up. We got history. That's all. I call him the gimp. I think he likes that I'm not all nicey-nicey to him. Gives him something to swear at."

The bell rang just then and we all crowded toward the doors. While we were shuffling along to get out into the hall-way, Danny said, "Did I tell you about Ordry and Morgan?"

"What? Are they still after you?"

"Me? No. I'm talking about Cindy. I clued in that I had some ammo against them. I went up and said, like, 'You better stop bugging Cindy. I know all about you starting that fire at Alvin's house. So screw off!' And that was it! She says they totally stopped!"

"Awesome. Good for you."

We got out the doors and went our separate ways to our lockers. As it turned out, Danny was completely wrong about Ordry and Morgan.

Not even a week later, the whole school was talking about Cindy getting suspended. Nobody knew exactly what the story was. But when I heard, I couldn't find Danny fast enough.

He was at his locker, totally stressed.

"Hey," I said. "I heard what happened."

"Oh, dude, he really bit his lip. Three stitches."

"What?"

"My dad trashed his jeep last night. He was texting and rear-ended somebody."

"What?" I spluttered. "No, like…with Cindy. Didn't she get suspended?"

"Oh, yeah," he said. "That was bad." He slowly shook his head. "Ordry Bruce, dude. He didn't stop. She was at the fountain just before lunch. Just finished filling her water bottle and Ordry passes her and makes this rude comment. Cindy takes her water bottle, follows him down the hall, grabs him and like, clocks him full force in the side of the head."

"And?"

"Oh, he was down, man. Gave him like, a detached retina. Parents are freaking out. Cindy's totally suspended. The guy might lose his eye, they said. I was like, *pfft*, you don't know Cindy, man. He's lucky she didn't kill him."

"Ha! Cindy's Rule, eh?"

"Huh?"

"Don't bug Cindy?"

"Yeah, no doubt."

Same old Cheevers house, I thought as I headed to my next class. Some things never change.

Two days later, I passed by the office and saw two huge cops standing by the secretary's desk along with a bunch of parents.

I asked the first kid I saw, "Any idea what's going on?"

He chucked his chin down the hall. "Three guesses."

When I turned, I saw Ordry Bruce and Morgan coming in from outside, followed by a teacher. Bruce had a bandage over one eye. They all went into the office.

I had to go to class. But that was literally the last time I ever saw those guys. They were gone from the school and gone from the neighbourhood. Maybe the info about them burning down Alvin's house got out. I have no idea. But I was really glad they were gone.

Grade seven was weird. It felt like we'd spent all of elementary school waiting for grade six so we could be the bosses. And then we got to a new school and *blam*, we're way on the bottom again. Ugh. At least we got new blood, new people from other schools to hang out with. That was the only good thing.

I visited my birth mom a couple times a month and we texted all the time. When I told her all about the stamps and Grantree and my big fail on his basement steps, she called me her 'bad boy' and shook her head at me.

Sadly, her freako boyfriend never made anything easier. He was always there when I went over, even when I tried my best to visit when he wasn't home. Somehow he always showed up and ruined everything by walking in on our private conversations. One time he even sent her to the store just after I arrived. I had to sit there with a full cup of scalding tea while he wandered around, pretending to be too busy to go to the store himself.

"What's your problem?" was his favourite thing to say to me. It was no great mystery he was like, incredibly jealous of me. Even though I'd just met her, I had a relationship with his girlfriend that couldn't be broken. And that drove him crazy.

Then one day in early December, he was gone. And I mean totally gone, like, permanently.

I had been invited to Madeleine's birthday. She was turning three and I was not keen to go over there, hating that guy so much. But my mom, my adoptive mom, bought this like, unreal cute dress as a gift for Maddy.

"You're her big half-brother. You can't not go."

So, with the gift bag under my arm, pink ribbons and all, I got on the bus to my birth mom's place, dreading seeing that freako and hearing his "What's your problem?"

But he wasn't there. His skateboard and bike weren't in the hallway when I went in. And my mom was like, floating, she was so happy. Her hair was all curly and awesome. She was wearing makeup and smacked a great big red kiss on my cheek, which she had to wipe off with a kleenex. Cassie and Jake were there, and these two cousins, Talia and June, who barely said ten words between them. They kept trying to get the cousins to be excited about me with stuff like, "Isn't he handsome?" and "Doesn't he look like his Uncle James?" It was lame, but still pretty cool to meet more people I was related to.

Then, halfway through the party, as Maddy was opening presents with everyone's help, Cassie said, "Isn't it nice Keith isn't here?"

Cousin June, who was next to her on the couch, said, "You can say that again. Breath of fresh air."

I heard my mom and the cousins talking about him in the kitchen later. But Jake was blabbing at me about his Batman comic website, so I really didn't hear what had happened.

Later, I managed to stay behind when everyone but my mom left the kitchen. I had to ask. "So where's Keith? He's not here for his daughter's birthday?"

My mom smiled. She was filling a little jug with cream for everyone's tea. "It was amazing. I kicked him out."

"What? Really?" I had thought she was way too chicken to stand up to the guy.

"You wouldn't believe what happened. I got talking about him at work. There were some customers at the front and one of the guys in the shop, his wife was there to pick him up. I've known her for years. She says, 'I'm so tired of you crabbing about Keith and doing nothing. You gotta get rid of that guy.' I was like, whatever; same old. Then this customer pipes up. He says, 'Don't listen to her. Saying and doing are two different things. What you need is a practical plan.' And he launches into this like, whole step-by-step. And not just, 'Oh, kick him out.' It was like, how to get him to *want* to leave and never come back. There was no blame, no nothing. Just a great plan. I was like, wow, nobody had ever talked to me like that before. I went home and cried for two hours in my bedroom. Then I did exactly what he said." My mom began to tear up and had to hold onto the back of a chair. "And he's gone! I still can't believe it. He's got a job and he says he's going to pay child support and everything." She looked down and blinked about five times. "I still can't believe it. I owe that man everything."

"Do you know who he was?"

"No. I'd never seen him before. He was an older guy. Big chest. He was carrying a cane. Said he was getting new cabinets for his daughter's house. Didn't want them too fancy 'cause he had to sell it for some reason. I asked him, 'How do you know this stuff?' And he's like, 'Well, it's kind of what my ex-wife did to me. And don't get me wrong, I totally deserved it.' Weird, eh? Anyway," she said, "can I give you some cake to take with you?"

After that, I did not need a bus to drive me home. I could have floated the whole way there.

Days passed and I really wanted to thank Grantree. I actually went to his house one day. But he wasn't home. Then Christmas rolled around and I bought him this thing of chocolates at the grocery store and left it in his mailbox. It was pretty lame for what he'd done for me, but I didn't have much money and it was better than nothing. I just put a Christmas tag on it and wrote, *Merry Christmas, from Brian.* I hope he got why I was doing it.

Speaking of Christmas, I was excited about buying my birth mother a gift for the first time. I agonized over it for like, weeks. And then after I bought it—it was this handmade bracelet I bought at a craft sale—I lay awake freaking out that I'd bought the wrong thing and I couldn't take it back. Mom gave me heck because I got real crabby. "Please calm down. She's going to love it. It's from you—that's all that matters!"

I even bought Maddie a cool toy. And when Christmas

arrived, it turned out that Mom was right. Alicia totally loved the bracelet and put it on right there. It looked awesome and even matched this sweater that Cassie gave her.

A couple of days before New Year's, I was watching TV after the boys had gone to bed. Dad was snoring in his easy chair. A commercial started and Mom hit Mute and asked me, out of the blue, "Whatever happened to that boy who slept over here?"

The question totally caught me by surprise. "Alvin? Oh… he's staying with Mr. Grantree's daughter."

"The greenhouse man? How did that happen?"

I suddenly realized I was on the verge of making a huge mistake. "Uh…Grantree met him and…his daughter helped him out."

"Why would she do that? Is there something you're not telling me?"

"No."

And that was all it took. Two days later I got this text from Danny: *whats with ur mom?*

what?

I'd barely finished typing when Danny phoned me. "Dude, your mom is on the phone talking with my mom about Alvin."

"No way."

"What did you say?"

"Nothing. She asked about the kid who slept over and—"

"So it was you! Arrgh!" he growled, and hung up.

I sat there staring at my phone, my heart racing madly.

On New Year's Eve, there was a huge snowstorm. Giant flakes piled up and up so that the news was full of snow-plows and reporters on the street, their coats dusted white with snow. It was already pitch black out when somebody knocked on our back door around six thirty. It was Danny.

"Dude, we gotta talk."

I got my coat and boots on and we went out to stand in

the cone of swirling white under one of the streetlights lining the street.

"Guess who's at my house right now."

I hadn't talked to him since the phone call. "No way."

"My dad went and got him from Sybil's."

"Whaaat?"

"Yeah. My mom totally found out we were all sneaking behind her back."

"How?"

"What? Idiot Randy. He blabbed the whole thing! About Cindy cooking for them and my Dad buying wood to fix their porch. She totally lost it. I thought she was going to have a breakdown."

"Yeah?"

"Oh, it was bad, dude. She started yelling at my dad, saying he'd betrayed her, and he lost it, too. Everybody's slamming doors and crying and like, wow, I thought they were going to get divorced and everything. Then Cindy gets home and everything like, flips."

"How do you mean?"

"My mom goes on about her cooking for Auntie and everything and Cindy just stands there with her arms folded. Mom's like, 'I pay the mortgage and blah-blah-blah! You wait till you have children, then you'll understand!' And Cindy's like, 'What are you talking about? I do all the cooking and everything. You're never here, so what do you care?'"

"Ouch."

"My mom tried to defend herself, saying her baby got injured, or whatever. And Cindy's like, 'So? Get over it. That was years ago'."

"No way."

"Yeah. Then Cindy tells her what it was like over there. The mess, the toilet flooding, Auntie getting sick, Alvin starving. Then Cindy says, 'If that's all okay with you, then you're just a heartless cow.'"

"Ho-oh," I laughed.

"No kidding. That was it for my mom. Out the front door! She was gone for like, two hours. We were all like, wow, divorce for sure. But she gets back and she's all like, cried out and calm. Something snapped, for sure. All she says to my dad is, 'Go get him.' She doesn't apologize or anything, but we don't care. It's done, man."

"Wow."

"Yeah, really."

"So he's at your house. Doing what?"

"He's in the kitchen with Randy, being annoying. He's trying to teach him how to put his foot in his mouth and they're all farting and laughing. I couldn't take it. I had to get out of there."

"Well, happy New Year."

"Yeah, no kidding. Thanks, I guess."

We walked back toward my place through the snow. A few people were out shovelling. Cars passed us, completely silent. Everyone still had their Christmas lights on and every house looked warm and cozy. When Danny and I parted ways, I stood there watching him trudge off down the avenue. I stood there for a while. I guess he didn't know I was watching. Two streetlights away, he did this little skipping hop. And man...that told me everything.

After the holidays, the weather turned like, crazy cold and I didn't go anywhere other than school for weeks. Which was fine, since Dad had gotten "the family" a little laptop for Christmas and I discovered the joys of a bigger screen. I tried hogging it, but that didn't work. I ended up showing the boys and Mom how to do stuff on the Web, just so it wouldn't leave my grubby little hands. That totally backfired. The next thing you know, Mom's clicking *Like* like the rest of the world and the boys are going crazy for Mitzy Pits games. Ugh. It felt like the walls of the house were coming down, one cat video at a time.

And then all of a sudden, right at the end of January, a great big freaking bomb dropped on our little house. It was so stupid, people at school would come up to me, wanting to hear the story. I was very popular for about four days straight. We finally figured out what was causing Kyle's drippy nose.

Chapter 24

I shouldn't say *we* figured out what was causing Kyle's drippy nose. I didn't really do anything, other than notice something weird. But it kick-started the big discovery.

One night after supper, I went back to my school for this big awards thing for all the teams and clubs and stuff. I only went because I'd heard this hot girl was going. Turned out she wasn't even there, but they had like, free pop and I ended up chugging about a litre of it. Whatever; no biggie—but I had to get up in the middle of the night to pee, which I hate.

Anyway, I was in bare feet and got up to the landing without making a sound. And there was Kyle, rummaging around under the kitchen sink. He spotted me and freaked out and ran back to his room.

I'd totally forgotten about it the next day, until I caught him watching one of my recorded shows. I was ticked and wanted revenge. So during dinner, I asked, "Hey Kyle, so what were you doing under the sink last night?"

He just frowned at me across the table.

But Mom was interested. "The kitchen sink? What do you mean?"

"I got up to pee at like, eleven and he's got the cupboard open. I was just wondering why."

"Kyle?" Mom asked.

"What?"

"Brian asked you a question."

"So?"

Mom put her fork down. "Okay, now I'm asking. What were you doing last night? What's under the sink?"

"Nothing."

Dad got involved. He brought out the big guns. "You want to go to bed?"

"Huh?"

"Answer your mother. What were you doing under the sink?"

Kyle mumbled something that no one could hear.

"What was that?"

He repeated it as a shout: "I was getting a potato!"

Dad looked at me as if I had an answer. I shrugged. He put down his fork. "Why were you getting a potato?"

Kyle mumbled again.

"Speak up, would you?"

"I was hungry!"

"Okay. Didn't you have enough dinner?"

As usual, the kid had barely eaten two bites. "I don't like dinner," he said.

"Why not?"

"You said it would make me big and strong."

"So?"

Kyle shrugged. "I don't want to get big."

Dad looked around the table. Then he asked, "Why not?"

It took Kyle a second to answer. "If I get too big, I can't play with Jayden."

"I don't know what that means," said our mother.

Kyle mumbled at his plate. "Brian doesn't play with Jayden. He's too big."

My parents looked at each other, trying not to smile.

Dad scratched his head. "But what's that got to do with potatoes?"

"You don't see me when I eat potatoes." Kyle sniffled.

"Um…?"

Then Kyle burst out, "Mom counts all the crackers and cheese, but not the potatoes."

"Counts?" Dad said.

"I think he means," I threw in, "she would notice crackers missing, but not potatoes."

"Is that what you mean?" Dad asked him. Mom had a hand up to her mouth now.

Kyle nodded.

Dad suddenly addressed Mom. "You count the crackers?"

"Well, with your pension and salary…I can't just—"

Dad waved her away. "We're not that poor. Don't you have snacks or something for them? How about cookies? The kids have cookies and milk, right?"

Mom's hand went down. "I don't buy cookies!" she said, outraged.

"What? What do you mean? Why not?"

"Well, they'll just eat them!"

Dad's hand went to his forehead. Then he gave his head a shake. "Okay, whatever. Kyle."

"Yeah?"

"So you eat raw potatoes?"

"Yeah."

"How many?"

"All the time. But they make me poop."

Dad laughed. "I imagine they do. Do you wash them

first?"

"No, it makes too much noise. Can I go now?"

"Just…hang on a second. Do you poop more than usu-al?"

"Yeah."

"How many times a day?"

Again with the shrug. "I don't know. Sebenteen?"

"Seventeen? Do you know how many seventeen is?"

Kyle nodded.

Dad turned to Mom. "You didn't notice this?"

It was her turn to shrug. "He goes when he needs to go. I don't pay attention."

Dad leaned forward a bit more and asked Kyle, "Do you feel sick? From all this potatoes and pooping? Or is it okay?"

"I like potatoes. But pooping makes my nose run."

Everyone at the table sat up another two inches.

"Excuse me?"

"Whenever I poop, my nose drips. I can't stop it." The kid was on the verge of tears.

Dad sat back in his chair and looked at Mom. "Seventeen times a day." Then he sat forward again. "You eat the peel and everything?"

"Yeah, except for the green ones. Jayden has those."

I had never in my life seen my father laugh out loud. A guffaw, sure. A snort, you bet. But this was the first time I'd ever seen him double over and chuckle till the tears rained down his face. When he was done, he pushed his plate away and got up to get a second beer from the fridge. "I give up," he said, still laughing. "Now I've heard everything. Buy the kid some damn cookies, would you? Jesus." And he grinned his way into the living room to watch the news.

They clued in a few days later that Dad's cereals—bran flakes and bran buds—probably weren't helping. And magi-cally, oatmeal and cheerios appeared in our cupboard.

Then another bomb dropped. Dad admitted later that he

284

had the same problem as Kyle. It was totally genetic. Dad just honked his nose before he left the bathroom and no one ever noticed. Ha! Mom's reaction was priceless when she heard that one. She went into the cupboard where they kept their vitamins and medicine and threw Kyle's plop splay in the garbage. Then she slid a box of kleenex across the table at my dad.

"What's this for?"

"That's for you. You can show him how to blow his nose."

"Me? I'm at work all day. How am I gonna—"

Mom's arms were folded across her chest. "That's your problem. I took him to all the doctors and specialists and stood in line for all the stupid medicine. And you never saw him have a fit when I had to spray that stuff up his nose. I'm done. You two figure it out."

The whole thing was still amusing to Dad. He picked up the box of kleenex and put it on the counter behind him. "All right. You've got a point. I'll teach him."

And true to his word, he sat Kyle on his knee before dinner every night and showed him how to blow his little honker, laughing the whole time. It was the first real bit of parenting I ever saw him do.

I guess I never clued in before that kids could inherit stuff like that from their parents. Hair color? Sure. Buck teeth? Totally. Which made me wonder, what else didn't I know about me?

Solving that ridiculous nose-drip mystery changed everything in our house. Yes, Mom bought actual cookies, and not from her freako discount store. She doled them out for snacks and magically, when they were finished, she bought some more. But that wasn't all. I started getting two big, thick sandwiches for lunch every day. That may not seem like a big deal, but I was growing like crazy. Two inches in five months. I could have eaten twice what she gave me, but whatever. I felt like giving Dad a hug every time I saw him.

I thought, *Yay! Everything is turning out awesome!* But slowly, over the next two weeks, my mother slipped back into being her usual stingy self. My sandwiches started getting thinner and thinner. The fresh, awesome cookies were replaced by discount store cookies. Next time she went shopping, all she brought home was crackers, and the time after that, nothing. The boys complained loudly, but nobody listened. The next thing you know, Kyle's nose was dripping again.

When February arrived, Alicia started dating new guys and always seemed to be busy on the weekends. I was like, what the heck? Is the world out to get me? It was too freaking cold to go anywhere or do anything outside. Mom put a fresh coat of her fake frost stuff on my windows and my room just felt claustrophobic. The only thing that stopped me going completely crazy was my plasticine. Maybe I thought that if I could sculpt something awesome, I could impress people at school and Alicia would make some time for me. Who knows how my weirdo brain worked.

I found all these videos on technique. I decided one day to try to do a real, actual human being, head to toe. It took me two days—a whole weekend—to get my little man to the point where I was doing ears and abs and everything. I even put a little wiener on the guy, just like a real sculptor would do. When I was done, the thing looked amazing. But it felt like it was a total fluke. How did I know how to do that? On Sunday night I stood it up on my dresser, thinking I would never be able to make anything that awesome again.

I went to school the next day feeling like that little sculpture had given me a fingernail grip on sanity. It was a rough day. I got teased about a zit beside my nose. Ordinarily, it wouldn't have bothered me. But that day, it just crushed me. I don't know, maybe it was hormones. Anyway, I couldn't wait to get home. *I may not have nice friends,* I thought, *but I do have my awesome little plasticine man.* It was like it was evidence that I was worth something.

I was starving for dinner and went downstairs to dump my backpack. As I reached the last step, I suddenly got this horrible feeling like, out of nowhere. When I opened my bedroom door, the first thing I noticed was that my sculpture was not on my dresser. The next thing I noticed was a pile of folded laundry on my bed. With a jolt, I realized my mom had been in my room. For sure, she had seen my little naked man with his little wiener out. Was she such a prude that she had wrecked my sculpture? Was she thinking I was some kind of perv now? I had this vision of all my work lying crumpled in the garbage, covered in crumbs and dust bunnies. And I freaking lost it.

By the time I'd stumbled to my dresser, blind with tears, I was imagining going upstairs and screaming and yelling, "Where's my plasticine? What did you do with it?"

And Mom answering, "I took it. What a filthy mind you have. How dare you have that dirty thing in this house. What is wrong with you?"

I dropped down on my bed, completely crushed, tears pouring down my face. But as I drew a big, shaky breath to sob again, I saw my little man on the floor between my dresser and the bed. He had just fallen over. No big deal.

It was then that I really clued in what an idiot I was. I dried my eyes and held my little guy for a long while, smoothing his shoulder back where he'd bashed it on the floor. Then I went upstairs and took an apple without even asking. I needed some fuel in my stomach or I was going to pass out.

That night, I asked Dad if I could have a lock on my bedroom door.

He looked at me for a long while over his beer. Then be blinked and shrugged. "Yeah," he said. "We'll see."

I didn't now what that meant, so I just gave up.

That week at school, there was a rumor going around that a kid in grade nine had tried to commit suicide. Yeah, that sure lifted my mood. Right after that, this guest speaker woman was going around to all the classrooms teaching us about SAD, Seasonal Affective Disorder. She said we all go to school in the dark, we come home in the dark, and the lack of sunlight makes us all depressed. *Yeah, thanks,* I thought. *I feel so much better.* I wandered around like a zombie for days after that, an emotional flatline, just empty.

Summer felt like a million miles away. It was the middle of February and the weather was still crazy cold. There was ice fog every morning and about six inches of hard-packed snow on the ground. On really bad days, there was this wicked wind that felt like it was trying to tear your face off.

Mom chewed me out for not visiting my birth mom. "When was the last time you talked to her?"

"I don't know; couple weeks ago."

"I can drive you anytime, you know. There's no excuse."

So I texted her just to say hi and she invited me over the following Saturday. I was totally dreading meeting some new boyfriend, but that didn't happen. The house was super quiet, with just her and Maddy there. We watched a movie and ate like, six pounds of cheetos. When it was time to leave, she handed me this blue post-it note with like, gibberish on it.

"What's this?"

"Directions."

"To...what?"

"I did some digging and found out where your dad's buried. Your birth dad."

"No way."

She got serious all of a sudden. "Brian, I'm so sorry. After I first met you, Cassie gave me such heck. My thing with Devon, your dad—that is what it is. But it's not fair to you. You probably want to visit his grave."

"Yeah, totally."

"Oh, that's so sweet," she said, blinking a couple of times. "It's just over on 107th Avenue."

I stared at the piece of paper as if it was some kind of

magic carpet that would transport me somewhere amazing. "So what're these numbers?"

"That's how they do it. Like, the groundskeeper guys. It's which row he's in and all that."

"Cool." I didn't tell her I wanted to go there like, right that minute.

"Well, when you go, let me know. Some relative wants to meet you there."

"No way. Okay." I was blinded by emotion for a second. I stuffed the paper in my pocket. I couldn't wait to get outside, and said my goodbyes to her and Maddy a little too quickly.

As soon as I was out on the sidewalk, I just about lost it. I kept my hand in my pocket, covering the piece of paper. This like, tsunami of emotion came over me and I actually started walking crooked, as if I was getting blown off course. Thinking of the grave and my birth dad underground was bad enough. But now I'd get to visit the grave, and I was going to meet a relative of my birth dad's! It was too much. When the bus arrived, I must have looked like a total freak, racing to the back so no one saw how worked up I was.

When I got home, the first thing I did was ask Mom, "Is anything going on tomorrow? Can I go out?"

"No, just a normal Sunday. I'm going to clean the oven when I get back from church. Why, where are you going?"

"Oh…just a friend's."

Twenty seconds later I had Brian-lunged all the way down the stairs (without clobbering my head) and was texting my birth mom.

im going to go tomorrow around eleven

She answered right away: *ok ill let him know & he can meet you there*

I literally vibrated the whole rest of the day and all night. "Him," she had said. So it was a guy. An uncle of his? A brother? I woke up at like, five and couldn't stop thinking about it. Why had I told Alicia eleven o'clock? I could have made it earlier. It was going to be torture, waiting that long.

I tried playing games for most of the morning. I killed like, forty-five minutes googling how I was going to get to the graveyard. Since it was so cold out, I decided to take the bus even though I'd still have a ten minute walk from 124 Street to the graveyard. The problem was the stupid Sunday bus schedule. I'd have to leave at like, ten. By the time I figured all this out, it was quarter to ten and I had to race to get ready. I practically flew out the door without saying goodbye to anyone.

Waiting for the bus felt surreal. The ice fog was so thick, you could only see a few blocks in either direction. I'd worn my nice thick birthday hoodie under my parka and these old winter boots that were too small for me. Still, I was shivering—not from the cold, but from excitement. And I could feel sweat dripping inside my shirt.

By the time the bus got me all the way around to 124 Street, I was a mess. I got off into the cold and headed east up 107 Avenue. The wind from the passing cars was killing my face, so I jaywalked to the other side. I totally knew I looked like an idiot, hurrying up the street, vibrating from my out-of-control nerves.

Anyway, when I got into the graveyard and amidst the tall trees, I totally calmed down. I was out of the wind and the giant spruce trees were all peaceful and awesome. The place just got to me. I stopped shivering so darn much and pulled out the blue post-it that Alicia had given me. On my phone I had the cemetery website up. It showed all the sections and plots and all I had to do was follow the numbers.

I had this moment, as I got closer and closer, cluing in to how important this day was in my life. My own birth father was lying just over there under the snow. This wave of like, pining came over me. I would have killed to meet the guy, just for like, two minutes. Shake his hand, look into his eyes. Say, "Hey, thanks, I'm alive because of you." But the sadness of him being gone was too much and I had to stop thinking about it.

I found the grave without too much trouble. It was one of those granite markers that was sort of lying almost flat and because of that, the snow had crusted and hardened on it. I bent down and began rubbing away the hard snow with my mitt. After a minute, I saw the name.

DEVON JAMES ALEXANDER. Ever in Our Hearts.

Oh crap, I thought. Was I supposed to wait for whoever was supposed to meet me here? I dug out my phone. It was only ten to eleven, so I had time. I was still on my knees. I decided to brush away all of the snow from the gravestone.

There was some kind of scene etched underneath the words, across the whole bottom and up the sides. When I cleared away the left-hand side, I saw something that made me honestly, completely, forget how to breathe. It was a polar bear. He was standing on the shore under these trees. There was a lake or river all along the bottom of the gravestone. The bear was looking at the far shore, which had nobody on it, like he wanted to get over there.

I kid you not, the tears jumped out of my eyes and splattered on the stone in front of me. *What the hell?* I thought. Was my crazy aunt in England psychic or something? What was the polar bear looking for across the water? Whatever it was, it felt like me. And I knelt there, blubbering like a baby for like, five minutes straight.

Then I got all self-conscious and looked around to see if anyone was watching. But there was no one. Still, I thought, I really had to get my act together. I was supposedly meeting someone in a few minutes. So I dug out my phone again and took a whole pile of pictures of the grave and all the trees around it.

It got to be eleven and then five after. I found myself wandering around, sniffling, and running out of things to wipe my eyes and nose with. Then I got an idea to google

Pizza the polar bear to see what had happened to him after the big fundraising campaign. It took like, five seconds to find the answer. And it was not what I expected.

I guess they got a million signatures on a petition and with all the money from the fundraising, they were able to move him out of the shopping mall. But they did not ship him back to the Arctic and set him free. He had lived alone in a cage his whole life, they said. He wouldn't have survived on his own in the wild. But they did send him back to the ocean park where he was born. And there, in a much bigger enclosure, able to smell the flowers and feel the sun on his fur, he was reunited with his parents.

Okay, so I'm an idiot. That set off a whole other round of blubbering. For sure my aunt was psychic. I was now convinced.

At quarter after eleven, I started to get cold. Whoever was coming was seriously late and I was not keen on getting hypothermia. *Should I leave?* I wondered.

The very second I had that thought, a very crappy old van pulled up on the nearest road. It sat there for like, ten seconds before I saw anybody move. Then this absolutely huge man came out and walked around the front of the van. He was maybe thirty-five or so, with this tiny touque that didn't even cover his ears. He had huge fur mitts and like, monster winter boots, as if he worked outside or something. The guy waved at me and all of a sudden the van doors slammed open behind him. Two more big people got out, swearing and arguing, and started to slog toward me through the snow.

Before I could really register what was happening, a small red car drove up and parked behind the van. And after that, another crappy old vehicle. I swear, they were like clown cars, because eight or ten people were crammed into each one—crying children and women with fur-trimmed parkas, helping old grannies out into the snow. Then two old men got out and lit cigarettes and exchanged this little flask, which I figured contained brandy or something. The whole mess of them came charging toward me. Some moved fast, passing the big man with the tiny touque. Some lagged behind, busy with their own things. Three kids, all younger than me, got to me first. They just stood there staring.

The big man came right up, removed his giant mitt and held out his hand. "Hey, I'm Don, Dev's brother."

I pulled off my mitt and took his hand. It was huge! It felt like I was shaking hands with a Yeti. "I'm Brian."

"I know, eh? Nice to meet you. We didn't know nothing about you till the other day. Welcome. I guess this is your new family."

The whole crowd of people came up. There must have been like, twenty or twenty-five of them. This one woman came running up and smashed into me—like, hard—for a hug that shoved me back off my feet. She didn't seem very old, but she just kept saying, "I'm your grandma. I'm your grandma. Oh my god! I'm your grandma. You look just like him. Oh my god!"

This other woman came up and pried her off and sent her off, sobbing and tripping over Devon's gravestone. "Oh, it's so great to meet you. I'm your cousin Jess. My god, you're handsome. These are my kids, Joel and Megan. That's just their friend Tom, from next door. He's living with us till his mom gets out of rehab."

To tell you the truth, I got lost in the crowd for like, the next fifteen minutes. I got so many hugs and shook so many hands, I lost count. And I had no idea what anyone's name was. There were just too many of them. It was a whirlwind. People started telling me stories about Devon. They'd get interrupted by someone else. It was complete chaos.

I was totally overwhelmed and I'd be lying if I said I didn't love every second of it.

I don't even know what happened. Somebody borrowed my phone and started typing their contact info in. It got passed around and passed around and I ended up with like, sixteen new contacts.

The first woman who came up had her hood up now and urged this old guy toward me. He was smoking and had the most incredible laugh lines beside his eyes. "This is Grandfather," she said.

"Well, look at you, young man. You must eat dinner with a shovel. How old are you?"

"He's twelve, Grandpa," somebody said. "Don't be an idiot."

"Well, young man, looks like you'll be as big as Don someday. Good for you."

"Your great-grandad's over there somewhere. I think he's looking for a place to pee."

"Isn't he always?"

I started to tell them I'd never had grandparents, that my adoptive parents were old. But somebody fell against me, trying to avoid a snowball.

"You guys stop that!" the grandmother yelled. "What are you, brain-damaged? Come here and say hello."

Two teenagers came over and shook my hand. Then they ran off between the gravestones, tossing chunks of ice at each other.

Then some lady came over and totally talked my ear off. "You have to come fishing up at Max's in a few weeks. Oh, you wouldn't believe the whitefish. Make you cry into your parka, it's so tasty."

"So it's ice fishing?"

"Oh, heck yeah. Got to eat it outside. Something about the smell of the snow, you know? And see your uncle over there in the scarf? He'll take you up in his plane sometime. You coming for Edna's anniversary next week?"

She went on like this for five minutes straight and eventually wandered off when all these people came crowding around me for selfies.

The rest was a blur. Half of them weren't even dressed for winter and stood there shivering and smoking. "I'm cold," one of them said.

And that was all they needed. "We'll give you a ride home, eh, boy? Come on, Rufus has the best car. Won't break down on the highway like *somebody* we know, eh, Johnny? You get in with them."

The big guy, Don, had been talking with one of the old men the whole time, sort of watching me out of the corner of his eye. When everyone started tearing toward the vehicles, he walked up beside me.

"You all right?"

"Yeah, totally."

"I got lots to tell you about Devon. He was my brother, but he was my best friend, too. I got lots of his stuff you can have. We'll get together after all this craziness, eh?"

I was about to say something, but his great big fur mitt came down on my shoulder right then and I just about lost it. "Okay," was all I could choke out.

Everyone was yelling at me to get into the last car. Don returned to his van and by the time we all got in, I was crammed with three other people into the back seat and Tom, the neighbour kid, was lying across us. "You fart," the guy beside me said, "I'll kill you. These are my nice pants."

"Ew!" someone else said. "Is it going to be wet?"

We got like, ten feet and the driver complained, "You guys quit breathing. You're fogging up the windows!"

"Don't be such a crab, Rufus. Get out the scraper."

We pulled out onto 107 Avenue. I couldn't see a thing out any of the windows and I'm sure the driver couldn't either. My grandmother in the front seat began scraping the windshield with the lid from a Tim Hortons cup.

I don't even know how we got to my place in one piece. The whole way, the guy and girl on either side of me kept asking me questions while the three people in the front kept cracking the rudest, most hilarious jokes. I swear, I was related to a circus family—and half the monkeys in the zoo.

When we pulled up at my house, two guys had to get out before me. I literally fell out of the car into the snowbank. Before the door was even closed, the car started to drive away, people yelling. They got the door closed, but halfway down the block, they opened the windows and waved and shouted at me till they drove off, laughing and screaming around the corner.

Oh…my…god, I thought. *It is a new day.*